Sapphires of Hope

Gems of Australia
Faith Series
Book 1:

Sapphires of Hope

Olwyn Harris

Dedication:
For Rebekah,
whose enthusiasm for Mum's stories
at a young age started this journey of hope

.

1.

Andrea sat on her bed and looked at the basket in disgust. "There is no way," she thought, "that I am going to use this!" She had desperately searched their cupboards for something, anything that would come close to what she needed for her catering project. She found only this old dilapidated breadbasket that looked like the sort of junk that comes from one of those tacky jumble-sale stalls… the type where hopeful vendors scrawl the words 'bargain' and 'treasure' on the same price tag.

This wasn't classy, classical old. Faded, tattered raffia flowers sprawled embroidered over the brittle old cane. It was lined with greasy brown paper. The torn flowers were padded out into lumpy, bumpy, faded, coloured bulbs. It was obviously someone's attempt to brighten up a rather plain basket, a long time ago, and it was well past its use-by date. Andi hated it. She hated what it meant. She hated that her classmates always seemed to be able to have whatever they wanted. She hated that they would get a better mark, just because her parents didn't see this as important.

"Andi, Joanne's here," her mum called from the kitchen. Jo bounded up the stairs to her friend's bedroom door.

"I need help with my maths homework. It's stupid," said Jo dumping her bag on the floor. Andi didn't move but sat with her hands laced through her dark hair, looking despondently at the basket.

"Oh gross! Who dumped this?" Jo gasped in horror. "Andi, if you were this desperate for a new hat you only needed to tell me. I have spare ones at home!" Jo plonked the basket on her head and stood up on the bed striking a super-model-on-a-catwalk pose.

"Not funny. It's disgusting! It's all I could find. I have to use it for the table setting on my catering assessment. *And* I'm supposed to invite a guest of honour! How could I? If I put that on the table, they'd throw-up before they could eat. I don't even know anyone who'd want to come! Mum says I have to use what we already have. This is *so* ugly! I hate it! It's horrible!" She snatched the basket from Jo's hand and flung it against the wall.

Jo looked at Andi through raised eyebrows. She didn't often see her friend venomous over something so… so well, tacky. It was just homework... and it wasn't even maths. Andi glowered and grunted some more.

"Well, maybe..." suggested Jo tentatively, "if you ripped off the gross stuff – it might be kind of more… I don't know… classical rustic? Shabby Chic? Kind of? Look, I'll help you start before we do maths. It won't take two seconds to do a make-over on this."

They sat poised with their instruments of surgery laid out beside them. Jo grimaced. It was so yuk. They started snipping the raffia and pulling it through the cane. They were careful not to cut the fragile woven basket as they trimmed and unthreaded, slowly dismantling the flowers and lining.

"They sure went to a lot of trouble," said Jo, sucking her finger when she nicked it. "Who did this?"

"Dunno. It came in some stuff that June gave us after her mother died. Mum said she was 'processing memories'," said Andi. "Mostly it moved from her garage to ours."

"Check this out," said Jo unravelling a tiny screwed up little wad of paper that padded out the centre of the flowers. "It's got writing on it!

Hey, that's cool. Help me get this off..." She attacked a different faded blossom with renewed vigour.

"This one is just… well, just a whole stack of numbers. Probably doesn't mean anything at all… Maybe this was all they had to use, and had to make do. Like I've got to."

They dismantled the flowers. Bits of faded raffia scattered like confetti over her bedspread. Carefully they smoothed out the pieces of paper. Some were blank and some had old-fashioned cursive handwriting. As they pulled the last of the flowers off the outside, the brown paper lining peeled away, revealing more documents underneath. They carefully placed the pressed out crumpled pieces side by side. Somehow Andi felt this collection was more than the work of a resourceful home decorator, merely making something out of left-over bits and pieces.

Maths was completely forgotten. They pieced the fragments from the flower-centres together like a jigsaw. They became letters handwritten in a rudimentary script that was difficult to read. One letter was signed "Sally" at the bottom. The numbers became part of an inventory tabulating uninteresting items like baling twine and bags of oats. But it was the other letter, water stained and blurred, that gave them a queer sort of nudge...

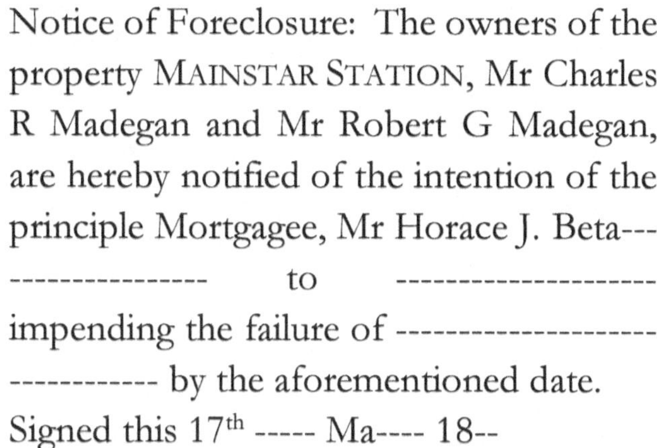

Notice of Foreclosure: The owners of the property MAINSTAR STATION, Mr Charles R Madegan and Mr Robert G Madegan, are hereby notified of the intention of the principle Mortgagee, Mr Horace J. Beta--- ---------------- to --------------------- impending the failure of -------------------- ------------ by the aforementioned date. Signed this 17th ----- Ma---- 18--

There were sections that were smudged and illegible, like a censoring pen had gone over the document. The year was smeared right through the middle and the signature at the bottom was signed with an extravagant flourish. Andi screwed up her face with intrigue. "Who puts official documents into a basket? This is just weird."

Jo picked up a letter, pieced carefully onto a sheet ripped out of her Maths' book. Together they tried to decipher the smudged ink and odd shaped letters.

"My dearest ------------ I regret that circumstances ----------------- the future without Mainstar -------- -- I am no longer in ------------- will be gone as you --------------

Sincerely yours,
Charles.

Andi swallowed the unexpected lump that caught in her throat. She was romantic to the very core of her being, and this read of thwarted love. Jo looked at her and rolled her eyes. "Don't be daft. "Sincerely yours"? He probably didn't even put up a fight," said Jo reading her expression.

Andi turned to the fragments scribbled by 'Sally' and read the little note…

"My Robert,

------------ aware that ------------- I have never had the opportunity ----------- pursue. I am taking two weeks ----------- I pray God's blessing over everythi---------------- Soon--------- and trusting---- --------- taken ----------- forever devotedly yours,
Sally.

There was a newspaper clipping, yellow and fragile, with an article written by a Thomas

Betancourt with the headline: 'Old station, New Enterprise'. Most of the article disappeared into the creased paper, but the photograph of the group could still be made out. Even if the detail of the picture was lost in the crumpled folds of newsprint, they could read parts of the caption underneath: "------ *Mainstar* ----------- *with Mr Frances* ---------*ick, who recent------------- in Sydney* ------" and the writing disappeared into a ragged, ripped edge.

Finally, Andi carefully unfolded the lining of the basket; her hands trembling slightly as she gently pulled apart the needle-pricked holes that had stuck the folds together. It was a poem, by an unknown writer, beautifully scribed on a bordered sheet of paper, now yellow and old and fragile. The poem was called 'Sapphire Blues'. It was not very talented work, but it touched a chord in Andi's soul that she could not explain. She desperately wanted an explanation for this.

"I wonder if June remembers who owned the basket?" she whispered.

* * *

2.

They waited under the tree outside June's place watching a bowerbird hopping around, threading himself in and out of her overgrown garden that had long been taken over by underbrush. They smiled at his industrious rearranging of his trinkets, creating the very best effect. They always thought it was amusing that June had a bowerbird in her yard, and bowerbird tendencies inside. June didn't throw anything away. That was another reason the basket was a mystery. Eventually June drove up in her old muddy brown EJ Holden. She gave them a tired little wave with arthritic bent fingers and ground the gears as she drove into the carport. She struggled out, slamming the stiff door of her car she affectionately named 'Esmeralda-Jane'

"Oh, thank you so much, Dears. This is an unexpected pleasure. Come in while I kick off my shoes and have a cup of tea," June balanced her handbag while she jangled the keys in the front door and gave it a perfunctory shove. She dumped her bulging handbag beside a wilting planter that stood in front of a cluttered sideboard loaded with discarded envelopes, paper-clips and dusty old-fashioned photos of old men dangling bonneted ruddy face babies on their knees. June lit the gas burner and positioned the kettle carefully as it popped and spluttered.

Andi and Jo were charmed by June. She was as eccentric as they come, but her heart was a treasure of willingness and generosity. Her diligent assistance to all the 'old ones around' especially amused them since they knew that many of those visits were to people younger than herself. She sat down heavily on the chair.

"So, my Dears," she sighed as she closed her eyes and sipped her tea, her arthritic fingers curling sideways through the handle. "It's been a long day; a long week, in fact. I still look forward to a Friday. What about you Dears? How was school?"

Andi and Jo looked at each other. Jo just bowled in. "We found an old basket that was with some stuff you gave Andi's Mum. We wondered if you knew who made it." Andi pulled the basket from a shopping bag and sat it on the table. June looked at it blankly.

"I hope you don't mind..." said Andi quickly, "I need it for a school project so I took the flowery stuff off."

June picked it up and turned it over. She blankly shook her head. Then suddenly she registered something. "Oh! The basket. Well I never!"

She quickly covered her shock with a grimace. She paused and sipped her tea again, inhaling the aroma as if her drink was a link with the past. "Didn't recognise it without all the stuff on it. It became a bit of an icon in our family. Mum used to give me big talks about preserving our heritage. All those years my family spent at that place... and they kept this basket and that candelabra over there. The basket was kinda dull, so I didn't put it out any more. I didn't even realise it had gone. Well! Goodness me… where did you get it from Dears? I'm sorry – I have been quite over taken with prattling."

The girls looked at each other. She didn't know! The story in the basket had been hidden very well. Andi hesitated. "Does 'Mainstar Station' mean anything to you?" she asked finally.

"Well sure you must have heard me talking about Mainstar: it is where I grew up. What do you know, all these things jumping out of the past… and our anniversary tomorrow! And I told myself I would not even think about it today. Well, my Dears, some things cannot be helped."

"What anniversary?"

"Mother made me promise she was to rest beside her parents and grandparents. I don't get out there as much as I used to, but I do try and visit on her anniversary… which is tomorrow. Well, my Dears, it is a long drive and I don't mean to be rude… but that's what I need to do."

They left June clucking over the unexpected disturbance of the past their visit had made.

* * *

The girls knocked on June's door early in the morning. The sun was still cool, peeking up over the gum trees that lined the street. Kookaburras were laughing hilariously in the gum trees that lined the street. June was bustling about, getting ready for her urgent appointment at Mainstar Station.

"June, we want to come with you. All your stories are really interesting. We thought… since you are going for the day… we might…" Jo started out boldly but petered out. Finally, she stopped and waited. June stared at her.

"You asked your parents about this?" she said sceptically.

They nodded enthusiastically.

"You want to come and see where I grew up?" she asked again staggered. "But Dears, it is really a very ordinary place. Surely you have been to farms before?"

Andi looked down. In truth she just wanted to see what sort of backdrop could create the untold story that the basket had kept under wraps for so long. "We would really love to. We don't want to intrude on your private grieving of course…" Her voice trembled slightly; she did not want to appear too eager. June misread it completely.

"Puddlewash my Dears! I do this every year, and I could go more often if I wanted, so don't you go being distressed. I do declare! Go and pack a lunch and we'll get going."

Even June's eccentric down-to-earth, nothing-is-ever-extraordinary attitude could not dampen Andi's excitement. She tucked their cut sandwiches wrapped up in a little checked tea towel, in the basket beside her on the backseat. It just seemed so appropriate to bring it along.

They left suburbia behind as they headed west, the morning sun quickly warming as it shone through the back window. June balanced a big bunch of flowers in half a bucket of water beside her on the front seat. The flowers had started to wilt already.

They travelled through a couple of small towns interspersed with scrub and undulating paddocks where cattle grazed or which were cultivated with summer crops. Andi stared out the open window and tried to imagine who's who in the world of the basket. The trip was uneventful and even Andi got listless looking at more trees and more cows and more paddocks. Maybe June was right. Maybe nothing special ever happened, except in the recesses of active imaginations.

Eventually, June turned onto a small gravel road where a large log fence announced 'MAINSTAR STATION'. As they slowly rattled their way over the cattle grid, Andi sat up and looked about. "Well, my Dears, here we are." Nothing did look particularly special. They drove along a barely visible track through low scrub until they saw a lone bottle tree standing like a bushman's vase with a tuff of branches stuffed in the top. June parked the car by a gate and pulled out the bucket of flowers, and a shoulder bag that had a water bottle poking out the top. "We'll go and see Mother first and then I have something to show you. Bring your picnic. I hope it is still there," she said mysteriously.

They could see the Station's little cemetery on a small rise, shaded sparsely by a few solitary gum trees and bordered with a low, faded picket fence. June went to open the gate and then suddenly stopped. She looked across the paddock to the cemetery and cloudless sky, then turned towards a bank of trees running down into a gully. She stood undecided, and then firmly put down the bucket beside the gate and turned on her heel and went straight down towards the trees, muttering as she went. "Come on girls. I have to see. Mother, we won't be long, I promise."

* * *

They followed the tree-line down into the gully. The heat evaporated as they stepped down onto the cool gravely-sand at the bottom. They followed a fresh trickle of water that appeared. The creek banks became steep as they walked deeper into the mini-gorge. Moss grew in the shady recesses of the rocks. Maidenhair ferns peaked out from under logs. Cicadas sang lazy summer songs. Wild flowers nodded gracefully in response to their admiration. It was like they had stepped through a door into another world. "This is so beautiful," whispered Andi. Some finches bounced on a low branch and drank from a shallow quiet pool with their bright red beaks. A lizard, sunning itself drowsily in some mottled sunlight, quietly watched them with blinking eyes and then disappeared behind a rock.

June stood transfixed. "It has not changed… in all this time, it is still the same. We used to call it *The Gully*. Quite the imaginative name hey?" she chuckled. "I would come here whenever I wanted to escape. Come on Dears, just a bit further."

They scrambled over some rocks and followed a narrow little goat track up the bank, which opened onto a little clearing. It was warmer up here. The sun was high, making hazy patterns above the grass. There, in the shade of a curtain rock wall, snuggled a little slab hut. Some secret played around the creases of June's mouth. "The hours I used to spend here with old Uncle Billy. He died when I was just a wee thing,

but I still remember. Mother would not…. oh!"
She glanced at her watch involuntarily and tapped
its glass case and held it to her ear. "Oh, that
can't be the time. Well I cannot show you now
Dears. It would have been nice, but maybe
later…"

Jo looked at her bewildered. Honestly,
June's dithery ways frustrated her to bits.

"What a cute little place," said Andi gazing
at the little hut. There was a spindly old
Kurrajong tree beside the tank at the back, its
bell-shaped flowers splashing red colour around
the eaves. Wild bluebells danced in the wind that
rippled over the bleached grass towards the old
verandah.

"Does anybody live here?" Jo asked. This
place had a genuine feel of Goldilocks about it.
She cleared her throat. "You know June, we
could wait here…while you go and place your
flowers."

"Oh yes, June. That is such a private
thing. This is the perfect place for us to have
lunch. It is fantastic!" Andi sighed, clutching the
basket that carried their lunch.

"I'm starving…" added Jo not too subtly.

June hesitated again. "You know Dears, perhaps you are right. It will not take me long. Now don't go wandering… stay on the flat near the hut until I get back. It will give you a chance to eat. You might even want to take a peek inside…"

"Oh June, you're the greatest! We'll be right here."

"Well, then Dears, I'll be back in a jiffy. Those flowers won't hold out much longer." June turned on her heel and disappeared down the side of the hill, with surprising agility. The girls looked at each other, slapped their hands together and pulled out their sandwiches!

* * *

3.

They swallowed hard on their bread and took a swig from their water bottle. Even if the hut was deserted, the whole thing seemed quite daring now as they walked towards the old wooden verandah. The roofline drooped rather oddly in one corner and weeds grew through cracks in the compacted dirt floor at the front. A broken-down seat-swing was heaped in the corner and a brambling dog rose climbed around the posts and up onto the roof beams. Eerie, sinister fingers reached out to grasp the girls' hair as they ducked under and brushed it aside.

They pushed at the door, their hearts pounding audibly in their ears. It creaked as it swayed limply on a broken hinge and jammed on bits of rubble inside the doorway. They squeezed in and waited for their eyes to adjust to the dimness. They looked around. This had been somebody's home. They had eaten meals here, washed and dried-up… laughed, cried, had fights and made up. The normality of it began to seep into their hearts. This was a home, like their own living room, and curiosity burned questions into their minds. Who had lived here? What were they like? What did they do?

Dust coated everything in a warm comforting blanket. Cobwebs hung like decorations from a hurricane lantern that swayed from a hook in the rafters. The earthen floor was cracked and uneven. Walls were papered in newspaper and the pictures from faded old-fashioned Christmas cards were glued in patterns around the sill. Tin mugs and enamel plates sat in a jumbled mess on a wooden shelf. An old metal drum had been split in two and folded out like a book to make a double washing up basin. It was inserted into a wooden plank bench in an original designer bush kitchen.

Even with everything in disarray, it felt homely. Hessian hung in shreds from a board precariously nailed to the roof; presumably once a dividing curtain to the next room. They pulled it aside, cobwebs taking up where the hessian had given out. There was a double bed, made from roughly sawn timber, and a baby's cradle. Another bunk, heavy and bulky was jammed in the corner. A teddy bear, made from old flour bags with large, blue, button eyes and a circular stamp printed across his tummy sat there waiting for his owner to return. Andi picked it up and looked at it curiously with a thoughtful frown.

There were holes in his legs and arms and a gaping wound in its side showed matted wool-fleece as the stuffing. She gently sat him back on the bed and adjusted some torn rugs crocheted out of an oddment of coloured wool, that were draped over a lumpy mattress as a cover. Mice had moved in and made it their playground. A mat was made out scraps of rag pulled through a hessian backing giving it a scruffy pile, now faded and threadbare, worn out over time and the traffic of mice.

Andi studied the wallpaper of newsprint. She read little advertisements for handcrafted silky oak furniture and solid silver hairbrushes *"beautifully ornamented"* for 8/6, or 15/6 for a flashier model. Another page promoted goanna oil rheumatoid remedies: *"goodly, proven therapies"* for next to nothing. A cartoon of a granny clicking her heels with glee, artistically expressed the delight of saving the frail elderly from the endless pain of aching bones. Andi smiled. Maybe she should get some for June. Even though she never complained, Andi suspected her arthritic hands ached.

Jo was noisily munching on an apple when she saw the crack of lightning and heard the low rumble of thunder outside. She thought she heard steps outside and briefly looked out the shuttered window to see if June was back so soon. That change in weather had certainly come up fast. The light outside was sort of weird. "I hope June doesn't get caught in the storm," Jo said, glancing towards where Andi continued to study the wallpaper.

Andi was staring at the wall looking really confused. "I was reading this article on the newspaper on the *virtues of engaging in written correspondence*, but I can't find it now. It was so funny…" Andi turned back to Jo. "I don't understand… it really was just…" She screamed. A big hairy arm was held high over her.

"Goldilocks has a friend," growled a deep, unfriendly voice. She screamed again as her forehead split with pain and her whole world blacked out.

* * *

Andi could hear herself moaning. Her head throbbed and pounded in time with her pulse. She tried to move but that sent sparks of agony shooting through her eyes. What happened? It was dark. She attempted to open her eyes, but they were bound tight. Her shoulders and neck were stiff and aching. She could feel a cool breeze on her arms, but when she tried to move her wrists, she couldn't. Was she paralysed? What was going on? Her mind started to spin. A dark panic circled, as she tried not to breathe too quickly. Slow. Breathe slowly. "Oh God! Help me!"

Another breeze puffed over her shoulder and patted her cheek. It helped sooth her panic. It must be late for it to be so cool. Slowly she remembered: June; the car trip; the farm; Mainstar Station; the old hut. June! What happened to June? Was she mugged when she returned to join them for lunch? Jo? Her foot touched something soft and it responded by kicking her forcefully in the shin, accompanied by a muffled yet definite commentary on her opinion about the situation. She pulled away. Huh! At least Jo was okay. Oh, her head hurt.

Slowly she wriggled around and propped herself against the wall. A kookaburra laughed at her predicament and she felt tears wetting the binder on her face. How could this have happened? June was so sure no one lived here. Unless they unwittingly had fallen into a den of criminals. But the house was deserted, and unlived in. She felt like she was slipping off the end of a rope. She clung onto it for dear life. "Oh God. Please help us."

A quiet voice in her throbbing head seemed to say, *Bless those who persecute you.* Andi groaned. She wasn't going to bless any thug who bashed her head in. "No! That's unfair. You know, God, he's probably into drugs or stuff. You wouldn't want to bless that! That's insane!" And the quiet voice went away… but so did the comfort she sought.

She gritted her teeth. No way! "Besides, my head hurts and what about Jo? She's kicking mad so she's obviously not hurt – why don't you ask her to do it?" Tears stung her eyes as she tugged at the straps that held her hands and she could feel them biting deeper into her wrists. She felt sad that Jo didn't really believe that God was interested in the details of life… even the panicked details. "Oh, God! Help us! Please… we need you. Help us get out of here…" Andi leaned back against the wall, weakness seeping into her tense muscles. The screaming inside her head fading through exhaustion. Silence. Jo stilled beside her.

She jolted awake as she heard a woman's voice, edgy and distraught, outside. Andi strained to hear what she was saying; her words muffled by the binders around their heads. Now she was yelling. The door opened with a gust as footsteps ran closer to them. "Whatever were you thinking? They are only girls! You are much bigger than they. If you told them to sit, they would obey you like dogs." Hot, dry hands struggled with the cloth on her face.

Warm sticky blood trickled down into Andi's eye and she blinked as it smeared her vision. A woman lifted a lamp and wiped at her face with a cloth. She muttered distraughtly under her breath. "Go outside," she snapped, "while I clean up this mess! I can't believe you did this. You are so much better than this Billy. Go! I will talk with you later."

Andi toppled and swayed ungainly as she stood up. The woman supported her and slowly helped her over to the table. Their basket was sitting on the red checked tea towel, where they had been in the process of sharing her lunch. Their sandwiches were gone, and in the dim evening light, even the faded brittle wicker didn't seem so tattered. The woman covered Andi's forehead with a cool damp cloth and sat Jo down on an opposite chair. She had dark hair that was pulled back straight into a bun. Her long dress was faded and ordinary. She was not old, but she didn't seem very young either. She came back with a bowl of water and carefully wiped their faces with a well-worn scrap of sheeting. Jo's cheek was bruised and her nose started bleeding again. She ripped off a section of the clean sheet and made a pad for Jo to hold over her nose.

The woman started muttering again as she gently wiped the grime from their faces and arms. "I'm so sorry. I didn't believe them. I really didn't. But perhaps they are right. Maybe I should... Pa said I could do it, and I did promise him."

Tears were streaming down her face, and she swiped at them angrily, smearing dirt and blood down her face. Strands of dark hair fell loose and straggled in her deep blue eyes. By the time they were cleaned up, it looked like she had been in a brawl. They both stared at her. She was no enemy, but she was at battle with something they had no idea about.

Andi felt her conscience explode. *"Oh God I am so sorry! Forgive me for arguing. Of course, you know all about these people… and I know you know how to work things out. Bless them God — bless them big time! Don't let my disobedience step in the way of you blessing them!"* And immediately Andi felt a peace flow around her. The sense of doing the right thing was comforting… even when your head hurts — really badly.

* * *

Jo stared around the cabin with a weird look in her eyes. It was already dark outside. How long had they been here? The dim yellow light from the hurricane lantern cast distorted shadows into the corners of the room. Although it was not tidy, the evidence of the weathered disintegration of time had disappeared from the hut. Had they imagined that? The dust and the dirt had disappeared too… and although there were dirty mugs on the bench, it was the regular, day-by-day dirt, not the powdery layers of unused years. Andi did not seem to notice. Her eyes were glued to the young man that stood beside the woman.

"Well, I will introduce ourselves since you are guests in our home. My name is Sally. This is my brother Billy." Sally's slight frame seemed tired and frail as she fought back more tears. She had his dark hairy arm in her thin hand. The body that grew on the end of that thin hairy arm was also thin and hairy. But Billy's eyes told Andi so much more. They were big, wide blue eyes — the same colour as his sister's, clear like sapphires, but innocently repentant as he scuffed the ground like a schoolboy caught playing truant. "Now Billy," continued Sally, "say what you need to say."

"Oh Sal, I is sorry. I didn't mean that they would get hurt. But they were just like the story… that girl… and they were eat'n all our food and could've broke all our stuff and I caught them just before they went to sleep in our beds." Billy's voice had broken into a deep man's tenor, but his thoughts were like a child protecting his toys.

"Billy – that was their food. You ate with Molly, remember?"

"I's sorry Sal. I thought maybe…" His eyes were sad and anxious. Suddenly he spilt out the most important explanation that he had. "Besides they are dressed like pixie-people – all weird like!" Still he had made Sally cross. It was such a bad mistake.

It seemed ludicrous to Andi to think that she had tried to pigeonhole him in some drug-lord crime ring. Story about a girl? What was it he had said before she was knocked out? She struggled to remember and then smiled reassuringly.

"Billy, do you mean the story about Goldilocks?"

He nodded mutely.

"Billy, I know that story too. And you think our clothes are weird?"

He nodded again.

"We are not from here – that's why our clothes are different. But we didn't know that you lived in this house. It was just like the story; we were only looking and didn't think we would be in any one's way. I'm sorry we gave you a fright. We were not going to sleep in your bed."

"Really?"

"Honest."

"Does it hurt much?"

"Yeah, a bit. Well, quite a lot really."

"I didn't mean to hit hard. But I was scared. Sal was away."

"Can we be friends?"

"Really?" Then he added… "But you're a girl. I know that now, even though you dress like a pixie-person… or a boy. You didn't trick me." He grinned at his cleverness.

"Ahuh. But I can still be your friend. I'd like that." But when he eagerly spat in his big hairy paw and thrust it forcefully in Andi's face, it was all she could do to spit on her own hand in return and take the offered peace token. She closed her eyes and swallowed. Yuh-ck! Her mouth went dry and she tried to inconspicuously wipe her palm clean on the back of her jeans.

Jo looked from the room that she had been gazing around in amazement to Andi with equal astonishment. She seemed so calm and natural with the big, hairy, grown-up kid. He had hit her on the head and she had a cut on her forehead from when she fell, and now she was spitting in her hand and exchanging body fluids! This was really freaking her out. Okay, that was enough: time for a reality check. "So, Andi – where do you think June is?"

"June?"

"Yeh, June… why didn't she come back?"

"She might of… got scared and left. Maybe…"

"June would never do that!"

"Billy, did you see a lady come around here? She was wearing…" Andi's voice trailed off.

Jo impatiently continued, "… a yellow hat and a green dress with flowers on it. She would have come up along the creek and trees. She was going to meet us." Billy shook his head. "Did you see anyone?"

He shook his head again. "Nope, just Goldilocks and you," he said directly to Andi.

"Well, we'll have to go to back to the car and see if she's okay, I guess," said Andi apologetically. "I'm sorry we were a bother – we honestly thought no one lived here."

"Andi. It's dark."

"Well, we'll take a torch. I'm sure they'll lend us one."

Jo looked at Andi. Her eyes did look a bit dazed…or fiery maybe, like the throbbing in her head was worse. "Could I talk to you outside Andi? We won't be long. Honest." She grabbed Andi's hand and pulled her out onto the cool verandah.

"What? Jo let go… my head hurts enough without you yanking at me like that."

"You don't get it, do you?" Jo said in a harsh whisper as she grabbed her by both cheeks and moved her head around so they were looking out past the verandah.

"Jo! Stop it! It hurts!" Andi pushed Jo's palms off her face and turned away holding her head. Then she came back and stood by her friend. "I'm sorry; it just hurts still. I don't get what?"

"Tell me what you see," said Jo anxiously.

"Darkness… stars… grass… what are you getting at?"

"What else?"

"House… verandah… garden… I don't know…"

"What about the house and verandah and garden…"

"Jo you are right. We have to find June. My head really hurts…"

"Andi just tell me what you notice about the house and verandah and garden."

"I don't know… oh the rose… they trimmed back the rose… it was climbing all over the rafters."

"Hmm. Where have they cut it?"

"Oh Jo, since when are you worried about gardening? Why does it matter where they cut it? You are acting really weird."

"No Andi, this is weird. Look, there are no cut stems. This rose climber hasn't been pruned this afternoon."

"They ripped the old one out? What a waste. It looked healthy enough…"

"Andi – listen to me! I think this is the same plant... only when it was young. Look at the verandah… it was falling down… don't you get it?"

"They mended the verandah as well? They should have visitors more often."

"Andi don't be dense! This is really weird… it is like we have gone back into the story of this place. That's why June did not come back… she's not here."

"Really? We can't have slipped in there... that's not possible..." Her voice trailed off again.

"We must have. Why else would they dress like that?"

"I just thought they were farmers… or some of those religious people. Oh, what do I know? They could be…" Andi's head hurt more. The pounding in her forehead felt like some little green man was hitting the inside of her eyeballs with a mallet. She was struggling to mentally keep up with what Jo was saying.

"Well, I dunno. You're the one who had all the questions about this… the basket and stuff. Maybe this is the chance to find out."

"Jo, I…" Andi did not finish. She melted in a heap onto the compacted dirt that was their verandah. It reminded Jo of a chocolate bunny her little brother had left out in the sun one Easter Sunday hoping it would find all the eggs their Mum had hid in the garden. Jo panicked as she tried to gather up molten heap that was Andi. "Help me! Sally! Billy!" she screamed, "Help! I need a hand!"

* * *

4.

Dr Hollingsworth straightened up and put some strange instruments back in his bulky black leather bag. He took his handkerchief from his vest pocket, rubbed his balding head with it, polishing it to a high gloss. He had examined Andi as she lay on the starchy white sheets in the Homestead guest room. Her face was pale and colourless. The cut on her forehead had been bound together. Bits of her dark hair jutted out between the bandages, making her look a lot like the peculiar rag doll that sat on the dresser beside the bed. He looked over at Jo. "Are you her sister, Miss?" he said resignedly. Jo shook her head. "Where are her parents?" Jo shrugged. It was a bit absurd to try and explain what she suspected.

He sighed, "Look, I don't know what it is you two are up to, and quite honestly, I don't have a mind to pursue it. But this little girl is seriously ill, and her parents have every right to know. Now when you can pull yourself together and start thinking of something else besides your own hide, you had better talk. Get Madegan to send for me when you're ready," he snapped his bag firmly shut and left the room. Jo could hear him talking in the hall outside the door. She heard him say something about Billy before his horse left.

Jo was bewildered. She was so sure she would know, deep down, if her best friend was in danger… and yet all she felt was like she was walking above the whole thing. It didn't feel real at all. She went over and gently placed her palm over the bandage on Andi's head. She kind of wished she believed in Andi's God right now. Then she could pray. But she didn't and she wasn't going to throw herself desperately at some god because she needed help. That would not be right… just because she needed something. So, she whispered positive thoughts, knowing there was little else she could do. She was stranded in a very strange place. The clothes Sally insisted they change into did nothing to make her feel like she could fit in here. She couldn't explain that to anyone.

The door opened and Sally came in. She had washed and changed her clothes and was wearing a long plain dark skirt and a white top with starched cuffs, and an apron trimmed with frills. Her eyes seemed tired and there were lines about her lips that Jo hadn't noticed before. She held out her hand and gave Jo the little wicker basket that had held their modest picnic. "You left this at our place." she said.

Jo took it, staring at her. "You're the maid?" she asked amazed.

"I like to think of it as housekeeper. It is a way to keep us in our home and gives Billy some work. No one else would ever offer him a job. He helps on the farm and around the garden. My father arranged it. Mister Robert and Mister Charles are kind bosses. It works for us here."

"Where's your father then?"

"He died in an accident at the Mill about five years ago."

"Oh. I'm sorry."

"We do okay."

"Sally, what are we going to do? Andi needs a hospital, but I suspect that is not going to happen. I know the doctor thinks I'm hiding stuff, but it's just too hard to explain. I was wondering maybe if I could stay with you and Billy, and then Andi could stay here? I'll help out."

Sally looked torn. The idea of company appealed to her, more than anything. But the expense of an extra person… it was a scratch-and-survive life they had. Would a visitor want things they didn't even have for themselves? And Billy. How would he react?

But Jo was desperate. She needed Sally on her side. "Well, I could talk to your boss. If he gave me a position, it might pay for Andi to be here, and a little bit of board." Jo continued without drawing a breath. "I really need somewhere to stay. I can't leave Andi here alone and I can't move her. Please. I promise not to sit on Baby Bear's chair and break it all up. What if you said I'm your friend visiting or something?"

Sally smiled. It was a worn out, tired sort of smile. "I couldn't tell Mr Madegan that…"

"Why not?" said Jo.

"I've lived here all my life. They know everyone that I know."

"Didn't you go away to school or anything?" She was exaggerating if she said she had no outside friends.

"Why would I need to go to school? My Dad taught me and I've been working since I was eight."

"But… eight?" Jo stopped. Things were different here. The glaring reality of social flaws seemed to be flicking up and stinging her face like someone was slapping her.

Sally smiled. She liked this Goldilocks person. She had always thought the way the story ended, with the girl running away, so the bear-family never saw her again, spoilt the story. This was much better. Suddenly she felt like she did have a friend outside her life at Mainstar Station. It was a new sensation and it felt strangely empowering. "I'll think of something," she said. "Besides, someone will have to stay with your friend overnight."

* * *

5.

Jo entered the room and stood quietly by a large, dark leather chair. Mr Madegan sat at his writing desk with numbered accounts in his hand. He glanced up as she entered and quietly finished the line, he was working on without pausing. Jo had no idea if this was Mr Robert or Mr Charles. They were names that Sally had mentioned only briefly.

Finally, he put his pen down near the ink well. His moustache wriggled when he spoke, like a big hairy caterpillar that was feeding off his top lip. His voice was deep and friendly, but sort of washed out, like a favourite pair of jeans. "Just so you know we will not be pursuing any charges against Billy. We only have your word against his."

Jo blinked. She hadn't even thought of that. Could she really sue? Andi was seriously hurt. What she needed was a real hospital, not this… but what else could she do? She had no idea. Who would pay the bills? She swallowed hard but before she could formulate something to say Robert continued. "Likewise, I will not pursue charges of trespassing or theft or whatever. Sally said you were here after a position so you can continue to nurse your sister. That seems fair." Jo looked at the caterpillar when he spoke. It was doing a hundred-leg tap dance. "We wouldn't normally be hiring, but with shearing coming up, the extra hand will be needed."

"Fair?" thought Jo in disgust, *"He seriously thinks this is fair?"*

"So? Can you actually nurse?" he sighed wearily.

Jo was jolted back by his question. "Nurse? You mean sick people? Like Andi?" asked Jo.

The grub continued dancing. "Yes, sick people. Usually the only types I know that get nursed: around here at any rate."

Jo shook her head. "My grandfather got sick last year and died. But my mother mainly looked after him." Tears started to pool in her eyes. Did this mean that Andi was condemned? She had no idea what to do.

"Not a strong recommendation. We might just leave that to Sally then. What can you do?" he asked quickly.

Jo stared at the caterpillar again. She almost said 'algebra and accounting' just to shock him because she wanted to be able to say she could do something, anything, even if it wasn't nursing. Then she remembered that she hated maths and accounting was one of her worst subjects. She thought of her school bag still unpacked near Andi's bed, waiting for help with her homework, and almost laughed as she wondered how she would explain her way out of detention when it wasn't done. The excuse *'I was visiting the last century Sir"* probably would not be considered reason enough.

Jo refocused on the caterpillar crawling along his top lip. "I like animals Sir, and I have done accounting." She couldn't help it – she just had to. And the reaction that Robert gave was pretty much worth it.

"Accounting?" he repeated carefully. Whenever he raised his eyebrows his moustache twitched and wriggled. "As in book-keeping and accounts?"

"Oh, but I prefer animals," she said quickly.

"Well, it is the animals that make the accounts," he said slowly. He almost seemed to doze off. "Very well. Sally will attend to Andi's nursing. You'll have to help her of course, as well as her other duties. She will explain what needs to be done. And we'll to talk about Dr Hollingsworth's bill later."

"His bill?"

"He charges like a wounded bull – just like every other bloke around these parts. He made a house call… all the way out here. So yes, there's a bill."

"How much?" And when he named the amount Jo tried hard to remember what her Grandfather would have translated that to be worth. She couldn't work it out. So much for accounting skills. "How long for me to work that off, on top of what I'll have to do now?"

He looked at her steadily. She was obviously thinking things through, but her story about accounting lost credibility.

"Probably about three to six weeks." He wasn't going to tell her that he would probably pay the bill anyway. He had argued with Charlie about it before he left to go to town this morning, but his sense of responsibility was genuine. If Billy had smacked the kid on the head with a stick, technically it was not their problem, but morally, he felt it was the right thing to do.

"Three weeks!" Jo exclaimed. "Did he say how long before Andi gets better? What if he has to come back?"

"It'll take longer, I guess."

Longer? She felt like he had just tossed a huge net over her. Her instinct was to fight in panic. She groaned silently and started to give herself a pep talk. "Don't lose it! Don't lose it. Be calm. You can do it…" and she suddenly thought of Andi telling her the story about Jacob in the bible. She said he was stuck in a job for seven years just to be saddled with the wrong bride. And then what's more, he happily went back to work for another seven. Andi said Jacob could have been peeved, but he chose to make it work. So… she would choose to be positive.

"Well," she said brightly, "That just about accounts for most of my time. Ahh, Mr ….?"

"Robert," he said without pausing. He was used to people not knowing him from his brother.

"Mr Robert, could I ride a horse sometime?"

"Ah yes, the animals. We'll see," he said good-humouredly, as he dismissed her to Sally's supervision. He could see she cared desperately.

Didn't she come, cap in hand, willing to work for her sister's care? She had not demanded anything. He had interviewed girls before; he had no doubt she was from some wealthy private establishment – hence the line dropped about accounting, and her soft hands and neat nails. He noticed the shock that flickered across her face when she registered the time frame, even though he thought he had been exceptionally generous with only three weeks. Rich people are used to things happening much quicker.

Perhaps Sally's explanation, freely volunteered and convoluted with information, had some truth. She had said the girl was a relative of an acquaintance her father had made from his Sydney days: running away from an abusive situation, looking for work. Still, why all the detail? The story sounded trumped up. Certainly, Jo had not been abused. There was no pain or the look of being hunted in her eyes. Underneath her anxiety about her friend, she was relaxed and free and unsullied by care. If Sally wanted to go to so much trouble to help, there was merit in that alone. Sal would have her reasons. And if nothing else, he was open for her to stay, just because he wanted that freshness to breeze through their life for a little longer. He hoped that the curses of Mainstar would not settle over Jo's face. Was it possible that some of that light would blaze them away? And he had no idea why he would even hope it could be possible.

* * *

6.

Jo was quickly introduced to Sally's life at the homestead. Every morning it seemed another film of dust came to coat any evidence that they had been there the day before. Although Molly did all the cooking, it was up to Sally to set, serve and clear meals. She tended the vege-garden with the help of Billy. He would water the seedlings, dig the next patch, and weed the beds. They ate their meals in the kitchen and at night after a light supper, they took turns in sleeping on a mattress in Andi's room, while the other walked Billy home to in the little slab worker's cottage over by 'The Gully'.

Andi's care was demanding. She fluctuated between periods of restless and feverish sleep, muttering incoherently, to lying glazed almost unresponsive and still. Molly made her fresh chicken broth every morning and they fed her with a spoon as she lay, propped up against cushions and pillows.

Sally tried to get her out of bed, but she collapsed again. So, they washed her in bed; toileted her in bed; massaged her and turned her in bed; wobbled her arms and legs in bed; changed her bandage in bed. Sally seemed to know a whole lot, for someone who had never stepped inside a hospital. "You have to do these things. Otherwise she won't move very well when she wakes up. Had a stockman once, fell off a horse - they all left him for dead, excepting his poor wife. But by the time he was strong enough to get out of bed, his legs had seized up and he couldn't move. That's not going to happen to Andi. Not while I have a say," she said determinedly.

Jo was amazed. She knew from when her Grandfather was sick that nursing was far more than just wiping feverish brows. The skills that Sally had were far beyond those of an illiterate housemaid. Jo quizzed her a bit more. "I nursed old Mr Madegan, for a long time before he died. And Mrs Madegan." Sally admitted. "They had proper nurses come, but they couldn't be here all the time. They would show me things and tell me why they did them. It is all just common sense really. Nothing very clever." Jo didn't think so. She thought it showed a great deal of skill. She watched her with Andi, and noticed how the gentle, persistent care seemed to come naturally to Sal. "Had a nurse tell me once that I should go and learn properly... about nursing.

She said I was natural like. But I never could. Still, it is nice to think someone thought so.”

“Why couldn’t you?” And as soon as Jo said it, she felt foolish for making such an obvious blunder. She hadn’t even been to school.

“Because of Billy. I couldn’t leave him. He’s my kid-brother and he needs me, and… well I need him. We are good together. Just sometimes, sometimes I would like a break.” Sally sighed. She stared at Jo, wide eyed over Andi’s bed; she was confessing her most dreadful secret. “I feel so tired. And when he hit you girls, I thought that would be the end. I almost believed I would give in and send him away. Just like all the people about have been telling me since Pa died. But I promised him… and I know the importance of a promise kept.”

Jo had no response. She was beginning to put Sally up there with Mother Teresa. Having a break sounded fair enough to her. “Would you like to do nursing though?”

Sal laughed: a light gentle tinkle that sounded like the wind chimes on the verandah at the hut. “I get all the nursing I can ever want here. Andi isn’t the only one. I’ve had others:

mainly workers, or their family ones. Mr Robert has a kind heart. He would never turn a sick one out. Sometimes they are taken to the Shearers' quarters when it's not shearin' time. Here is easier though. Things close to hand. Mr Charlie calls it Mainstar Charity Hospital when *he* gets sick of it." Sally straightened the sheet over Andi's shoulders, and she moved restlessly.

Jo gently placed her hand on her bandaged head and tried to gently calm her restlessness. "Andi" she said, "Me and Sally are going to look after you really well, until you are better." Then it was time they moved on to the next job. There was always another job.

* * *

On Friday, Mr Charles came home from town. Jo saw him get down from the sulky, as she hurried along the verandah to the dining room with fresh water. She nearly dropped the pitcher in her hand as she did a double take, looking back over her shoulder. He looked exactly like Mr Robert without the hairy-grub moustache! He had a thin pencil line that was sculptured up at the ends. Sal had already told her, "There could be no two identical twins less alike on God's own Earth… and the hair on the lip says it all." Jo had assumed that meant they didn't look identical at all, but she was looking at two peas in a pod. She had to mean more than just lip hair. Sally point blank refused to be drawn into explaining exactly what she meant by her comment.

Beside Mr Charles, in the sulky was a portly man with a high stiff collar and flashy red vest, and a young lady. Rumours flew amongst the homestead staff like brush fire. This man was the primary financier: Mr Horace J. Betancourt who had numerous interests in real estate. He was known for his hard-nosed business deals. He had a slogan that he cited to those who walked around with him: *"Need a deal to be done? Bet-on-your-life, Betancourt is a son-of-a-gun"*. It was always said with a patronising laugh. It made Jo gag. It was confirmed that he was here representing the interests of *Betancourt Enterprises* and he had designed this visit to coincide with the shearing that was due to start next week. Everyone was put on a Best Behaviour Alert.

* * *

7.

Mainstar Station activated. Sheep were rounded up from the back paddocks. Mobs were mustered and herded into the holding yards near the shearing shed. Even the sedated and silent homestead now constantly buzzed with the background of bleating sheep, barking dogs, agitated workmen and horses, and people coming and going.

A shearing team appeared out of nowhere and the lonely quarters became a hive overnight. The shearers' cook was a rough, toothless man called Bluey. He had wild ginger hair that stuck out everywhere. Even his ears and the rudimentary tattoos on his arms were framed with coarse red fuzz. His uniform consisted of a holey blue singlet and a pair of well-worn moleskins. He was top hen in the chook house, and no one questioned his authority.

Jo had no time to think through the arrival of Mr Horace J. Betancourt. Shearing was upon them and they were busy with extra work. Wherever Horace Betancourt went, there was a trembling frenzy of bowing and scrapping that followed in the wake of his generous figure. Jo watched the display in disgust. Only Robert seemed unaffected by his booming voice and over loud laugh. He had retreated into his office and rarely appeared. Jo suspected it wasn't because he personally despised the kind of person Horace was. It was more that he seemed resigned to the fact that fate had already decided his future and no amount of nose rubbing would change it – so why bother?

Jo tried to piece more of the puzzle together, and she didn't know whether getting away to process her thoughts or getting close to the action would help her do this best. However, in the end her schedule decided for her, because all she could do was to sneak a quick look from the servery during pauses in mealtimes. She watched Horrible-Horace Betancourt eating his meal, checking his chained watch, as his bushy beard snagged on his high collar, dabbing at his fat, cleanly shaven lips with a linen serviette in a peculiarly pompous way. He was just like a stray dingo sniffing about a weak, lonely lamb. He wasn't ready to eat, but his circling presence made everyone nervous. He would put down his spoon and laugh at one of his own jokes, by throwing back his jowls and howling at the moon. He gave Jo the creeps.

And then there was that young woman with him! Jo knew her name was Sophie. She was a flirty little piece that would wander past Mr Charles unnecessarily and find a way to concoct some disaster that needed his urgent assistance. Then she would coyly tell him how clever he was and how wonderful it must be to live in a beautiful place like Mainstar all the time. She looked like cheese on a rat-trap to Jo.

Sally stayed in Andi's room at the homestead every night now. Before Jo made her way back to the cabin at night, Jo always went in and said goodnight to Andi. Every evening she would tell her all about the day. She sat on the wooden chair, slowly drawing up her tired legs and hugging them. She felt so bushed. How could these people keep going? Sally must be made of iron. She sat in the shadows beside the bed as the candle flickered slightly from a whisper of a breeze that crept in through the double French doors that opened onto the verandah.

She closed her eyes as she held the limp hand of her friend. If it weren't for Sally, she would have gone completely bonkers by now. "Andi… I just wanted to tell you about this man Horace who's come to check out the farm. He looks around at everything and I can see in his eyes he is already packing everything up and adding a price-tag. Sally says he doesn't even want the farm. He just works out how to liquidize them into the most money possible. This is so unfair. Mr Robert is the nicest fellow. I really like him…I don't know Mr Charles much yet, but they're identical twins you know. Except they're not very identical – Sally says they are completely not like each other. They do look the same though… if you get what I mean…and tomorrow… they start shearing... and everything is..."

"Jo, Jo, it's time to start…" Sally stood shaking her shoulder gently. The grey streaks of dawn were filtering though the gum trees that stood guard outside the fenced Homestead yard. Jo opened her eyes. Her cheek was creased from the folds in the sheets on Andi's bed where she had rested her head as she sat beside it last night. Sally had packed away the mattress and the household was already up. Billy was bringing in the firewood and the sounds of horses and tack being readied outside jangled in the stillness of the morning. When would she ever get to go horse-riding instead of doing housework – again!

Every morning she had to do the disgusting dunny duties and then just to give this monotonous life some variety, they designated certain house duties to a weekday. So instead of Monday, here it was "Wash-day". It consisted of boiling a large over-sized soup-pot called a 'copper' set outside in a brick barbeque. They would boil the sheets until they were pristine white and then cook the other dirty laundry. Tuesday was dust-the-entire-house and scrub-the-floors day. That included beating out the floor rugs as well. Then she would go through the house and polish the brass doorknobs until they gleamed like glass Christmas balls. Wednesdays had Jo sitting with Molly in the kitchen and scrubbing the silver cutlery until it mirrored her reflection. Every day had an allocated duty.

"Jo! We are really late – the first day of Shearing and all. Mr Charlie will really not be happy!" Sally quickly tidied the toilet things she used for Andi. "I've done breakfast; go and see Molly and check what to do," she called as she flew from the room.

Cleaning up after other people definitely got old very quickly. Jo was totally over it! "Why did I get stuck with the maid-stuff? I'd really like a horse ride," she muttered sulkily.

* * *

Jo looked wistfully up at the open double French-doors, longing to don her jeans and hard helmet, and jolted as her eyes met Sophie's. She had on a pretty blue riding habit with a smart little jacket. "I could organise a break for you... from the *maid-stuff*," she giggled hideously.

Jo couldn't believe her audacity. How dare she step in here? She felt a territorial tremor. Mainstar was Sally's home! Her's even: for now. She had no right to come in acting all high and mighty! "I don't think so!" Jo spat out, "I have to help Sally."

"Oh yes, I know," she re-joined smoothly. "But the gentlemen need some morning tea."

"Before six in the morning?"

"...and some lunch freshly made - delivered to the shed. We wouldn't expect them to eat what the Shearers have, now would we?"

"Well, feel free to help out and take it to them. You know the way."

"Oh, that is ridiculous. I'm not the House Help.   Besides, you're the maid who so desperately wants a change."

Jo looked at her again. She felt violated that she had overheard her personal gripe. Sophie wasn't much older than herself. Her dark wavy hair was braided up ready for her ride. She would have been quite pretty except for the arrogant twist of her mouth. She reminded Jo of the snobby clique at her high-school. If they were at school Sophie would be their ringleader. She was obviously used to getting her way. "Give me a break! You're unbelievable." said Jo exasperated.

"And Molly said you were to come with me. There is no one else. It's shearing time," Sophie said with a tilt of her head, as if she had engineered the whole thing to her complete satisfaction.

Jo realised she wasn't being offered a choice. Great. "I'll have to go and see Molly." Jo left the room in a twirl and got to the kitchen in double quick time. The pretty blue jacket was right behind her. It was like she thought she was already mistress of this house.

Jo paused at the kitchen door. Sitting at the huge table was Bluey, the Shearers' cook. The thin, faded blue singlet didn't seem big enough for his bulk. Holes had worn through across his back. His ginger red hair stuck out at wild angles like it was trying to jump off his head. "Molly, ole-girl," he said as he was slurping through a mouthful of some delicacy, "My Molly – you just gets besser and besser every year. This is the bess pie I has ever tasted!" He shovelled in another humongous mouthful and continued talking around it without pausing for breath. That was quite a feat when Jo realised, he was missing his front teeth. "Now no use s-trying to get me the recipe, Mol'… those brutes don't appreciate real classy grub like this. And even if that were the case… I couldn't none handles it like you – you're a genius – yes ma'ams!" he declared with a lisp.

Molly stood coyly by him, her bulky frame balancing yet another plate of sliced pie in hand. "Oh, I know you. You're just say'n it to have the best feed you get all year. Now you try this. It's Mulberry pie with my special pastry. The mulberries were a bit dry this year so it may not seem so sweet…"

Bluey grabbed it with both hands. "Well Mols. You know I'm honest. They don't just say I's the best taste-tester these parts knows for nothin'." He paused as he savoured the bouquet and rolled the first spoonful delicately on his tongue. He looked thoughtful; he was choosing his words.

Molly was becoming agitated. "Oh dear, I was right. I reckoned we should have thrown them to the pigs. Well, never mind – they can have it now!"

"Hangs on there, Mol. You don't rush an artist. Yours the painter, I'm the looker," he said with a twinkle in his rough eye. "And you also know I's likes to looks slow." Molly stopped half stride to the pig-bucket and waited. "A hint of lemons… nah, it's has to be's lime."

"Yes, that's right. The limes were good this year. Nearly half a cup from each one."

"And… cinnamon … hmm … who would 'ave thought…" Molly listened expectantly. "Oh Mol. Yeh, you might be right. You might want to give it to pigs," he shovelled another mouthful of pie, as if it was not yet quite decided, winking at the girls by the door. Molly looked completely ashamed that her pie was caught out. She resumed her trip to the pig-bucket, pie poised on her hand. "…yes siree, them swine at the shearing shed would be right appreciative. Nah Mol, that would be wrong!

You can't throw away art. You feed it to the bosses. It's them mulberries. Plumped out nice they 'ave."

Molly was so relieved. Her shoulders relaxed and her face slowly beamed a glorious smile. "You think so – it's okay?"

"*Okay* it ain't. Pure art it tis," he said definitely as he chased the last crumbs around the plate.

"You know Bluey, I have a dozen of these pies…"

"No way! Them blessed lucky blokes. Oh, to be a boss-man."

"I'll treat your men. They work right hard…"

"That they do ma'am. That they do. You are like an Angel of Mercy to 'em."

Molly put the pies already packaged up, unceremoniously on the table. Jo was amused. These pies had been in the pantry from the cooking frenzy yesterday. She understood now why there *had* to be so many. Molly looked up and saw her grinning. She hustled Bluey out the door like she was sweeping the floor. "Now git your ugly face outa here. We has work to do!"

He disappeared so quickly with his arms piled high with pies, that Jo was not really sure they had really witnessed their flirty game, except Molly's round face was flushed pink.

Molly turned to Jo; her voice grumpy. "Now where have you been? Miss needs you to ride down to the sheds with her. I have the tea things here. All hands are welcome, even if Sophie is a Betancourt, so take these and get moving."

"Sophie *Betancourt*?" Jo looked at the blue jacket with fresh eyes. She hadn't actually realised they were father and daughter.

"Yes," she said triumphantly, with a toss of her dark eyelashes. "Who did you think? Of course, I am Sophie Betancourt."

Jo gaped at her. The villain's daughter was a spoilt, dark haired beauty with more arrogance than a proud sea-going leisure cruiser. "It wouldn't be proper for me to go anywhere without a chaperone."

"To visit your father? That's completely dangerous."

She laughed delightedly. "Didn't you realise that shearing sheds are full of… shearers?"

"Oh, give me a break! Get someone else to baby-sit you." Jo said again, and she turned to leave. Jo felt she was being treated like a kid. She paused at the door, "Molly, what time do we have to deliver the morning tea? It's early yet." Jo eyed Sophie curiously.

"The first run finishes at half-nine. So, you need to have it to Bluey half before. Give him a hand to have the kettle boiled and tea things ready. This being your first time though, you go down now and have a look around and get a feel of how it is. You won't have time later. Then you come back and help Sal before you get the lunch things. Then smoko is at three. Get back here pronto for Dinner. All things are *go* at Shearing Time Miss. They don't mess with waiting around. Blue'll show you how things are down there. Mr Robert left a horse at the stables for you with the one for Miss Sophie." The door clanged shut as Molly shoved a bundle of stuff into her arms and pointed around the back to the stables.

"I know you're new here," said Sophie quite mysteriously as they went to their horses. "But you won't work your way into this place."

"I get worked into the ground, that's all," mumbled Jo. She turned to Sophie and said, "Why are you so sure?"

"Because I know. I've heard you talk to your vegetable friend."

"Andi's sick and she is not a vegetable!"

Sophie shrugged. "Irrelevant really. My father is here to offer some solutions for Mainstar's affairs. What is going to happen is going to happen. You are not in that picture."

"Yeah, I bet you know so much because your father always consults you on business!" said Jo tartly. She couldn't see Horrible-Horace consulting anyone.

Sophie was taken aback. Briefly. Quickly she smiled at Jo. "You're not so dumb really. I like that. Even in the house-help. Of course, he would not consult with me. He has no idea I am even interested in business. But I am. More interested than my brother – who couldn't earn a dime to save his own life! Thomas has only one concern: writing stupid stuff for the newspaper. Besides, Father leaves things around and I just happen to see them."

"That's not very good manners – reading confidential stuff."

"Poo. I have to learn somehow. Mainstar is going to be my tutorial. That is why I talked Father into letting me come. It's not for the fresh air and horse riding at all."

"How inspirational," said Jo sarcastically, "someone who believes a female is capable of more than cooking, cleaning and looking ornamental." Jo tugged on the saddle. She had to get on the horse. It turned around and nipped her thigh and then shied away as she struggled to heave herself up. Her boot evaded the jangling stirrup as the saddle edged further and further away. The horse suddenly seemed to grow far beyond his fifteen hands high.

"I'm no good at cooking or cleaning. And I'm not going to let them even realise I am *more* than ornamental. They would never believe me anyway… well, not until I own all this! Then they will understand what they missed by not investing in me!"

Jo looked up from where she was juggling the saddlebags Molly had filled with the things she needed to deliver. If nothing else, she felt she had to give a begrudging measure of merit for her uncompromising confidence. She tried to look confident also. This horse was obviously retired, the only one left in the paddock that was not needed for work. It was not taking kindly to being put back into service by a novice jiggling tea bags around his flanks. It shied again. Sophie grabbed the bridle.

"Thought you said you could ride?"

"Never did. Said I would *rather* ride than being stuck inside cleaning all the time."

"Riding is so… simple! You really only have to stay seated. The horse does all the work. So… you have no idea?" She raised her eyebrows as if she found that insight quite compelling.

Sophie strapped the bundle of saddlebags on the back and held her steady as Jo struggled into the saddle. Sophie even led the horse around the yard a couple of times, giving basic instructions about stirrups and bridles. She tossed the reins over its head and told Jo how to hold it. Sophie was an accomplished horsewoman. She didn't even ride side-saddle – she sat astride.

Jo turned to ask her a question and saw a particularly sadistic twinkle in her eye. Sophie slammed her riding crop down on the old horse's rump and it retrieved every ounce of energy it had been storing up for a greener pasture. It took off like the space shuttle launching. It tore through the gates as if the whole human space mission was reliant on this one successful lift-off. It galloped over the dusty track leaving a trail like space pilots tracking through Earth's atmosphere. Jo clung to its mane, hanging on for her life as it took off down the track and over a farmer's specially engineered culvert of side-by-side roughly sawn timbers. It jumped a bumpy ditch and Jo felt her whole awareness reduce to slow motion.

It veered off the track under a low hanging branch, as it loomed closer. Jo tucked her head down low beside the horse's neck and clung on grimly. "Evil beast! You saw that coming. I'm not going anywhere!" yelled Jo in its ear. The retired nag surged forward in a conceited attempt to be youthful again. Jo had lost her footing completely and squeezed her knees tightly to gain traction. She felt the throb of the horse straining under the saddle. The leather strap entangled in the mane registered with her fingers and she cautiously tugged the reins. Unaccountably he seemed to exert himself to go even faster. She closed her eyes and wished a stop button to appear. When no panel of electronic controls manifested between its ears, she lessened the tension on the reins and surrendered to a full rip-roaring gallop. So much for riding! Well, at least she was aware enough to realise she was staying on.

They tore past the Shearer's quarters and Bluey lifted his head from the buckets he was filling from the tank to shake his head in amazement. He knew a run-away horse when he saw one. He noticed the leisurely canter of the Betancourt girl riding casually up the track behind the dust cloud. He gathered his things inside and dried his rough hands on a faded grubby tea towel. Bluey jumped on his own horse and cut across the paddock to the shearing shed.

As Bluey reined in his saddle horse at the yards near the shed, he spotted the retired nag. It stood in a trembling lather beside the wooden fence underneath a shady old Pepperina tree. Jo was lying frozen on its neck, clinging to its mane. Bluey gently prized her off the saddle. She hit the ground on her feet and her knees gave way. He caught her and steadied her stance. "Now Miss… let me just say that was the smartest class of riding me's seen in a while. That young fancy Miss wants to bully you right out of her picture. Be cool and jus' look like you enjoys the challenge." He winked and gave a toothless grin. "We'll just go about getting the tea things out 'n ready. It'll drive her nuts to thinks she didn't win."

Jo nodded mutely. The half sniff of toleration she had almost allowed *Miss* Sophie Betancourt was torn off by the wind that ripped through her hair on that maniacal horse ride. Forever. She was never to be trusted. Bluey handed her a canvas bag hanging up under the tree. "Here Missy. Takes a drink and we'll gets all set up before her ladyships can even turn around."

* * *

8.

The smell of sheep arrested Jo's senses. Dogs were barking and men whistling directions. She was looking at a sea of white, bleating unhappy sheep. A thin brown dog with a white patch over his eye jumped up and ran over the backs of the sheep to the shade of the shed and helped itself to a drink. "Rusty – ya mutt! Get over 'ere!" Someone yelled and whistled at the kelpie. He obediently ran back over the woollen carpet of sheep's rumps, eager to do his master's bidding.

"See them jumbucks – come straight here from the washing pool. Once they dry out, their job's to get the wool off their backs – into the bale, as quick as they can. That's it. Our job is to keep everyone fed with the least fuss possible. If they don't see us, we done our job."

Jo smiled. Sally was much better at being invisible than her. She went to walk inside and Bluey reined her in with his big ginger paw. "Naah now Miss. You won't be going inside. That's not allowed."

"I just wanted to have a look around. I won't get in anyone's way."

"Nope. This is as close as you get. They have rules. We stay out here," Bluey said patiently. "Shear'n's the most important time of the year. The bosses all have short fuses and they'll blow like a stick of dynamite as quick as look at ya. So, don't take it none too personal. We just keeps the food coming and their tea hot. Mostly I handle that, but Molly — she'll be sending stuff down for the bosses' smoko every day. Just giving you the lay of the land."

* * *

Suddenly Sophie appeared in the doorway wearing an exhilarating wind-blown look. She stepped boldly into the shed, straight into where the workers were running to and fro. Shearers were lined up on the board, calling for this and that. Some were dragging sheep from a small pen behind where they stood, while others were shoving cleanly shorn sheep down the chute. The shearers were all were at various stages of removing the fleece at lightning speed using antiquated hedge trimmers. Some were yelling for a roustabout to keep their pen full. "Sheepo!" they bellowed as they tossed the shorn sheep down the chute and added one more to the tally.

They dived in to retrieve the last sheep in their holding pen.

A shout went up: "Duck on the pond!" and everything came to a screeching halt. The shearers down their shears and stood still. There was a woman in the shed! A couple of men went outside and pulled out smoking pipes, perching on the yard-rails like birds. Sophie flicked her hair in disgust and went out the back to the wool classing area. She stood at the door watching the workers sorting and picking through the fleece tossing tangled burrs and daggy bits into baskets. A large boxy contraption dominated centre stage. It had swirling ornate pin striping featured on the sides. Two men heaved on levers pressing the clean fleece into an enormous canvas lined box. There was growing mountain of canvas bales with "MAINSTAR" stencilled on the side waiting to be loaded onto the drays for the wool markets.

The overseer, a mean looking fellow in a broad brimmed hat quickly accosted Sophie. "Ma'am! I am going to have to ask you to leave!" He looked as if a carrier of the pox had infested his shed. "You cannot be here. You must go now."

"I am not hurting anyone. I am only looking around," she said curtly.

"I would have to disagree Ma'am. You are disrupting the whole operation. The men won't work with a lady in the shed. You have to go."

She huffed and grunted and flounced outside. She looked suspiciously at Jo and said accusingly, "You didn't wait for me!"

Oh, she had to be kidding! Jo suppressed a growl and turned away so Sophie would not see her face as she held onto the uneven timber rail, her knuckles turning white. A rough splinter dug into her palm. She hardly noticed it; she really wanted to slug her lights out! Bluey's advice echoed in her ears: *"You jus' look like you enjoyed the challenge and be cool. It'll drive her nuts to think she didn't win."* Jo took a deep breath and said quietly, "Molly said we were not to dally. I had somewhere to go – so I went there," and then she busied herself helping Bluey. The men would arrive any second with their minds full of business and shearing. They would want their cuppa tea.

* * *

Jo walked the horse over to the Shearer's quarters with Bluey. "So, where's the high and mighty town-girl?" he asked.

"Sophie? Oh, she decided she needed to learn more about shearing sheds." Jo said with deliberate nonchalance.

Bluey nodded. "She needs to learn well enough… but not about Shearing sheds."

Jo smiled. She made a private pact to stay right out of Sophie's way. Bluey looked at Jo with an appreciative eye. "Now, I was just wantin' to tell ya, you have a natural seat for that horse. To stay on that there 'ol nag was quite somethin' to get an eye full of. Now no offense intended, but I was wondering if you'd be like'n some hints for next time you to go galloping past when the bosses need their smoko so urgent like?"

Jo looked surprised. She never expected this benevolence. The tough old nut was as soft as butter. "If you could teach me to ride properly, that would be so great!" Jo enthused. "I love horses that's why I asked Mr Robert if I could ride sometime. But I had sorta meant like a lesson, because I only rode a pony on holidays...and not very often."

"You don't needs teaching… I say you a natural. Just a few pointers and you's be good as any 'round 'ere."

"All right!" Jo glowed with delight! She knew Bluey was exaggerating through his toothless front gums, but it felt nice he was willing to protect her self-confidence.

"Well, I know you's busy and 'ol Molly will get her draws in a tangle if you don't show on time… so here's the plan. Every time on your way to the shed, stop in 'ere for a second and we'll go down together. I'll tell ya a few things to practise on the ways."

He went through an abbreviated Bushman's Riding Lesson: the mount-dismount – without the Sophie launching plan. He told her how she should bear weight on the stirrups, toes forward; stopping and getting him to canter. And then finally he said, "Now just you remember you are in charge here. Not him. If ya want's him to stop, you make sure he stops. Horses are just likes kids they is… never too old to thinks theys can get away with anything that takes their fancy. And if he charges off again, ya pull the reins 'round tight so he's got to eat da saddle. Can't be taking off in one direction, if he's facing the other way, now can he?"

With that final undignified advice Jo pointed the old horse's nose towards the homestead and he reluctantly returned to the homestead. The first thing she would ask Molly is what the old horse's name was. Jo felt he deserved the self-respect of being called by name, given the morning he'd had.

* * *

9.

Every day Jo grew more confident. Musket unofficially became her very own horse. No one else could be bothered with him. He was old and grouchy. "Too long in the tooth" was their unanimous opinion, but Jo adored his enduring spirit.

She talked Billy into pulling a carrot or turnip from the kitchen vegetable garden, so she would have a treat in her pocket every morning. Billy was very generous in his gifts for old Musket. His growing affection for Goldilocks made him devoted and loyal. "Billy, Molly said we could only take the old tough turnips," Jo said to him as the tender shoots of a baby carrot found its way into her hand. "I'm sure Musket will love this, but we better stick to the rules… just old tough ones… for a tough old horse. These little ones might give him a belly-ache…"

Somehow Jo found time to groom Musket's dull coat. He began to look less dishevelled and surly. She had restored him to his rightful place in the animal hierarchy of the Station, and the old glue-pot began to sense his useful days were not over. They had a unique understanding, and her ride with Musket became the bright spot in Jo's day.

The sheep-station routine was constant. Jo continued to help Sally nurse Andi, spooning her broth as she talked about the stuff she had to do in helping at the homestead. Nothing could hold up the shearing routine. She'd wave to Bluey as she rode past the quarters or stop to give him something Molly deemed he could not do without. Only occasionally did he give her hints on riding now. "You'se got a good seat Miss. Done right well. Ol' Bluey knows a natural when he sees one."

Sophie hung around like a bad smell on a hot, still day. Jo made no effort to pretend to get along with her. Sophie was constantly asking questions of the men, pretending to be really dumb and then turning away, looking so smug as she clocked up another answer on her private tally board of things to research. "Not that asking questions is bad," admitted Jo to Musket one day on her way to the shed, "it's just she is so under-handed. Sly – that's it. She's definitely got an agenda... and the blokes have no idea they're helping her play her hand. Just wish I knew what her game-plan is." Jo suspected it would include more than just exposing herself to the wonderful masculine world of sheep farming.

That night they made their way over to the little slab hut to settle Billy in bed, and Jo asked Sally what she thought. Sally said nothing until they got inside. She lit the lamp and hung it on the hook above the table. She sat down on the rough bush timber chair at the table and ran her hand through her hair in a tired gesture. "How is what you are asking any different from Miss Sophie's questions? We're above the likes of her and her methods."

Jo was stung by the rebuke. "Well, I don't want to see Mr Robert hurt!"

Sally shrugged. "Oh, don't be ridiculous. Mr Robert would see through whatever her agenda is. She is a spoilt little girl. And not a very clever one!"

"That's just what she wants people to think. But she is smart. She is too clever to let anybody know exactly how it is."

"How could she hurt Mr Robert?" Sally obviously thought the man was invincible. She stirred uncomfortably. "Do you think that she is not after Mr Charlie after all?" she said recalling the meal-time flirting.

Jo looked at her. Could Sally really be so innocent? "Well, I was thinking more like she was after… Mainstar Station."

"Of course. Who doesn't want Mainstar? But she's a woman." Sally's eyes held shadows of resignation. This was a painful reality of life. There was no threat here.

"So? I think that for Sophie, maybe it is especially because she *is* a woman. It's like a dare; and she'll do it just to prove that she can. I understand that part, you know."

"What part?"

"The part where people think just because we're female, we're incompetent and have no potential. Don't you get sick of that?"

"Why – no one thinks I'm stupid."

"But we get stuck with all the lousy jobs, because we don't wear trousers. I think that's unfair."

"Which jobs would you prefer?"

"Well, more of the outside ones, maybe."

"You ride every day – and you don't have get all filthy and sweaty because you are a 'girl'. That's a benefit, not a handicap."

"Sally, how can you really like what you do?"

"I like what I do because… I don't know. Well, it keeps Billy and me in our home. My family's important. Besides, I'm good at what I do. Not many women my age get to manage a station household. Mr Robert respects that."

"Mr Robert?"

"Well, Mr Charles too, of course."

"O'oh! You're sweet on Mr Robert!" said Jo with a grin. Sally blushed and squirmed a little. "You are so! It's written all over your face."

"Well, nothing can ever come of it, so don't go 'n make a big deal of it. At least I can look after his homestead."

"If it *is* his homestead – for much longer," said Jo firmly. "Betancourt has shown up here because he can make a killing." Jo was ruthless in her honesty. "But I reckon Miss Sophie is ambitious enough to try for the whole thing herself. Not just to pull it apart necessarily, but to run as her own."

"How can you really believe that? Sophie knows nothing. Besides, everyone knows Betancourt's speciality is stripping places bare and selling them off. I don't believe he'd help Miss Sophie buy Mainstar when he can get more money pulling it apart."

Jo looked at Sally quietly for a while. Her mind was whirling with all these thoughts. Sally shook her head bewildered. Change was always hard, but when it was painful, rotten, displacing change, it almost seemed impossible to handle. Suddenly Jo jolted upright. "I have been completely wrong about this! You are so clever. I never saw it!" Jo looked as if she had just completed a thousand-piece jigsaw puzzle.

Sally looked at Jo blankly. "You mean he *would* buy it for his daughter. My father would have done anything for me, I know... but...."

"No that's just it. Horace the Horrible hasn't got a clue what his little girl is about. He's completely underestimated her passion for business. He's never given her any opportunities so Sophie wants to prove she is as clever as any of her father's associates... or her brother. Better in fact. She'll show him that she can do it... with or without him! But I bet she is working on doing it without him. She wants to impress *Daddy*!"

Sally visibly flinched. "Wow. I've heard of a woman doing a business like this down in the city. But I wouldn't be game – not by myself. It can get so ugly..." It was like Sally was trying on a new pair of shoes. If Sophie could think about it… perhaps… just maybe… Sally got up shaking her head and readied her bath. She poured cold water from an enamel pitcher into the metal tub. Jo left her to attend to her ablutions.

Jo had a nightly date with Billy while Sally had her bath and then went back to stay overnight with Andi. They would sit on their rough bush timber twin-seat swing on the verandah. He would show her some treasures he found on his daily trips around the scrub and farm, then they'd read a story together. One day he brought her some emu feathers and an old emu egg he had blown out. Its dark emerald shell, dimply smooth, felt cool as she held it against her cheek. Another day, he presented a mat of velvet mosses he found in The Gully. Jo looked forward to seeing what wonderful treasures he would bring her next time.

Sally dipped the soap and mused as she lathered her arms. Why couldn't things stay the way they were. Secure and comfortable… where people knew where they stood and there was no subterfuge. Jo was probably bored. Her imagination had to think up exciting plots to stave off her upper-class appetite for amusement. Life was not like that here. Sure, there were tough times. But people got through them: intact, together. She was living testimony to that.

Tough 'stick-ability' was what Sally was good at. It was part of her Irish heritage. Her father told her so many times; especially after the accident, when he realised, he was not going to make it. "Sally-girl," he would whisper through fever-hot lips, as she moistened them from the thick brim of a mug, "You're like your mother, tougher than iron and softer than down. That's more precious than sapphire jewels, my girl," he said as he gave Sally her mother's ring with a sapphire he had prospected before they got married. He had it made into their wedding ring. "Just you remember, Sally-girl. You're my 'Blue-eyed Irish belle' – you've got what it takes: stick-ability. Don't let anyone tell you otherwise. You're a gem. God's got good plans for ya girl. He's your Father now that he's ask'n me to come home. He won't let ya down."

She sat, knees bent, soaking in the water, gently pouring cool rivulets over her body, relaxing in the quiet of the evening. Funny, she had not thought about that in a long time. God was very real to her tough Bushman father. He taught her to read from the Bible, his finger tracing the words on dog-eared pages. "Words of life — they are, Sally-girl. Better than spring water when you're feeling right dried out and cracked up like an old empty dam."

Other fellas used to call him the poet-parson; he was an artist who put his thoughts into little pictures painted with words. They would go to the little bush church once a month, and he would read to the modest congregation a poem he had written. She would be amazed as the ladies would go up to her father afterwards and dab their eyes with their Sunday-best linen 'kerchiefs, "Will McBride, God has given you a gift. He just touched my spirit so, when you read that poem." She remembered the little pedal organ that her Mum used to puff and paddle her way through the hymns. That was before Billy was born. The whole world changed after Billy was born.

"Oh God," she prayed quietly as she poured water over her hot flushed face. "I have not been remembering You. Pa said You had plans for me… good plans. I want to see them come to be. I want to be the kind a person my

Pa would been proud of. And God… please God, protect us. Protect us and our home."

Suddenly Sally sat upright in the bath. "Oh my," she gasped with a revelation. "I never!" She hurriedly grabbed a towel and yelled to Billy who was outside on the verandah with Jo. They had been reading a story from Billy's precious single volume of fairytales, by the light of a hurricane lamp. It became a nightly routine that they really enjoyed. "Goldilocks and the Three Bears" was still his favourite. Jo finished the story and closed the book. She turned and growled at Billy with fake ferocity. "…and now I'm going to gobble up all your food!"

Billy grinned. "Goldilocks, you don't scare me… I made your nose bleed everywhere," he said gazing at the stars, and he pointed out The Big Dipper. "We could make a lot of porridge in that saucepan," he said. "Enough for everyone!"

"Billy, your bath is ready. Better come — early start tomorrow." Sally dried herself and slipped on her coarse yellowed nightgown, and sat down with Jo under the stars, while Billy dragged himself inside.

"Now, I don't know if you're imagining this stuff or not, but I'm thinking that Misters

Robert and Charlie would handle things alright. But I know he's stressed and he's spend'n hours over books and figures. It's just I remembered something that I hadn't thought anything about before… but your Miss Sophie wanting to prove herself and all, made me think…" she paused as if just thinking such thoughts was scandalous.

Jo shook her head. "*My* Miss Sophie. I don't think so."

Sally took a deep breath as Jo's eyes riveted on her face. "Well, the other morning early, when you were so dead beat, I let you sleep beside Andi's bed. That morning… I was coming back from the tank out back o' the homestead. I saw Miss Sophie talking with a shearer. It was hardly light and they hadn't started the first run at the shed yet, but by his get-up he was one of 'em."

"Who was he?" asked Jo curiously.

"I don't know. I don't have much to do with the Shearing gangs. But I do know that they looked right friendly together," said Sally.

"A shearer wouldn't be able to buy a station. Wouldn't she want to link up with someone with money?"

"Shearers do okay. The good ones, anyhow. Most of them blow it all on booze and two-up, just as soon as they cut out of a job. They hit the pub and it's all gone before they start the next job. Have heard of a few doin' good though. If he was one of them types and he'd been workin' for a while, he'd be able to make a good deposit. 'Specially if we had to sell up cheap."

"Huh." Jo sat swinging the bush seat, musing over this new perspective on shearers. "That would make sense hey? Independent backing for Sophie."

"Then why is she all over Mr Charlie, if she already has her heart set on a shearer?"

"Well, it could be she's fishing for information. Mr Charlie has no money, so it's not like he's an option, is he?" said Jo matter-of-factly.

"That's all very well, but it doesn't change the plight of Mainstar. The likes of us can't do anything. We're like ants..." Sally rolled her eyes in despair.

"No! You can't think like that! Something good might happen. It's got to."

Sally looked at Jo amazed. "Really – out of thin air? My Pa would tell me God has good plans for us… but it doesn't seem good to me. He loved to pray to Him… used to sit with him for hours sometimes… down there overlooking The Gully."

"Huh." That was freaky. Another person with faith like Andi. Was she some sort of religious magnet that attracted these types? It wasn't lost on Jo that Andi was in bed barely able to move, and Sally was on the verge of losing her home. "Do you talk to him?"

"God? I try. But I haven't in ages. I just get so busy… I'm not like Pa."

Jo looked at her friend in the quiet of the bush night. The yellow dim light of the lantern cast faded shadows around where it hung. Her heart ached for her, and the life she led. Sally never complained and she counted her blessings. "It sounds like your Dad was a wonderful man. I doubt he would give you a bum-steer, so I guess you can trust that if nothing else."

"I haven't read the Bible in a long time," she said as if that explained everything. "Pa used to say they are words of life."

"Yeah… God's words." Jo quickly got up. She didn't get it when Andi went on about 'The Words of God' being alive and powerful. So much for that. She was the best Christian Jo knew, yet she was lying in the Homestead barely alive. And now here was another person who said the same thing… or her Dad did. "I gotta have my bath: Billy's finished. Any time you think you could talk to God, say a word for me and Andi too." Jo stood up stiffly. Her arms and legs seemed weighed with lead. She needed sleep. She left to ready herself for bed.

Sally sat still for a while in the quiet of the bush night and soaked in the warm evening air. She stood and gave Billy a goodnight hug before she grabbed the lantern and made her way back to the homestead. She trod along the dark track that was familiar and worn and whispered a shy prayer. She was quietly amazed that she felt comforted by an awareness that God had been there all along, waiting for her to talk again.

* * *

10.

When the shearing finally cut out, it was over as quickly as it had started, and Mr Robert gave the girls the morning off. Jo rode Musket down to the deserted quarters to say good-bye to Bluey as he was finishing up. She wanted to thank him for the help he had given her. She suspected she might not have survived her first shearing experience quite so painlessly if it wasn't for his support.

"Another shed, another pound," he lisped philosophically. "I don't suppose you got much idea of what goes on behind the scenes hey Missy. Not that ya needs to know either," he concluded. He seemed down in the mouth.

"Bluey, "she said, "Thank you for saving me from dying an untimely death. Your lessons helped me with Musket more than you will admit. And, hey! I've brought you something that'll make your day. The best for the best. Molly gave me this to give to you." She handed him a large, plump, sweet-crust apple pie. "She said she would've given it to you herself, but she is really busy."

"Yeah, and flies don't hang around dead meat," said Bluey disgustedly. He didn't even seem to want to try the pie.

"What do you mean?" Jo knew it was a favourite.

"She's right shamed of this coarse old brute. If she'd wanta – being busy would not stop the likes o' her. She'd never be seen dead near this 'ere shed, or its coarse 'ol mess cook and that's the truth. But this shearin' has given me more than just money in my pocket. It is who I am."

"You're kidding – right?" He grunted and went back to stashing some things in his wagon. Jo persisted. "You reckon she won't come because you're a shearer's cook?"

"Well, she got her respectable Homestead and her respectable bosses. I reckon she just can't swallow the likes of me."

Jo stood up and laughed at him. "Bluey, I reckon Molly's right! She said you were as dense as two planks! Bluey! How could you miss it? She's as sweet on you as that apple tart of hers. She cooked three before it was good enough! How's that?"

"Well, the only ol' tart around 'ere, ain't the eatin' kind. She won't come and tell me her case."

"You're kidding – of course."

"Do I look like I'm kidd'n'?" he responded indignantly.

"Well, you should be! Molly's been muttering since you landed here…" Jo picked up rolling-pin from a wooden box of stuff and started waving it about. She emulated a very Molly type voice, "I's not been a chasin' floozy type and I ain't gunna start now. A man's got ta earn his rewards. The state of courtin' petticoat, ah – I mean, etiquette, now-a-days will give our dear Queen Victoria a real ugly seizure that'd break her heart and die, if she knew the truth…and what's more I's buried one gentleman husband and I's'll die a poor lonely widow if it takes being down right cheap to be getin' another in these times."

Bluey hunched his bulky shoulders and stared at Jo in disbelief. "You think she'd want me to go callin' to the big house?"

"Yeah, why not. She really likes you."

"Why not – 'cause she gives a little, first up and then sweeps me out the door like dirt. Can't pick it ya know. Bein' doin' it for years."

"Well, no wonder. It looks like you're just after a good feed, when ya's passing through."

"Well, she does a good feed, that's for sure. And you can spin her around like a cat on a dark night…if you push and pull all her levers. She's good for a stir. Mind ya, she gives as goods as she gets."

"Do you want to know what I reckon?"

"Your goin's to tells me anyways – aren't ya Missy?"

"Molly reminds me of my Aunt Lindy… she just likes to be told… you never can't say it too often: how she does a good job and is a decent person. It makes her feel really special."

"You say'n I should tell Molly… what exactly?"

"Anything. All the time. Never stop… more the better. But you have to listen sometimes… what she's sayin' is as important as what you say to her. Aunt Lindy calls it being a 'Wordsie-person'."

"Well now that as good as stirring up a hungry cat without any cream – I ain't good with words… never bin educated like them dandies."

"Give me a break! I saw you two in the kitchen! Downright thick it was. Beautiful! Poetry in motion – how you was tellin' Molly how she could cook so well…that's all ya have to do."

"That's it?"

"Yeah. Why are you so worried? You do it all the time."

"Well, its different wringing out a piece of pie, to trying to tell her I just likes her for her."

"I don't think it's that different at all. Start with complimenting the pie… and then compliment her. Just try it Bluey. If you get no more apple-pie, my guess is..." She shrugged as she finished.

"Ahh, but if I don't bother – I don't fall on my face," he said stubbornly dumping some flour bags down so the powder puffed out of them like smoke. "…and I stay all together."

"That's really sweet Bluey. You're an ol' softie. You're secret's safe with me. But as they say: if you never, ever go - you'll never, ever know. You might be surprised."

"Wells, I can't go up there empty handed like, if she worried about what Ol' Queen Vic thinks… and I ain't got nothing like that. Can hardly take left over stew. Sometimes I don't even want to give it to me dog."

"Flowers are good."

"We're out in the middle of the scrub… where's am I gunna get flowers to go callin'?"

Jo could contain herself no longer. She laughed out right. Fancy being a romantic consultant for the oddest best-matched pair she ever met. She sobered quickly as she saw Bluey's thunderous look. "Hey, I'm just thinking you lack imagination."

"Imaginating isn't my card. I cook spuds and steak, or spuds and mutton, depending on the spread. That's it. It don't need imaginating!"

"You can feed a shed full of ravenous shearers on nothing but potatoes and haunch of mutton and they go away thinking it's the best feed they've had all season. That's creative talent if ever I've seen it. You just aren't used to thinking about this, that's all. I'm willing to give you a hand. I reckon I know where there's heaps of beautiful flowers. But it'll cost you! The bigger the quest, the harder the challenge."

"Git outa here, girl – you're chock-full of..." and he made a friendly swipe at her trying real hard to look annoyed.

"Now who's narky? Bluey, I'll get you the flowers… then you can call in on Molly real proper like. You'll have time to scrub up and everything." He stared at her wide-eyed with a filthy look, as if that extended the challenge beyond the boundaries of reasonable. Jo continued quickly, before he started to object. "You get me paper to wrap the flowers in, and I'll get you a bouquet that Queen Victoria herself would appreciate." Jo saw this as a perfect opportunity to do something for Bluey as a thank-you for his friendly support. He was an unlikely ally of the independent kind.

"Yeah, it's a deal." Bluey obviously didn't believe her resourcefulness extended to floral art – but he had no other ideas. "I'll git ya paper."

* * *

Jo grabbed a bucket, took a deep breath and dived down the narrow track to The Gully. With one thing and another, she just had never got back there. She felt the relief from the heat under the shaded trees and allowed her eyes to adjust to the dimness as she looked around; all she saw was a million green shades of coolness. Billy picked some exquisite flowers for Sally from his explorations so she knew there were flowers here. But then what? To do something like a floral arrangement seemed a little ambitious for her total lack of artistic flare. Usually Andi was the creative one. Where was she getting all these grandiose, creative aspirations? She was just happy with a ball, a playing field and her dog, Boof. Jo couldn't believe she got herself into this.

Jo followed the creek looking for spots of colour. She giggled as she thought about Billy calling her Goldilocks. The original bear's cottage hidden in the woods was found while picking wild flowers. She pinched off some long fronds of maiden-hair fern and stuffed the stems into the base of the metal bucket.

There were some tiny blue violets nodding quietly in the shade and added them to the fern. "Why haven't they invented Internet florist shops yet?" she thought looking despairingly into the bottom of the bucket. If all else fails, a pretty little posy might do. She stepped over mossy logs and walked on. A bottle-brush bush swayed over the creek-bed like a beacon. Its bright red flowers powdered with yellow on the end of its bristles, dusted the top of the water. "Oh yes, this is better!" she whispered excitedly. The fine red hairs were mutilated as she tried to break the stiff woody stems. She tried again, this time carefully snapping them off at the joints. As Jo leaned over to reach another branch laden with blooms, her foot slipped. She slid down the bank and splashed heavily into the creek.

She sat there stunned, sitting like some discarded rag doll out of Billy's storybook, with her knickerbockers and skirts floating in bubbles on top of the water. She abandoned herself to the absurdity of her ridiculous predicament and flung herself backwards, splashing in the water laughing. Her hair floated about her like river-weed and she closed her eyes enjoying the luxurious feeling of shallow water trickling over her as she lay on the sandy bed. Dappled sunlight threw patterns on her eyelids as she stretched herself out in a wide star as if somehow she could embrace all of the magnificence of this wonderful place. "How beautiful this world is. I feel like it has been made just for me," she whispered to herself. A tear trickled out of the corner of her eye and splashed unseen into the creek, as her heart seemed to rise inside her. "I want the world to be more like this…" and she knew she didn't mean just bush and nature, but how the place felt: more innocent; more whole maybe.

She opened her eyes and without warning Jo felt a blanket descend upon her, smothering the bubbles of happiness she had felt. How could she forget so quickly? What a dope to think she could do anything to ever make a difference in a world so hard and ugly drowning in trouble? Where was the hope? She blinked away tears as she gazed up into the thick strong branches of a great tree leaning over the water. Her eyes rested on the golden sprays of a bush orchid tumbling from the fork of a branch. Speckled dances of light flickered across the sprays of colour making them vibrate vividly in the breeze. A quiet voice inside Jo's heart said, *"I have made you with beautiful colours too."* She lay quietly in the water for a long time gazing at the golden spray and absorbing the implications that such a thought offered. She thought about it. Was the orchid worried about the enormity of the task even though it had delicate petals and was stuck in one place? Did it feel responsible to do anything more than to beautify its surroundings just by being itself? If there were no orchids that just did what orchids did, the world would miss an incredible amount of beauty. More ugliness would prevail.

She slowly sat up in the water determined to make the orchid spray the centre of Molly's bouquet. She slipped off her voluminous skirts and wrung them out. She couldn't move in them anyway. She draped them over some shrubs and then started to climb the tree. It felt so good to be scrambling up over the branches – hand over hand, branch over branch, keeping the orchid in sight. In no time three perfect sprays were within reach; so easy. She prised them free and lowered herself down backwards.

Jo paused as a movement caught her eye and steadied her balance by leaning her foot against a fork in the branch. Sophie and a young man emerged from under the dim shadows of the undergrowth. They were deep in conversation and talking very seriously. There were no coy glances and no giggly little flirtations. Jo watched fascinated; this was a different look for Sophie. She was dressed for an outing in a long blue skirt and the inevitable blue jacket, with just touches of lace over her cuffs and blouse. The young man was clean-shaven, good looking and obviously used to physical work. Was this the person Sally saw her with the other morning? Was this the financing shearer? He had on a starchy white shirt with a kerchief bulging over the collar as a tie. They made a very handsome couple. It felt like she was watching a silent movie.

Sophie stopped and started to raise her voice in frustration. It was obvious that whoever he was, he was not sharing her passion. He went to soothe her, but she pulled away, not willing to be appeased with anything less than her own way. Now she could hear snatches of conversation. "But we have the entire history at our fingertips. This gives us the advantage. You want your own place? Well, here it is… on a platter! Why should we wait? If we don't move, someone else will. Jack, I couldn't stand seeing this wonderful opportunity go elsewhere."

"But what about your father?"

"What about him? I've told you before he is not part of this. You don't want to be beholden to him for the rest of your life. And believe me, you would be. He would never let you forget it."

"Well, he's goin' to figure it out, isn't he?"

"That's why no one must know…"

"Oh great," thought Jo, "that instantly puts *me* in an awkward position…" How far Sophie would go to protect her secret? Jack stopped and said something in response, as he bent over Sophie. Jo looked down at her skirts draped over the shrubbery on the other side of the tree beside the bucket and calculated her presence would be exposed in exactly fifteen steps. She shifted her weight as her leg started to tingle from her position. She wriggled her foot, wedged deep and stuck fast. "Oh no," Jo squirmed desperately. "They are definitely going to see me."

Jo, still fresh from her encounter with the orchid spray that she cradled protectively in her hand, smiled at the irony: if I was inspired by these orchid flowers, I had not actually thought that meant grafting myself into the tree.

She leaned over and rubbed her ankle. It was aching now and had started to swell. She groaned. Again, louder. She thought it would be much better if they saw her before they got the feeling they were being watched. She leaned back and groaned some more, quite theatrically now.

Then she wailed, not very loudly, but a pathetic, "Help; please, someone help me…" By the time the couple did actually stop to try and locate the origin of the cries, Jo was genuinely feeling quite delirious with pain and powerless with self-pity.

"What *are* you doing? Why on earth are you up a tree?" Sophie stood staring up at her in disbelief.

"Sorry to bother you, but I have jammed my foot in the fork of this branch. It's swelling and I can't get it loose."

"And just how are we going to help you from down here? Stupid thing to be up a tree anyways."

"Point taken. Any ideas?"

A good-natured smirk played around Jack's mouth, but he said nothing, and quickly hid his amusement when Sophie looked to him. "Well just wriggle your foot around a bit…" Sophie was very good at telling people what to do.

"Ahh, would you believe I've been wriggling for quite a while now? I think I've just wedged it in tighter…"

Jack still said nothing… just loosen his neckerchief and handed it to Sophie. Then he slipped off his shirt and hung it carefully on a branch. It was quite obvious he found the whole thing very amusing. Sophie raised her eyebrows in scandalous disapproval. "Can't get my Sunday shirt dirty," he said by way of explanation, and scaled up the tree in his singlet.

When he reached her, she stuck out her hand. It was trembling and clammy. "Hi, my name is Jo," she said apologetically.

He took her offering in his massive calloused labourer's hand and said most courteously, "Pleasure ma'am. Jack Thacobee, at your service." His eyes told her he was completely relieved that her predicament had effectively extracted him from the heavy conversation he had been engaged in. "You're the Tea Girl helping Bluey at the shed – hey?"

"Tea Girl?" Her voice was trembling. That was a humiliating take on her job. "Yes, I guess so…"

"Come up here to escape the grind?" He suddenly became quite proficient at small talk as he slipped off his belt and started to slide it through a small slit of a gap underneath her foot. His voice was soothing… just as he might talk to a frightened horse, he was breaking in for a saddle.

"I was picking these orchids for a friend. Up was easy… the down part got me stuck."

"So, I see. Guess we'll have you back on your feet in a jiffy."

"Just be careful there," called Sophie from below. It seemed to frustrate her no end that this drama was not centring on her solutions.

Jack continued his quiet talk unperturbed. "Lucky we happened on… you could've been here 'til hell gone froze over, before someone found ya."

Jo tried to think of some clever response. She couldn't. She sensed he was not exaggerating her predicament. "Well, guess I am lucky then."

He looked up at her from where he was working the leather strap under her foot for extra leverage. "Huh. Or someone's lookin' out for you… now hold on to that branch there with both hands… tight now."

He gave the strap a sharp heave as her foot flew loose. Jo screamed with pain!

"Sorry 'bout that. No other way, short of chopping the whole tree down. You're right now. Come down."

"Could you take these? They are very precious." Jack took her orchids. They looked odd cradled in the palm of his large paw. He kindly coached her down branch by branch. Jo's ankle squealed with pain. She was sure it had fractured it into a million pieces. It throbbed, and every movement sent sharp stabs of fire through her leg. Finally, he eased her to the ground. She hobbled over and dunked her ankle in the cool water of the creek. Her whole body began to shiver. As she looked at the ripples in the water around her ankle, things started to curiously change colour like a photograph negative. Then they started to spin like she was inside a tumble dryer looking out. Almost immediately the pain faded into darkness.

Somewhere, in a dreamy place, someone was calling, "Jo! Jo!" She wanted to enjoy the softness of the haze that surrounded her just a little bit longer. Why wouldn't they leave her alone? But the voice was insistent, and she thought that perhaps Bluey was impatient for his bouquet. The orchids are pretty… so pretty… Sophie… Jack… Oh!

The pain in her foot swirled up around her head again. She rolled over and was sick. Gross.

That was so disgusting. It was completely unfair that Sophie saw her like this. Why was she was constantly being humiliated in front of Sophie?

She opened her eyes and tried to sit up. Jack was sitting on his haunches cradling her head in his rough hands. Jo's face went from pale white to a bright cherry flush down her neck. She was not easily embarrassed but now she felt hot and uncomfortable. "You're not doin' too bad really. Seen mates in worse shape," said Jack as if it would be a genuine consolation to realise he had mixed it with some really serious low life. Jo did not feel at all comforted.

"Where's Sophie?" she groaned as she tried to focus again. She may have missed the semi-digested bit after all.

"I'll explain later," he said matter-of-factly with a shrug.

Jo sat up, her embarrassment flaring. "I'd appreciate you explaining now." Jack dunked his neck scarf in the clear creek water, and passed it to her. She wiped the beads of perspiration from her forehead and leant forward on her knees. Man, she felt terrible! "Sophie..." Jo didn't want to play the innocent game. She held hope in her heart that Jack was actually a decent guy. "I know you realise I heard all that."

"Oh."

"Oh? That's not an explanation."

"Hey – our business is our business! Sophie and me... it's not that easy."

"Oh no, I'm sure it's not easy."

"What do you mean by that?"

"Only that perhaps you should take your blinkers off and see her for what she is. Then I'm sure it would be eminently easier."

He shrugged. "Well she insisted that I help you..." That wasn't exactly true, but Jack was sure she *would* have, if she had thought about it.

Jo grunted. "Now I've heard everything!"

"Me and her is complicated. I ain't exactly going to be callin' for rave reviews in the social columns. I ain't socialite material."

"You are *so* duped. She wants to have her cake and eat it too... that's the only reason it's complicated!"

"This is none of your business you know. You're just a..."

"Don't you dare say it!" said Jo accusingly.

"Say what?" Jack raised his eyebrows innocently.

"That I wouldn't understand because I'm the Tea-girl!"

"Okay, but… things are not always black and white. One day you'll see a whole stack of grey around the edges you never knew existed." Jack looked at her thoughtfully. He didn't wax lyrically very often.

"Oh, that's very poetic. When you start mixing right for wrong, you can be sure you are just in for a whole lot of murky grey. Doing good by people is never wrong. We always have the option make good choices." She winced when she realised that was her Mum talking.

"So, you're a preacher-girl as well?" This time Jack smiled. She was probably disorientated from when she blacked out.

"Oh no. Far from it. I don't do religion. But it doesn't mean I don't think it is good to do right by people"

Jack was very well aware that Jo was not just talking about a sprained ankle by the creek. He was starting to lose the entertainment factor in this encounter. "That's unfair. Sophie's a very smart lady."

"Well, smart does not make it right," said Jo emphatically.

He took a punt. "So how would you handle it?"

"I know I would look after those who were in a vulnerable position. Leaving them to fend for themselves is really – disgusting." How could he be so blinded by Sophie's snake-like charms? Jack was playing right into Sophie's flute-charmer hand: she needed a lucrative backer. If she could mesmerize him with her looks, it didn't seem to matter he might only tolerate her mind.

"Well, that's why I'm here... I'm looking out for you. I'll help you back to the homestead."

"This is not just about me; you know it's not. There are others. How can you take advantage of them?" These were her friends who were being cast out and discarded.

Jack looked at her. Why did he bother explaining? He looked at the reflections in the water and took a breath. He was never good at subtle. He preferred to be straight on. "Business is business. I ain't got no intention of pulling the wool over any ones' eyes or fleecing them dry." He smiled at his corny puns. He was a shearer after all. "When this Spread is up for sale then we've got as much right as the next bloke to put in a bid. It's all above board and honest like. I ain't goin' to cut anyone out… we need 'em to make the place run. The only secret here is that Sophie and me are partners… and that's because of her Old Man. She goin' to marry me when the deals all done, but she wants to do this as business… not like husband-and-wife. I don't get that myself… makes no difference to me… but it does to her, so that's the way we goin' to deal it out."

He took a breath. He had just finished the longest speech of his entire life. Jo looked down at her ankle. Perhaps he was right. Perhaps it was just a case of the early bird catches the worm… and too bad if you're the worm.

She struggled to her feet and winced at the tenderness in her ankle. "I've got to get these to Bluey. He'll be thinkin' I've forgotten him." She leaned heavily on his arm as he grabbed the bucket. "Guess this will have to do."

* * *

11.

By the time they hobbled into the Shearer's quarters, the bucket was over flowing with an assortment of grevilleas and callistemons. She'd even added a couple of dry sprigs of gumnuts she found near the shed. "This Job had better pay well," Jack said.

"Not everything is measured in pound and pennies," Jo said curtly. "Friendship and appreciation counts in my ledger as well." That was for his benefit.

Jack just grunted. Once he would've thought that would not be payment enough… but his relationship with Sophie had shown him that sometimes even *he* would do things for the sake of enumeration that could not be counted out into his money-pin. Not that her proposal was a poor business one: quite to the contrary. Left to his own devices he would have done things differently, that's all. Sophie changed everything.

The mess hall was empty and mopped out. There was a single canvas swag left in the corner. She sat down on a long bench and lifted her ankle up beside her. It hurt so much. Why had everything turned complicated?

The rough timber table was carved with years of graffiti; on it laid a folded sheet of brown paper. Bluey was no-where to be seen. Jo stared at it in dismay. Great. Molly will be over-come with the sentiment, thought Jo sulkily. "Brown paper..." For Queen Victoria? That was disappointing. The pain in her ankle throbbed pushing her emotions to the surface. She realised that she really wanted this to be special for Molly. Her gruff ways were kind and sincere. It would be nice for her to have the extravagance of being able to say, "Wow!" for no reason other than thinking life was wonderful! The Wow-factor was pretty low at Mainstar.

Jack hung around. He shifted his feet. "Not good?" he said obviously.

"That's an understatement. When I asked for paper… I didn't think it'd be just plain brown."

"What other sort is there?"

"Tissue, coloured, patterned, floral, foiled, cellophane... anything else would have been okay."

"Well, out here, paper comes in brown, or with the news on it."

"Oh." She'd forgotten that. Cellophane was probably coming with the invention of plastic cling-wrap for school lunches. *Huh. I know how Andi felt with that grubby old basket now. I am all out of imagination. What can I do with brown paper?* Jo took a deep breath. She lifted the paper and looked at it. Underneath was some brown string. And she burst out laughing. "Bluey's thought of everything! I even have matching ribbon!"

Jack sighed in relief. It was one of his unspoken philosophies: if you can laugh, solutions will come. Not that he was a laughing type really. Things just amused him… like before. While Sophie is trying to sort out major life decisions, a squealing tea-girl up a tree interrupts them. How to kill a moment – or revive it! The smiles make it tolerable. "So, it's okay then?"

"No, it's horrible… but there must be a way. Do you have any scissors?"

"Have a pocketknife."

"I've just had an idea. Don't suppose you'd have a needle or pin or something like that?"

Jack went over to his swag in the corner and pulled out a small canvas roll. He unravelled it and extracted his pocket-knife and a large bore needle. "Us shearer's make our own moccasins."

Jo took it and then with meticulous care started pinpricking scallops, making a fine lace pattern, within it. The thick paper popped as she jabbed it with the needle over the gap in the table. Little grooves from the shaft of the needle pressed and cut into the pads of her fingers. She kept going. She had a purpose now clearly in mind.

Jack disappeared, and then not long after he returned with a cork stopper. Wordlessly he took the needle from Jo's fingers and twisted the cork onto the end over the eye of the needle. He handed it back. She stopped every so often to stretch her cramping fingers. She flipped the paper to the reverse side and looked at the pattern.   Little pinpricks formed a raised dimensional effect along the edge of the paper. Not quite in the league of Aunt Lindy's scrapbooking   pages,   but   definitely   an improvement.

Jack went over to his swag and pulled out a wide thick leather razor-strap and hooked it over a thick nail on the wall. He slashed his razor back and forwards over the leather. He flicked the metal blade with the side of his thumb, testing the sharpness. After a few more slashes back and forwards, he shaved some hair off his forearm, and then he was satisfied. He showed her how to control the blade as she cut and scalloped the edges of the pin-prinked patterns in the paper.

Next step: the flowers. Jo tried to remember how arrangements looked. There were so many arrangements after her grandfather died. She could not remember one detail. Nothing. She pulled stem after stem out of the bucket and laid them on the paper. She had no idea so she just went bulk. Then on top of the colourful pile, she laid her three precious trails of bush orchids down the centre. The scalloped laced edge of the paper folded on the diagonal, edging it like a picture frame. She wrapped the string around the base and tied a cluster of gumnuts in a bow where the paper crossed over. She stood back and looked at the bouquet and smiled. Molly had no need to feel anxious about Queen Victoria's health after all.

* * *

12.

When Jo delivered the flowers into Bluey's hands, he pressed a ten-pound note into hers. She tried to argue with him, but he just grinned his toothless smile. "If Molly realises I ain't kiddin', it'll be worth every penny," he declared, so she let it be.

Jo hopped and hobbled her way to Andi's bed. She sat down and propped her leg up on a cane chair beside her. She stroked Andi's hand and unconsciously moved her fingers and wrist around, the way Sally had shown her. Her mind went around and around. *Come on Andi, this is going on too long. Sure, Sally knows some things, but seriously… she's not a doctor, who by the way, hasn't come back. Did that mean he figured Andi was okay? Or did it mean he was too busy, or he'd given out on her?* She just didn't know. Andi seemed to sleep all the time. And when she wasn't asleep, she would prattle incoherently. Her mouth sagged at an abnormal angle and there was drool seeping from her lower jaw. Jo's eyes brimmed over. Oh God! This seems so hopeless! What's the point? Oh Andi. I miss you. It's not fair.

That God of yours, who you say loves you, well: He has a great way of showing it! I'm sorry... but that is not love in my book.

She almost swore she saw Andi smile and she could hear her say... somewhere in the recesses of her memory, "God will work it out... his way, his time". Hmmm...

Jo's eyes filled up again and dripped onto Andi's warm, clammy hand. She had never known so many tears... so many extremes of emotions. When would she get back to normal? What *was* normal? She didn't even know anymore.

Sally came in and stood by her. "I've just seen Mr Robert, "she said. "He's going to town."

"Town? Oh, can I come? Please - Bluey just gave me some money. It would be so good to get out of here for a while!"

"Money? How much did he give you?"

"Ten pound."

"Ten pound! You're kidding!" Sally looked really worried, like Jo had just got involved in something criminal.

"No... I'm not kidding."

"What for?"

"Sally – it's all above board. But if you really must know, Bluey wanted to give Molly something special, so I helped him out."

"So, what did you get her? Molly's walking around ten feet off the ground…"

"I got some flowers from The Gully."

"Flowers! But they're not even yours. Bluey shouldn't pay *you* for them."

"He didn't. The flowers were free. He just wanted to thank me for getting them… that's all. I tried to give it back. What's the big deal?"

"Well, ten pound is the big deal! Shouldn't you put the money towards what you owe Mr Robert? I'm not going to town anyway… too much to do here. Staff going to town with spending money is not very usual. Though you could ask I suppose." She doubted even Mr Robert would be that flexible. Sally's blue eyes flashed angrily as she left the room in a huff. Jo looked after her bewildered. What had she done? It wasn't her fault that Bluey was feeling extremely happy with the world and wanted to share some of his fresh fat pay with her. She shrugged. She could have argued more, and she was going to pay for some off the debt that Andi had accumulated. That was before town was an option. Suddenly Jo was very tired of being here. She wanted to go home. She wanted to wake Andi up and walk back over The Gully to June's beat up old car… and drive back into town. She looked despairingly at Andi's feverish sleep and knew she did not have a choice. It would have to play out… as Andi would say… in God's time. She would have to do what they came to do… or they could be stuck here forever.

"It would help if I knew what You wanted from me," prayed Jo sulkily. It was an unconscious pout. And there was no way that she ever thought that it actually would count as a prayer. Her ankle throbbed and she knew there was no way she would be able to manage her duties around the Homestead anyway. She might as well see Mr Robert about going to town.

* * *

They readied themselves the next morning, as the sky was still pale on the horizon. Kookaburras laughed hilariously about all the prospects of the new day. The men had loaded up the bullock dray with the last of the bounty from the shearing shed. Giant wool bales stood three high on the flat top wagon, the stencilled insignia splashed across the side of each one.

Heavy ropes held them tightly in place as they were tested one last time for any slackness.

The driver, Tom, stood by his team, his long snake of whip coiled over his shoulder, calling to the bullock-leader, Cobber, by name. Jo counted sixteen beasts in the team waiting with patience for the command of their bullocky. They stamped in the dust, unperturbed and lazy, their thick heavy necks bowed slightly under their wooden yokes, tails flicking at flies gathered over their beefy rumps. Other teams would meet up to form a convoy onto the city wool markets. It was a long trip. Tom moved almost as slowly as his team.

Finally, the shout was given. It was time to go. With no fuss Tom cracked his long whip splitting the early morning with its loud thunderous clap. "Cobber!" Tom chipped. "Cobber!" Tom called out in rapid fire, the names of each of his team and a series of commands in Bushmanese that made absolutely no sense. Jo was amazed at their reluctant and yet unwavering obedience. Cobber dipped his head and pulled. Rippling down the team, the strain was taken up and slowly the large wooden spokes on the dray wheels began to turn.

Jo leaned on the gate, taking the weight off her foot, watching with awe as the massive load wound down the track on its way to market. Mr Robert appeared by her side. "That cargo is the telling of our future. We will soon know if it is enough. Until then, life goes on. So, to town. Charlie left with Betancourt and his daughter earlier. Now it's just you and me. Billy! Get the buggy from the stables. Take the back seat out so there'll be room to bring supplies home." He disappeared into the house in a few large strides. Jo looked around to see Sally glaring at her through the dining room window, the curtains pulled slightly to the side. Why would ten pounds be so violently offensive? Jo had no idea. She hobbled back inside and finished readying herself. She was still living out of Sally's wardrobe and borrowed things. She tossed her few toiletries into Andi's old basket and tucked it into Sally's worn tapestry overnight carry bag.

Billy brought the horse and buggy around to the front. Jo went up to him. "Sally's really cross with me. I'm sorry about that."

"Sall's not cross with you Goldilocks, she's cross with herself for not being you." And he muttered to the horses in gentle undertones something about how we all want to be someone else until we are really them. Jo stared at him. Didn't Billy have the mind of an eight-year-old? Had he really hit the nail on the head so accurately? Was Sally jealous? Of her flower-money? Or that she was going to town? But Sally lived here and belonged here. She, Jo, was just travelling through. And something she heard once popped into her mind… "Out of the mouths of babes…" …something… came out of their mouths. She couldn't remember exactly how the saying ended, but she thought with a rueful smile, that it was probably more than spit and puke. "Well Billy, I'm glad you're not someone else. You're very special just the way you are."

"Sometimes Miss Goldilocks, I wish I was smart… like Mr Robert. But he *is* smart and he gets so worried about not being smart enough some times. So, I just do what my Pa says… and tried hardest with the tools God gives me… and not worry about the tools he gives to the other peoples. I just a pick and shovel person. Mr Roberts – he's a whole station man. But I hope he does good with his tool. Cause if he don't, my Pa says God will take it away and give it to someone else. And then Sally and me won't have a place to stay. That does worry Sal' a bit…"

"Billy, you just keep doing good work with your pick and shovel tools, and God will look after you and Sally where ever you are." Jo turned away and blinked her eyes hard. She had never heard anyone say so articulately, the essence of what she had learnt down by the creek: don't be concerned that someone else is a rose… or a thorn for that matter, you girl, are called to be a bush-orchid! She turned around quickly and gave Billy a big hug, before he helped her into the buggy.

* * *

Sally watched from the window as Jo propped a cushion under her ankle. She leant back under the shade of Sally's broad-brimmed hat, waiting for Mr Robert to finish gathering his documents from inside. How Sally wished she had the audacity to ask to go to town like Jo did. Jo had no idea what was proper and it didn't seem to bother her whether she conformed or not. Sally felt ripped off. Hadn't she worked hard and not complained about her meagre lot? Hadn't she helped workers out and supported them through all sorts of revolting sicknesses? And not once, had anyone offered her a ten-pound note. The distance she could make that go…oh, the wonderful things she could pamper herself with, on such an amount.

Just then she saw Mr Robert appear on the verandah. He looked at Jo in the Buggy chatting with Billy… and Sally felt a twinge in her heart as a strange looked passed over his face. Quickly he regained his composure and strode out to the gate. Sally could watch no more. Robert was only a few years older than her, but sometimes the gap was far too wide to breach. Why wasn't she a well-connected like Miss Sophie or just plain brazen like Jo? Even Molly in her pastry apron was given flowers from an admirer today. Never before had she felt so familiar, like furniture, used and taken for granted. She went back to Andi's bed. She proceeded to strip the sheets and attend to the morning ablutions.

* * *

The buggy bounced and rocked along. The pair of horses settled into a steady gait and occasionally the wheels dipped into a rut so Jo grabbed the side of the seat to balance herself.

She tried to dismiss her altercation with Sally. It is a bit of a stretch to apologise for just being yourself. Sal would get over it no doubt. Jo determined to enjoy this trip. Perhaps it would help her discover something new. She smiled at the thought that she was learning all sorts of new things out of these old-fashioned ways. June would be so proud of her.

"You look like the cat who stole the cream. Have you got a secret worth sharing?" Mr Robert's moustache wriggled happily in response to the smile that played on Jo's lips.

"I was just thinking of a friend of mine. She really loves old fashioned things. She would just love all the stuff you have around here."

"Old fashioned? We actually pride ourselves on keeping abreast of modern innovations. You make us sound quite antique."

"Sorry – I didn't mean it like that. It's just different to what I am used to. I guess to me it seems… well, grown up." She cringed. Oh well, stumble along and dig myself into a hole, Jo thought carelessly.

"Grown up? I was thinking when I came out of the house, how grown up you looked. It took me a bit my surprise. I thought you were Sally for a moment."

Jo looked the other way and rolled her eyes. Must have been a very brief moment: her and Sally were like chalk and cheese. "Sally would be pleased to know that. She thinks you don't notice her much."

"Sally? I don't remember a time when Sally wasn't around. She reminds me of my aunt's Newfoundland St John's retriever in town. Faithful and incredibly patient... yep – that's Sally."

Jo laughed outright... and then quickly checked herself. "A dog? I don't think Sal would be very flattered by the thought that she is equated with a family pet!"

"Oh no. I mean it in the nicest possible way. I love that dog."

Jo was shocked by Robert's light-hearted comparison. A family dog? Really? It seemed callus even for him. "Yeah maybe, but you don't marry dogs."

"Marry? Who's talking about marriage?" Jo refused to respond and looked out over the paddocks as they drove on. "What has Sally said to you?" Jo became absorbed in the fingers of her gloves and said nothing. "Look," Robert said again, "I don't know what she told you, but I can't explain it to her."

* * *

Sally suddenly felt a real connection with Andi, as she lay frozen on her bed, her consciousness intermittently smothered by trauma. She related to that. It was like the real her, the Sally who wanted to run and dance and laugh and sing, was lying bound by the sheets on a pallet as well. She was unable to move. Why was that? God – why is it so difficult? Why can't I be comfortable in who I am? The routine was so familiar, and as she strode through the motions, tears fell unheeded into the sheets.

Sally had taken on Jo's habit of chatting to Andi. Jo said she had read somewhere that people could still hear even if the rest of them were unresponsive. Sally had never heard of such a thing, but even if Andi was asleep, she would talk to her. It was good, having a confidential listener to get things off her chest. "Andi, you know I feel like you, so weak and unable to really be me… and yet in another way I want to be even more like you… unable to feel this pain, this rejection. I feel awful that I want that… yet I'm standing by the window and I'm watching Jo in *my* hat and *my* town dress and hugging *my* brother and sitting next to *my* Mr Robert and all I could think is: this is *my life*! She's stealing my life! I don't want to be resentful and I don't want to be mean about it, but I feel so protective. It is like I *should* be gracious and I *should* be happy that she is happy – but I can't. I can't!"

Sally was facing the window as she dipped the face-cloth in a tepid bowl of water. She angrily swiped her nose on her sleeve. She didn't see Andi open her eyes, blinking in confusion, but no longer clouded. Andi tried to say something, but the dryness in her throat made it crackle.

"Oh Andi," Sally groaned with an internal pain, "sometimes I can't work out how to keep going. I know I can't marry Robert… just because of who he is and who I'm not… but to see him with someone else would be like a form of ancient torture. I couldn't do it. First Miss Sophie comes fawning all over Mr Charlie and now Jo! It's all changing. Sometimes I wish we could stay in a time lock… just the way things were. What if Mr Robert falls in love with her and I have to end up having to be in service to them both? What could be worse? Nothing! I would rather live in the town gutters. I would have to. I couldn't stay here. Losing the farm would be a blessing. Oh dear! What has come over me? How could I say such a thing? I am so confused!"

"Huh…" a faint sigh escaped from Andi's lips. She smiled wanly. Unless a lot of things had changed, she didn't see Jo playing a part in fiancé theft.

Inside Sally's head was screaming with a bottle of who she wanted to be and what she wanted to do, tugging against what was right and proper. Those dimensions did not mix. They could never mix. The way she saw it, she was the loser. She was always the loser.

* * *

"Explain what?" asked Jo as she looked at the caterpillar on Robert's lip quiver unexplainably. He studied the horses in the harness with concentrated intensity.

"I can't explain why we could never marry. My father expects that we marry… to …." He paused and swallowed.

"I thought your father died."

"He wrote it into his last will and testament. We are to marry women of means – he even specified the dowry. And if we don't – we will be cut out."

"You told Sally *that*!" Jo was mortified.

"No, I didn't tell her! *He* never even told me. I only found out when his will was read… after Sal had nursed him for years. She was always so good to him. He knew I had plans… after the funeral I was going to… well, I've just had to keep out of her way and that is that. Thank God I never said anything."

"But that was like years ago! You still have feelings for her!"

Robert's eyes looked out over the horizon, to a place that he didn't often visit. He sighed. "Sally? Sal's the sweetest, gentlest girl, yet at her very core she is made of cast iron. As kids we would plan how we would run this station together. It was only a game… but we meant it. We both did. We were made for each other. But now… it's not possible."

"Why not?"

"I just told you why not."

"But your father's dead!" To Jo that obviously meant his involvement was over.

He jolted at her lack of correctness. "Some people reach beyond the grave that's all."

"You don't seem mad at him because of it."

"I can't change it. I went to every legal advisor around… they all said it was a standing legal document… completely unreasonable, but legal." Robert's resignation seeped out in a melancholy sigh. He was past fighting.

"But Sally doesn't *know* that's why you've given her the short shift."

"I couldn't. She'd leave. I don't want her to go."

"But you could leave together… do something else."

"I thought about that… heaps of times… but Sal loves it here. And Billy – he'd be lost anywhere else. I couldn't uproot them… not after all they've been through. It wouldn't be fair."

"Not giving her the choice is *not fair*! She's not stupid you know. And now you might lose the place anyway. Then what?"

"Well, Charlie invited Miss Betancourt to the farm for that reason."

"Invited! Ha! Sophie told me it was all her plan. So, Charlie marries her. It doesn't help you much."

Robert sighed with another impossible secret. "Charlie is already engaged to our second cousin. Eunice has money and if the clip sells well, the place is safe enough for now. Not many people know about the engagement. It is going to be officially announced while we're in town, at Eunice's birthday party. Miss Sophie was intended for me."

"Sophie!" Jo eyes opened wide. "You are supposed to marry Sophie? You're not serious." Jo was horrified. "You couldn't!"

"You're right. I couldn't. Charlie saw that instantly. That's why he took the fall for me."

"Won't Spohie be mad when she finds out she's been passed over for a second cousin! Or the maid!! How I wish I could see that!"

Robert looked concerned. "Do you think so?"

Jo screwed up her nose. "Sophie? Na, I'm pretty sure she'll cope. Robert? You're okay!"

Robert sighed another long sigh that seemed to start deep from within his tall leather boots, and he receded into the heavy melancholy that settled over him.

* * *

Sally drew herself back in from the window, back into the reality of the room that represented her life. "And then Andi, I look around and I see that I am so blessed. Really, I am… all that we have here is amazing for our situation and I know Robert is the reason for that. I truly do believe it… but something has changed. Once I really felt he was glad it was me who looked after the house and nursed his father and did things. Now? He does not know I am here. I… well… with Billy and all, it's not too surprising, I guess. Oh dear, sweet Billy…" A fear locked onto her heart that said the package was too heavy for any man. She was not an attractive option… and to be burdened with a disabled brother, made it more impossible.

"Billy… is a darling…"

"Yes, he's my darling. I love him so. I was just letting off steam. I don't do that very oft…. Andi? Andi!" Instantly Sally was back. She looked at Andi's ruffled hair and checked her eyes – the window of the soul, one nurse told her. Andi smiled back at her. She weakly lifted her wrist and smiled again before she took the drink that Sally quickly offered her and dozed off.

Sally flew out to the kitchen. "Molly! Molly! Andi just spoke – normally! She did! She's going' to be okay!" she shouted excitedly as she danced around the kitchen table, where a large bouquet of bush flowers stood featured in a bowl.

Molly looked up from crocheting milk jug covers with bottle green beads around the sides and smiled in amazement. "No end to remarkable surprises today," she said calmly. She wasn't even that surprised. It seemed very reasonable that many forms of impossible should happen all in one day. As Sally whirled back out the doorway, without a pause Molly lifted her apron and picked up some heavy grey woollen socks out of her lap. She was instantly absorbed in a knitting frenzy. The crocheting went into her apron pocket completely ignored.

Sally's dark head appeared back around the door-jam. "Just love those socks! Red stripes at the top would be very striking," she said cheekily with a grin as she disappeared into the bedroom.

Like a hearth-fire that had a fresh pile of kindling thrown on it, Sally's energy and focus revived and started to crackle. She got fresh water and soap and washed Andi's dark hair. She patiently combed and braided it to stop it knotting up again. She changed the sheets again, even though she had already done it for the day and clipped her nails. She massaged her skin with a homemade hand cream that she had made from lemon and lard. Sally threw open the side doors and windows and took down the curtains to wash. She sprinkled lavender water around liberally and went outside and picked a few bright red geraniums and mint from the garden underneath the tank stand and plonked them brightly on the dresser beside the bed. She stood back and looked at Andi sleeping peacefully. Lying there on the pillows any onlooker would say nothing had changed from how she had been for weeks. But to Sally… she knew. Hope stirred in her heart. That changed everything.

* * *

13.

As they drove into the town Jo was wide eyed seeing everything through the looking glass of last century. Gentlemen talked business, tilting their hats as passing ladies walked by sedately holding parasols or pushing large wheeled perambulators. Shop fronts modestly advertised their business… and she tried to think what that would be. A cobbler for example… did he make cobble-stones? The door was narrow and she could not see past into the dimness within. Her curiosity flashed onto the next thing: barber, farrier and wagon repairer; it seemed so normal that horses and buggies drove up and down the streets.

They pulled up outside a house that had a little sign "Overlander Boarding House: Mrs Hillary Mills – Proprietor" attached to the low picket fence. A climbing wisteria trellised an arch over the gate and Robert took their bags inside. Jo waited in the buggy, because getting up and down was an effort with her sore ankle. He returned shortly and stood by the horses, making no effort to get in. "I wanted to ask you… about your family." He paused and said nothing as if the question was completely self-explanatory.

"Hmm. What would you like to know?"

Robert shrugged noncommittally, but still looked expectantly for an answer.

"Well, my father left us when I was little. We lived with my Grandfather until last year. He died. I have a little brother. My mother…"

"You've gone to school?"

"Yeah – of course…"

"What is your house like?"

"Pretty ordinary…" Then she remembered what *ordinary* signified … and she couldn't help but elaborate what ordinary meant. "Well, the carpets were fairly new and there's heating in every room for winter and fans for summer. And we have running water on an *inside* bathroom…" She stopped. She didn't want to push it too far, but she couldn't help it. "And you know those new horseless carriages? We've got one of them."

"A horseless carriage! Your family owns one those?" He was amazed. Ordinary indeed!

"Yeah well – Mum owns it. Why? What are you getting at?"

He seemed satisfied. Jo felt she had passed some sort of test. "Charlie is going to announce his engagement tomorrow night, a dinner-party held at Eunice's parents' house. I would like you to come."

Jo groaned quietly and said nothing straight away. It wasn't a question. She had hoped to have a break from work. "I don't think I'll be much help with my foot like it is."

"Oh no... not to serve. Just to be there. You wouldn't have to work."

"Really?" That sounded pretty good.

"I will buy a dress, for you to wear."

"A dress?" That was interesting. Jo as a rule only wore dresses under protest. "Okay, on one condition."

Robert looked at her with raised eyebrows. Usually it was he that was able to enforce conditions. He smiled. Nothing this girl said would really surprise him. "Well?"

"If you buy me a dress, then you buy one for Sally too – one that you would really like her to wear if she could come with us."

Robert's jaw fell open and he stared at her stupidly. "A dress for Sally?"

"Yeah, you've seen her wardrobe. This is her best dress. It's pathetic. Something really nice. You pick it."

He shrugged as climbed back in the buggy. He hadn't counted on buying two dresses. Fair enough. He pulled up outside the drapers and went around and helped Jo out of the buggy. He tried to hold her arm but Jo shook him loose like a sticky fly. Enough was enough. She was okay.

Inside the shop was dim and there was clutter everywhere. Rolls of material stacked up against the counter. There were three dresses hanging on thick wooden frames in the window, and a couple of others hanging against the wall. That was all. Jo looked at the dresses critically. The first dress was severe and matronly: pass. The second was a dark sapphire blue, layered and frilled on the bodice, trimmed with elegant ivory lace: definitely, Sally. The third was unfussy and simple in plain burgundy, also with ivory trim. That would do her. Done.

She waited for Robert to catch up and browsed the shop looking in amazement at everything she found. There were hats and ribbons and stockings and other strange and wonderful items. She came across handmade doilies, knick-knacks, cottons and candles piled up high on a small counter. Not an inch of space was wasted, and most of it was used two or three times. The whole effect was a store jammed packed full of wonderful old-world charm.

Suddenly Jo had an idea. She embarked on a collecting frenzy. She chose three matching doilies, a couple of scented candles and fragrant soap, some bath salts, and a soft face cloth… some rose hand-cream and a little nick-nacky brooch. She piled them onto the counter and looked around for some other special little thing that she could put into their basket as a gift for Sally! It was a great idea – just to spoil her for being her. She wished Andi were here; she had such a way with natty things like this. She found an ivory looking hair comb and then had a fabulous idea. Chocolate! She chose a large piece of homemade chocolate fudge and tucked it in the pile. She tried to calculate exactly what the cost of the spoils from her treasure hunt had come to. She didn't want to spend all her money. She put back the rose hand cream and swapped it for a smaller, less impressive jar… then she swapped them back again and returned one of the doilies and candles instead. Finally, she was satisfied… she was done. She paid a bored looking clerk behind the counter while he wrapped up her package.

Robert was still busy, so she continued looking about. Jo picked up a hat that she thought might go with "her dress". A young girl with a snooty attitude immediately tapped her on the shoulder. "'Cuse me miss, we don't allow items to be handled until they are purchased."

"Sorry?"

"Would you like to buy the hat, now, miss?"

"How do I *know* if I want to buy it if I don't *try* it on?" Jo asked the girl with an equitable amount of snoot.

"The garments might get soiled," she insisted, "you best put it down."

"You're kidding?"

"No Miss. It is Mrs Cavanaugh's rule."

"Well, how am I going to make a choice without touching it? That's impossible."

"Perhaps your mistress could come in and help you sometime."

"Sorry?" said Jo with raised eyebrows. "Did you say "*mistress*"?"

"Yes Miss, she may be able to help you choose," she said looking down her nose at Jo in general and at her clothes in particular.

"Oh. So, this is an upper class – working class thing. I thought we were in Australia!"

"It is Miss, yes. But it is also Mrs Cavanaugh's Shop. She has her rules."

"Her rules stink!" Jo was completely disgusted. "Can you believe this?" she announced to the whole shop, "Are we supposed to buy things without knowing if it fits? Like how?"

Robert shuffled his tall legs around skeins of wool and attended her side, gently suggesting Jo lower her voice. But basically, Jo had no intention of doing it. "We'll go somewhere else – to some place that is civilized enough to allow us to fit things first. Pretty ridiculous I think!"

Robert wriggled his moustache, and said under his breath, "Ahem... there is no-where else. This is it."

"And that gives them the right to be rude and bigoted? The Consumer Affairs Ombudsman would have a field day with this. Just forget it. I'll go without. Thank you very much."

A matronly lady in a green suit that swept the floorboards with her hem came over and looked at Robert with sympathy. "I'm Mrs

Cavanaugh Sir. Can I assist you? Is this young lady… in your…. err, care?"

"Now *I* sound like the pet Newfoundlander!"

Robert ignored her. "Yes Madam. She is my friend. I came in to buy her a dress for a function tomorrow night."

Mrs Cavanaugh looked disparagingly at Jo's attire. "Oh, the Glossop function. Of course. I can see why she would need something suitable to wear."

Jo had enough! "Well, in your hat lady! What I wear is none of your business!"

Poor Mrs Cavanaugh was not used to such manners being tossed in her face. She gasped, closed her eyes, composed her demure temperament, and lifted her chin. Slowly she opened her eyes to find Jo had gone. Gradually she turned her head on the side to look around a display of fabrics in front of the window. Jo was sitting in the buggy, sulking.

Robert came out a little while later and tossed some large brown paper bundles tied up with string into the back. Then he went back inside and returned with four large boxes. He put them in and climbed into the seat without a word.

He silently passed Jo the package she had left on the counter. He clicked his tongue against his teeth and flicked the reins lightly. They went down the street. He stopped to drop a list in to the general grocer and proceeded to the boarding house. He said nothing.

He got out and tied the reins to the hitching rail and came around to assist Jo. "I will say one thing," he said conversationally. "Mrs Cavanaugh has a wonderful healing effect on people. You didn't limp once going out to the buggy."

Jo tried to keep up the offended look; but eventually burst out laughing. "Oh! Really? I'm sorry, but she was too much. Mrs Cavanaugh's rules! Just because I'm not dressed like whatever she thinks I should be dressed like! This is Sally's best dress. What if they had treated her like that! It's barbaric." Jo felt protective toward Sally. People shouldn't criticise her life. They didn't know what she had to put up with. "Too bad I won't be able to go to your dinner now. Sorry 'bout that." But in a way Jo was relieved. Robert said nothing as he unloaded the bundles into his room.

* * *

14.

They ate a light meal in the dining room. Jo was thankful not to have to rush around serving and cleaning up. It was a pleasant change to sit and chat. Their hostess, Mrs Hillary Mills joined them, while they made small talk about politics and local happenings. The names meant nothing to Jo and she switched off. Robert, for once, was making quite an effort to be engaging. He even started to talk about the farm and his growing up years, but after a while Jo was finding his stories all a bit dreary. She desperately wanted to go for a walk, but her ankle was aching again. Blasted thing! How long was she going to be hobbled like this? She asked to borrow a book from the shelf and retired to her room.

She sat down on the bed and rubbed her ankle. She didn't want to read. She wanted to go outside. She flicked the heavy pages restlessly and scanned the yellowed paper without interest. How boring. 'Wow,' she thought sarcastically, 'I can see why Sally wouldn't want to miss this! A trip to town is a real adventure.'

There was a gentle tap on the door. Mrs Mills opened it slowly and peered in. "Are you alright dear? A journey into town can be a touch draining. You look quite peaked."

"I feel fine really. Just annoyed that my ankle won't do what it is supposed to."

"Oh, I understand dear. I'm also finding many of my bits are not doing what they are supposed to now-a-days."

Jo grimaced. She didn't really feel that much identification with a middle-aged widow who kept an old boarding-house. She smiled and tried to be polite. "I'm okay – really. Thank you for looking in on me."

"Mr Madegan, dear, has asked me to bring these parcels to you. He asked me to assist you, so you can try these on. He'll exchange anything that needs doing tomorrow." Mrs Hillary stepped outside and brought in boxes and large brown paper parcels. She seemed quite impressed with Mr Madegan's benevolent generosity.

Jo groaned inwardly. Of course, he would have bought the dresses. Well, at least it would give her something to do. She nodded for Mrs Mills to put them on the bed. "You don't seem very excited my dear. To be invited to a function of the calibre of the Glossop's, dears, it is quite an honour."

Jo had asked to come to town, not to be thrown into some elite social circle. This was not her idea. She realised Andi would say this was a perfect "fact-finding" opportunity: in amongst all the people associated with Mainstar and the Madegan family. "Oh, Mrs Mills – you are so right. How ungrateful of me. Mr Robert is kind. Let's see what we have." Jo roused herself and forced a tight smile. She was privately disappointed she could be so fake, and justified just as quickly because she was acting proxy on Andi's behalf. She pulled at the brown strings and drew Mrs Hillary into her confidence. "I hope I like what he's picked..." she said a bit tongue-in-cheek. Jo knew very well what he had picked. It was so obvious there was no choice.

Mrs Hillary nodded knowingly. It could be quite difficult not to offend a prospective suitor. Jo unfolded the stiff paper wrapping and stared at the layers of sapphire frills and lace. "Oh no!" said Jo, "This is Sally's dress. It is not me at all!"

"Sally, dear?" said Mrs Hillary bewildered, "Who is Sally?"

"Sally McBride – she works at Mainstar. This is her dress!"

"The McBride girl? What would she want with a dress like this?"

"Mr Robert obviously picked up the wrong parcel. My outfit must be in the other one."

Mrs Hillary stood there confused. "But…"

"No – it's just a mistake. If you could get the other parcel, I'll try it on."

Shaking her head Mrs Mills went out to knock on Mr Robert's door. She returned shortly with the other parcel, still looking blankly that such a dress could be refused. Jo undid the string and tugged at a knot. She sat looking at the plain brown suiting in disbelief. She gathered herself. "Mrs Hillary… is this something one would wear to a social function? It looks like army garb."

"Normally something like the blue dress would be quite flattering," she said obviously. "Are you sure *this* was not for the McBride girl?"

"Sally! Her name is Sally. And this? I wouldn't put *this* on a dog…." And then Jo remembered the Retriever analogy and winced. Perhaps that is really all Robert thought of Sally.

Perhaps he really *had* given up. Whimp! She was disgusted.

Mr Robert appeared at the door. "Is there a problem?" he asked benignly.

"Problem? You promised that you would choose something really nice for Sally! I can't believe you think this is something she would wear."

"It is practical. Sally is very practical."

"Who wants practical? She's got enough skirts and aprons to be practical until the end of time!"

"Okay…it would be unseemly."

"Unseemly for whom? Wearing this is unseemly. I'm certainly not wearing this to dinner! I guess it is better I don't go after all."

He looked like he agreed. "What about the blue dress?"

"That is Sally's and you had better *swear* to me on your life that you never tell her that you picked it out for me."

He shrugged. "I'll collect the other one tomorrow. Will that be okay?"

"Fine."

He left the room and sat back in the lounge. He pulled out his pipe and fastidiously filled and puffed and lit it, while his moustache wriggled and twitched anxiously. He didn't get out his pipe very often. It was just that he didn't like the way Jo kept popping Sally's picture up in front of his face all the time. He had to put her aside. He couldn't do that at home, but he had determined to try while he was away. He had to move on. Why was it so hard? Why couldn't he just marry for money like his brother?

Robert knew Charlie didn't even like Eunice. Not really. But he would marry her anyway because there was money, made easier by the family connection. Her lacklustre father was their mother's cousin. He felt sorry for Eunice. She was small and fragile and hopelessly incompetent. Charlie would bury himself into more work. He could never imagine that they would laugh together or share any talk of common interests. They will probably have a family if Eunice's health hung out. If they weren't already engaged, perhaps Sophie would have been a better choice for Charlie. But then, Sophie would not like to play second fiddle. He had figured that much about her. With Charlie, it would always be second fiddle. He knew. He had done it all his life. He puffed some more on his pipe as he mused through the smoky fog that filled the room and his mind.

* * *

As the next evening settled in a glorious golden-rust sunset, a covered coach collected Robert and Jo from the boarding house and escorted them out of town to the estate of Eunice Glossop. An avenue of trees lined the drive to the long sprawling stone homestead set up on a rise. There, terraced gardens swept along a path to large stone steps leading to a verandah set with potted conifers and occasional furniture. The look was very aristocratic and somewhat counterfeit in the warm Australian evening. But apparently there were a number of things about the Glossops that were out of step.

Mrs Glossop was a slight lady who stood as if a fire-poker had been permanently shoved up her corset. She positioned her husband Jim by her side, as she welcomed guests into the drawing room. He was dressed in a grey suit with a gold pocket watch chain dangling lazily across his vest.

Jim was of medium height and said his introductions mildly as if the whole world was extremely tedious. Jo took his limp hand and looked into his bland face. The only notable feature was large brown birthmark peeking out from under his whiskers, and on him even *that* was uninteresting. She wondered if such a man as Jim Glossop ever got excited about anything.

Francine Glossop more than made up for his lack of enthusiasm. She was shorter than her husband but stood as if she towered over him. Jo watched with interest as she eloquently welcomed all her guests by name, ushering into her halls those who demonstrated the level of society that was due her family.

Her polished flow of introductions abruptly stalled when Robert and Jo arrived carrying a large box decorated with an extravagant red bow, for the birthday girl. Jo stood before Mrs Glossop in her cream and burgundy dress, gloves and hat included. She looked at Jo and paused. A flicker of disapproval was quickly smothered as she eyed the size of the gift and assured Robert that any friend of his was most welcome.

Jo took her hostess' hand and curtsied, copying the manner of the guests before her. It was unexpected that Robert would bring a companion, even if his invitation had been courteously penned to "Mr Robert Madegan and Friend". What was unusual was that this "friend" was *unknown* to Mrs Francine Glossop. She prided herself on the knowledge of all eligible singles and their families. Where had Robert Madegan found this girl?

The Madegan brothers had been known as "the Mainstar bachelors" since old Mr Madegan died. There were rumours about the old Codger's last will and testament, but the details were never confirmed. To Mrs Glossop it no longer mattered. Her daughter, at the sweet age of seventeen, had secured her hold on her second cousin's legitimate country status. She believed it gave her personal access to the Mainstar Empire. She was well aware, unfortunately, that the significance of any of this was completely lost on poor Eunice.

Jo threaded her way through the oodles of country couples that had come to enjoy the exclusive hospitality of Mrs Glossop. The room was large and sweeping. On one section of wall there was an array of ornately framed photographs of horses. There were sires and racehorses with their jockeys in their dated silk outfits, victoriously holding winning trophies in various shapes and sizes. Jo paused and admired them. Perhaps Mr Jim Glossop had a passion after all.

The guests huddled in their little cliques, elegantly waving their glasses of wine-punch as they nibbled on savouries. Jo wondered if Charlie's fiancé would be modelled after her mother or father. She spotted her standing with Charlie by the large ornate mantelpiece. Eunice looked like a frightened rabbit, her nose twitching and her eyes watering. She had her mother's stature and her father's manner. But where you didn't notice Mrs Glossop's height, with Eunice you could almost believe she had just swallowed a large amount of Alice in Wonderland's shrinking potion and any minute she was liable to fade clear away. Charlie held her hand reassuringly and Robert noted with pride that he almost looked like he wanted to rescue her from this public display of Glossop self-aggrandisement. Perhaps he had been wrong. Perhaps Charlie had more heart than he gave him credit for. He hoped so.

Robert reached out his hand. "Happy birthday Eunice," he said sympathetically. Jo could almost believe he was passing on his condolences for the passing of a dear mutual friend.

She smiled weakly. "Glad you could come Robert," she said.

"This is a friend of mine... Jo," he paused as he his mind went blank. He'd forgotten her full name.

"Josephine Stokes, please to meet you," said Jo without embarrassment. Josephine sounded so much more elegant than just ordinary Joanne, and it seemed much more fitting for a place like this. "It's a bit clunky – that's why I go by just Jo," she said, trying to lighten the moment as Robert looked at her queerly. Eunice stared at her with her startled rabbit eyes. Charlie gapped at her in confusion for a second and raised his eyebrows at his brother. Obviously, some mind-rending understanding was achieved because Charlie went back to scanning the room for the face of a particular business acquaintance. *Oh boy*, thought Jo, *these people are fun. Some party this will be.* "Well", she buzzed lightly, "have a wonderful birthday. We left your gift on the table. Ours is the one with the bow." Eunice nodded, and then was given attention from others that came flocking.

One older couple stood fast in their determination to pass on their personal congratulations. "My, my little Eunie, who would have thought that you are all grown up and such a young lady now. Happy birthday Sweet Seventeen…." The lady smothered her with kisses and left smudges of makeup on her cheek.

"Thank you, Mrs Fillips," said Eunice with a patient sigh. She looked around to see how many more millions of people would feel obligated to shower her with their sincerest greetings.

"Aunt Millicent, child," the lady gushed quietly, "call me Aunt… and Uncle Herbert… that is far more agreeable. We are practically family now." She winked conspiringly at Eunice who visibly winced.

Well, thought Jo, *I could never resist such a family!* Herbert took his wife's arm gently. His scruffy white hair attached itself in lumps to his scalp. "Come Millie… the girl has lots of well-wishers to attend to." Before Jo realised it, Mrs Millicent Fillips turned her focus on her. "Oh my, and you must be Robert's new friend. And where did you say your family comes from?"

"I didn't," said Jo flatly.

"Well of course dear... we've only just met," said Mrs Millicent Fillips sociably without any trace of unpleasantness. She was definitely trying to extract information that would give her the upper hand in any subsequent conversations regarding Robert's "mystery" companion. "But it is always such a pleasure to meet Robert's friends. So, where *does* your family come from?"

Prying busybodies, thought Jo callously. "Actually, I'm a born and bred African pigmy," she said tersely, and she turned her back and went in search of Robert. He had left to talk business with some stiff collared men with fat, short, neckties, and was deeply engrossed in some discussion on wool prices.

What had ever come over her to agree in being a part of a function full of snobby, old-fashioned, money grabbing worshipers who were polishing the shrine of their illustrious god "Connections"? What could the god of Connections do for her? Nothing. Robert knew all these people, and he still found his security wavered on a thread. Hence the engagement. She needed some air. She went outside onto the verandah and sat down on one of the chairs, willing a cool evening breeze to come her way.

She sat watching the night skyline and saw a shooting star fall behind the horizon. She wondered if Billy saw it as he sat on their porch recounting to Sally the things he had discovered that day. She smiled as she remembered some of the treasures he had shown her on their evening dates, before she read him his story. Sally called him their own resident Bower Bird… Billy-Bower-Bird. There were furry, fuzzy caterpillars with tiny yellow antennae that popped in and out; and petite purple flowers that spun their frosted petals around fine green stems. Billy would stuff them up her nose and demand she sniff, because they smelled really delicious. "Chocolate," said Jo amazed, "They smell like chocolate…" but she didn't think he understood. He certainly hadn't had much taste of chocolate. That was a luxury that Sally's careful budget never extended far enough to cover. She smiled as she thought of her gift basket sitting by her bed.

Robert came and sat quietly beside her, crossing his legs out in front of him. He said nothing for a while as he watched her stargazing. "I have always thought the stars looked like someone poked holes into a black velvet blanket to let the light of heaven shine through," he said quietly musing. He sighed again as he realised that this was also a Sally memory. They had laid on their backs on the rocks near the gorge late one night not long after Sally's Mother's funeral, watching the heaven lights twinkle, and tried to work out which star-hole would be big enough to let Sally's Mum look through to see them.

He paused and then hesitated again. "You know Jo, Aunt Millie is quite at loss to know how she has offended you." It wasn't a judgement or a reprimand, just a statement.

Jo came back with a jolt. "Who?"

"Aunt Millie. I saw the way you spoke to her. She is really quite upset."

"Well, really… all she wanted to know was whether I would fit into their snobby little circle… and quite frankly – I don't care whether I have the right connections or not." Jo sat on the other snappy words that wanted to slip off her tongue. Stuck-up, nose-poking hypocrites! She took a breath and glared out at the night sky.

"Joanne, you introduced yourself as Josephine. It suggests to me that in some way you do care. But Jo, regardless of how they are, does that give you license to be 'snobby' in return?" Robert was not finished. "Mrs Glossop has organised this function in honour of our family. I invited you to be part of it because I thought that you would help make it a happy occasion, not create more tension."

She was embarrassed that Robert called her on that. She had always considered she genuinely met her own exacting standards of authenticity. "Well, sorry to disappoint you. I thought this 'occasion' was for Eunice. Mrs Gossip obviously does just as she pleases."

"All of that is very true and given this is her home I don't believe we have any grounds to comment. For future reference: there is an "L" in Glossop."

Huh. He noticed that too. "Well it is a silent "L", and as far as I can see – it rubs off on a lot of people around here."

He stood up quietly. Nothing about Robert ever seemed to jar. She could see why Sally was so smitten. He was kind, even when he was *really* unimpressed. "This is who we are. We are not perfect, and I envy your ideals that can see so clearly where we need polishing. But courtesy is never wasted – even on the sophisticated roughness of our friends and family." He turned and walked along the sandstone verandah to the doors that led into the dining hall.

Jo sat quietly in the dim coolness. A mosquito buzzed around her ear and she slapped at it, squashing it without mercy. Robert was right. So much for being a bush-orchid beauty, she thought. Surely it is not such a difficult thing. And in her heart, she suspected it was the hardest thing ever: to glow even when no one else wants to shine with you. Oh boy. How could she ever achieve such an ideal? It was so much easier just to be cranky and intolerant.

Jo knew she would have to go and see Aunt Millie… and apologise. Robert was right. She was not there to drag him and Sally down. But she wanted to gather some courage first. Reminding herself about her resolutions was one thing. Telling snobby Aunt Millie would be another thing. She sat in the stillness and shrank into the shadows beside the walls a little more. Another mosquito buzzed and she slapped herself on the cheek as she felt it land and bite.

She saw Eunice slip out the side doors and lean on a verandah post trying to fill her lungs with fresh air. "Eunice?" She turned and tried to see who had trapped her catching a break.

"Come and sit here in the quiet. No one will miss you for a moment."

She seemed startled. People did not offer an escape often…ever. "Oh – you're Robert's friend: thank you." She sat down on the edge of the seat and looked as uncomfortable as she had inside. Jo went back to looking at the stars.

"I saw a falling star before – it went all the way down to the top of the hills. It was so clear."

Eunice peered at the sky and was uncertain how to respond, as all the stars she saw stayed glued in the night sky. "Oh," she said simply.

"Have you made 'the announcement' yet?"

"Not yet."

"When?"

"After dessert."

"You'll have a bit of time then – to gather courage…"

"Oh…"

"That's why I'm here – to gather courage. I have to apologise to Aunt Millie."

"She'll appreciate that."

Jo grunted and nearly said, "I bet," but checked herself.

"I know Mother intends this to be special. But honestly – I would have just preferred to put a notice in the Gazette." Jo was surprised that Eunice chose a perfect stranger to share that information with. She had only seen forced smiles and short plain responses. There was a stirring in Jo's mind that there was more to Eunice than half the population of the district gave her credit for.

"You don't like parties?" asked Jo simply.

"Do you?" It sounded like a sincere question…. perhaps to gauge her own response.

"Not much." Jo was glad she didn't have to think up clever replies to Eunice's questions.

"Me neither. But Mother does. She must be so disappointed that I'm not the social butterfly she was at my age."

"Butterfly wings? Oh, I'd love to fly out of here," said Jo with sudden feeling.

"Really? Would you like to see something?" The possibility of escape suddenly became a genuine option.

"Sure. What did you have in mind?" asked Jo curiously.

Eunice stood up. "We won't have long… but it would be good to get some fresh air…"

She carefully stepped down the stone stairs lifting her skirt high and waited for Jo to follow her in a hobbled hurry. Eunice supported her arm to move their progress along. They followed a dim path around behind the garden and out towards some impressive large stables, that matched the style of the house.

"How long before you get married then?"

"Next year… after my eighteenth birthday. Mother insisted. It gives her a year to do her social thing."

"Twelve months…"

"It seems like forever."

"I know what you mean. Hang in there, Eunie. I'm sure you'll be so busy it will fly." Eunice looked at her, her wide eyes darker still as her pupils adjusted to the dim light. She shrugged as if she really wasn't sure. Jo paused, "Do you love him?"

"Charlie? Oh yes. Don't think he loves me though."

Jo was curious. Eunice was not even upset or worried about that. "You reckon? How could you marry him then?"

"Because I love him. And he will marry me anyway. I can help him."

"You mean your money can."

"But he only gets the money if he marries me."

"I can't believe you talked about this. It seems so – calculated."

"Oh no, we never talked about it – Charlie has been a very polite courtier."

"Well, how did you know then – about him needing money?"

"Sophie told me tha…"

"Sophie? You know Sophie Betancourt?"

"Mother said I should ask her to be one of my attendants at the wedding."

"But…"

"Oh, look at me!" Eunice stood on the path, small and plain, even in the layers of fancy dress-fabric. "This is Charlie Madegan. He could have any girl around here he set his sights on. And he has set them on me. He asked *me* to marry him. I like that. I'm grateful I have an inheritance to make it possible."

Jo stood still and took a deep breath. "Whew. That's not how I'd want to do my marriage… but good for you. I hope it works."

"So, do you love each other?" and a look of wistful envy passed across Eunice's rabbit eyes.

"Me and who?"

"Well you and Robert of course."

"No way! We are not…"

"But everyone knows…"

"Everyone knows what?" Jo lowered her voice in panic. "What does everyone know?"

"How you must have money because of the way you are educated and Robert has found your family… and…"

"You're kidding right?"

"No – seriously. Sophie was…"

"Sophie told you this? What else did Sophie say?"

Eunice looked a bit dubious now. It obviously had not occurred to her that Sophie did not know all the facts. She had recently spent so much time at Mainstar she figured she *must* know.

Jo pushed her, "Come on – tell me."

"Well…" Eunice paused and then started walking again… as if she didn't want to stall any longer. "Sophie said you and your friend told her you were pretending to be paupers because that would get Robert's sympathy. That's why you are working as a house-maid. That it would not be long before you could… you know…"

"No. I don't."

"Well, marry him.

"Marry him!" Jo relaxed. Oh boy that was twisted. "Think about it Eunie. Why would I stage being *poor* to marry a man who needs *money?* That's stupid."

"Sophie said it was very clever. That you really…"

"And I don't suppose she mentioned my friend was really sick and she hasn't spoken to anyone since we got here?"

Eunice felt silly. Not that she cared that much about them not having money, but that she had believed the story so whole-heartedly. It had sounded so romantic, so different from her story. "She said you did have money."

"Yeah, my Mum gives me five dollars pocket money a week. I'm loaded."

"Dollars?"

"Pounds maybe…"

"Five pounds every week! That is quite an allowance." That Jo could be so dismissive of the privilege suggested to her that Sophie was not far from the truth after all.

"No it's not like that. Never mind. Listen, Eunie. I'm not going to marry Robert. He doesn't love me. And like I said – that's not the way I want to do it. But you don't have to tell anyone. Let them think what they like. Our secret. Okay?"

Something happened in Eunice's fearful rabbit eyes. They opened up and smiled. She held out her gloved hand to shake Jo's. "Our secret," she conspired. Suddenly she didn't have to believe everything that Sophie told her, or her mother's friends told her. Within minutes she would be engaged to Charlie Madegan and Jo had declared herself to be her friend – just hers. Not her mother's, not Charlie's. She could do this. She could! And she could do it the way *she* wanted.

"In here." Eunice opened the heavy door and went inside. The smell of hay and linseed and horses enclosed their senses. A stable hand was sitting at a table working on some gear. Another was rubbing oil into a saddle over by the wall. "Are they all settled for the night, boys?" said Eunice. Jo looked at her in surprise. The rabbit had transformed! She was perfectly relaxed and comfortable; no longer timid; no longer out of her depth.

"Too right, Miss Eunice. Not one of 'em a stirring…" The other stable-boy sniggered as he oiled the leather vigorously.

"Is there a problem, Wally?"

"You dressed up like a Christmas tree, Miss Eunice… ready to topple right over. No disrespect intended Miss," he hurriedly added.

"None taken. It's my engagement party. Mother thought I should make an effort." Wally just raised his eyebrows as if to say it was a pretty unsuccessful effort. "Never mind that, we're just here to see Prince Tyron. We can't be too long."

She took Jo down to the stalls, opened a door, and stepped back. A tall young black stallion stood lithe and energetic even as he remained motionless, watching them warily. "Meet the newest member of my family… Prince Tyron. He has fabulous lineage and… no don't go in – he's not ready. Had heaps of offers for him, but I will keep him as the basis for my own stud-line. My other horses don't come anywhere near him." She closed the door as she saw him getting restless.

"We'd better be getting back. Dessert will be served very soon," she said meaningfully. They walked in the cool as Eunice shared some more of her dreams of her life with Charlie at Mainstar.

"What does Charlie think about his future wife being an accomplished horse-breeder?"

"I don't think he takes it too seriously. I haven't shown him much. He just thinks I like horses a lot… and that it's Dad's business. Mum says men like ladies to be hospitable entertainers. They get threatened if women are too overtly businesslike. She won't let me talk horses when we are out. She says there are plenty of avenues without stepping into a man's territory."

"Your Mum said this?" she laughed at the idea of Mrs Glossop worrying about treading on other people's space. "She makes it sound like all men have marked their territory out like a dog!"

Eunice looked at Jo keenly. "Not everyone. It's been my Dad who has set me up and taught me everything. He's been a very strong advocate for me to start on my own… even at my age. He says there's plenty of room for quality horses from both of us!"

"I hope Charlie supports you just as much. Why haven't you told him?"

"Oh, I will. I just need to be engaged first, that's all." When they reached the verandah, Jo sat down and rubbed her ankle.

"Well, you're about to become engaged. Enjoy the moment," said Jo with a smile. "I'll be in soon," she said as Eunice braced herself for the plunge back inside. Jo sat in the quiet a little longer. Little Eunie was okay, and Jo was a little shocked to discover she was not the pathetic push-over everyone took her for. She may be quiet, but Jo suspected there was more of her mother in her than just the gene for height. It takes some finding out… that's all.

"Well, well. The house help has come out of the closet." Standing in the doorway was Sophie, in a predictable blue dress, not unlike the one wrapped up for Sally back at the boarding house. Jo grimaced. She didn't know if she liked the dress quite so much anymore. Sophie pulled herself up to full height. "I'm not surprised to find you here, although I would have thought kitchen duties would be more your style." Sophie had a long-stemmed glass in her hand and she took a slow drink.

"Actually, I have a sore ankle. But then you would not know about the ankle… because you didn't stay around to find out."

"Whatever are you talking about?

"I'm talking about how you conveniently disappeared while *Jack* was helping me when I hurt my ankle up that tree. Of course, showing all the tender-hearted care I would expect from you."

"You were up a *tree*." She laughed as if this was a novel little cocktail story, told to make the evening entertaining. "Why were you *up* a tree?"

"Yeah right. I was the one who passed out… and funnily enough, I don't have amnesia."

"Oh dear… I think the Glossop's good wine has quite gone to the house-help's head." She giggled sillily and took another long drink.

Jo sat there. Surprise, surprise: Sophie wasn't going to acknowledge anything. She remembered Bluey's advice after the horse-riding incident: *Be really cool about it and it'll drive her nuts.* Okay, thought Jo, I can be cool about this. So, she giggled sillily in return and said nothing.

It was obviously not what Sophie had expected or wanted. She was a bit light headed from her drink. "Tut-tut. She's going to give me the silent treatment. How very un-country. We share all our secrets in the country!" and Sophie wobbled slightly.

"Whoa! Sit down Sophie, you've gone a tad over-board… take it easy…" Jo guided her to a bench, and gently took her drink from her hand so she wouldn't spill it on her dress.

"Charlie Madegan… loves *me*…" Sophie picked up her glass and started talking to it.

"…not," volunteered Jo. Jack was too good for her.

"…*and* I am going into *business*.…"

"Right…" Jo raised her eyebrows.

"…and *every*one will know that I am… Sophie Betancourt."

"Information we already have."

"You don't believe me… but I will. *And* not you or her or Madegan or Daddy will stop me. I *will*."

There was a sudden sound of clinking glasses from inside. Jo stood up. "I think it is time for the guests to assemble," she said.

* * *

The moon was high when the coach pulled out to take them back to town. It spun silvery messages over the broad paddocks of grass along

180

the road. Jo pulled her shawl in tight as she looked out of the side window, trying to read the moonlit memos.

"Thank you for talking with Aunt Millie. She came to me just before she left. She seemed so much more at ease," said Robert in the shadows of the coach.

"You were right. I was not polite and there is no excuse. I'm sorry."

"You should meet Carey sometime."

"Carey?"

"That's Aunt Millie's St John's… actually she's an old dog now."

"Aunt Millie owns the sure and faithful Sally-Retriever-dog?" Jo had not made that connection before.

"Carey. The sure and faithful one? True. That's her."

"Oh."

"Just … thanks. Much appreciated."

"Robert?" Jo paused. Great. Did she really need to get into this? But she couldn't see a way around it.

"Hmmm?"

"There seems to be a general misconception that you and I intend to get engaged."

"Oh. Really?" He did not sound at all surprised.

"Yes really. And I was wondering why you would let such a misconception persist?"

"Would you mind, a lot – really?"

"Mind what?"

"Well, marriage."

"To you?" Jo nearly choked. He was trying to be serious. She wasn't even fifteen. She wasn't getting married. Not now. Maybe never!

"Yes. Surely it is not such a terrible idea."

"Well, one - you didn't ask;

two – you are in love with Sally;

three – she is my friend;

four – I'm not sixteen yet, and

five - even if I was, not likely!"

"Many ladies would consider it a compliment…"

"Well, gee – pick one of them!"

"I thought you might reconsider…"

"No way!"

"Can I ask why?"

"Like, five reasons isn't enough? Get over it!"

"According to my father's will, you would meet the criteria."

Jo could contain herself no longer: she burst out laughing! She figured if she didn't break the tension, she would strangle him with his pompous ugly necktie. "Criteria! My – the romance is killing me!" she gasped between the rollicking laughter.

Robert's moustache twitched and wriggled. He seemed unable to grasp that anything was funny or inappropriate. Jo quietened down. "You think I am rich? That I am your ticket to save Mainstar?"

Robert didn't deny it. "You're obviously educated. Your Mother has property…and a horseless carriage! It shows position and means."

"She owns a house and a car because she works at a hospital. Hardly landed gentry."

"But she owns it."

"She owns a mortgage, big deal. Even if she owned it outright – I have no access to it. It is… like, tied up in a time capsule in another century. Right now, I am seriously disinherited. Nothing. Zip. Zilch."

Robert looked thoughtful, but completely unperturbed. "I know the clauses in that blasted document like the back of my hand. It says nothing about access to assets… only that they are there."

"But why? Why marry for assets, if you can't get your grubby little hands on them? Oh, you are sick!" Boy, she was annoyed. "Besides… why would you consider marrying anyone when you and Sally go way back? Like – *why* would you?"

"I've told you why. There is no way. I have tried everything… and there's nothing. It's a dead end. I have to move on."

Jo shook her head. "Not with me you don't! Why should *you* move on and not give Sally that option? You selfish, pigheaded, self-absorbed chauvinist! You only talk about how stuck *you* are in this. You don't think about *her* at all. You don't deserve her! You should at least release her with a valid reason… but not the one about her not being good enough. That stinks!"

"Thank you."

"You're welcome."

"Thank you for not spilling all that at the party. It was very respectable."

"Well, you tell her, or I will. She is my friend. She should know how it is..."

"The bit about being pig headed or the will?"

Jo grunted. He was pathetic. "Take your pick."

* * *

15.

Jo said nothing further all the way back to the boarding house. She went straight to her room and lay down. She wanted peace. She had put far too much weight on her ankle all evening. Her foot throbbed… but it was her heart that ached more. Jo couldn't believe this. Sally would end up hating her. If she ever found out Robert had proposed – even if it was because Jo met *contract criteria*, she would lose her only friend in this place. How thick could some people be? Specifically, how dense could Robert be?

At least Sophie was out of the picture now, because Eunice had come to the rescue. Jack was obviously a red-herring, and had nothing much to do with the big scheme of things. The wool clip was on its way to market, and there would be no need to put Mainstar up for sale. At least that was good.

She just wanted to get back to Mainstar and see Andi. She was her only connection with the real world. What was the point, to go through all this just to put Andi's life in jeopardy? Jo rolled over and cried into her pillow. "Oh God. You have to heal her! She has always been good. God?" Huh. Stupid! It was like talking to the ceiling… and the cornice work was not replying. Of course. The rest of it was like looking at a page of maths problems. There was obviously a solution but getting there was impossible. And it all seemed very pointless anyway. She rolled over and pummelled her pillow in frustration.

When Jo woke up the candle beside her bed had burnt out and there were grey pre-dawn streaks of light around the edges of the curtains. She thought she heard people talking, but she crawled under the covers and collapsed back into an exhausted sleep.

It was really warm when she finally stirred, and the quilt was in a crumpled heap beside the bed where she had kicked it off. Her long dress she had worn last night to the party was creased and crumpled. She struggled out of it and hobbled over to the washstand. She poured water out of the ceramic pitcher and flushed her hot face. She looked into a silver-plated hand mirror on the washstand. Her eyes were red, her skin was blotchy, her hair hung in lumps and her mouth smelt like a gorilla's armpit.

She felt vulgar. "Boy! This look is irresistible!" she said to herself, and she smiled in spite of how she was feeling. "Even if I meet 'contract criteria', I doubt anyone would go for this. *'Contract criteria'!* I still can't believe he said that! I'm so glad I don't have to look great to be Andi's friend. God, I wish she would wake up!"

She attacked her hair with vigour and determined to scrub out the cobwebs. The first thing she'd do when she got home would have the longest, hottest, soapiest shower in the whole of recorded history! She scraped her teeth with a frayed piece of twig, and then slipped outside and scanned the kitchen herb garden. She picked a few sprigs of mint and chewed them vigorously before she spat them out and rinsed her mouth to get rid of left-over green bits. She was learning to be inventive in the absence of fresh-mint toothpaste and spearmint chewing gum. By the time she got inside, she felt she was ready to mark time. Eventually she would find out what to do. She was not good at waiting. She was an all-in, get-it-done type of girl, but she was learning.

* * *

Sally took Andi's arms and supported her carefully as they moved slowly along the homestead verandah. "You're doing so well! That's wonderful! Keep coming!" Slowly her legs swung forward, her face concentrating hard on the movements. It seemed like her muscles had forgotten what to do. Andi set her jaw as she moved the other leg. The effort was too much and her body began to give way. Molly slipped a chair behind her and she collapsed into its arms. Andi's face beamed. Sally jumped up and down! She did it! It worked! It was hard, but it worked!

* * *

Mrs Mills met Jo at the servery. "Oh, my dear, dear Miss Josephine! Mr Robert said not to disturb you…" Jo looked at her. *Mrs Hillary* was obviously quite disturbed by the fact she wasn't permitted to 'disturb' her.

"Mrs Hillary, is there something wrong?"

"Wrong dear? I would say so! Oh yes my… wrong it is…" and she wrung out her long calloused fingers that had spent years looking after other people's needs.

A slow panicky feeling began to grow inside Jo's chest. "Andi? Is everything okay with Andi? Or Sally? Billy? What's wrong?"

"Oh dear, I don't know about them… but Mr Robert…"

"Something happened to Robert? Is he okay? I know we didn't finish our night on really good terms, but I figured he would understand…"

"Oh dear… I've got you all in a fluster… I am so sorry my dear; I should just come straight out and say it without letting your mind dream up all sorts of unimaginable terrors… I do just get so…"

"Mrs Mills!"

"Yes dear?"

"Tell me what happened!"

"Oh dear." Mrs Hillary paused. "A messenger came really early this morning… nearly banged down the door he did… it was most distressing dear, to be disturbed like that… barely light it was…." She shivered as she relived the shock.

"And…?" Jo raised her voice.

"Oh, my dear… how terrible for you… I keep forgetting… the man… barely a boy he was… just a young lad… came from along the track… saw the whole thing… was sent along to give Mr Robert the news… awful shock… just awful…"

"Mrs Hillary! What did he find?" Jo was a bit relieved to realise it wasn't news from

Mainstar Station. Still, what could be so terrible? She wished she would just spit it out.

"The lad… such a brave boy… the wooldrays… terrible, terrible accident: they went over the edge of the range. Two drays went over… the Mainstar clip is gone. Just like that. Gone. And the bullocky… old Tom…. known around here like a faithful pair of moleskins… just always been here, dear… looked after them beasts like they were his own family. The lad… he said old Tom, said he tried to stop it going over… with his hands… as if he could've done a thing… whole thing… over the edge." She sat down shaking visibly.

Jo sat beside her and took her hand. She didn't know what else to do. She tried to absorb the implications. But her mind just swirled with graphic images of the horrible accident. Old Tom was gone. So was his team. So was the clip. She pictured them in the morning light… stamping in the dust – patient and eager at the same time, to get into the day's work. And now they were all gone. Their work would never be finished. Jo swallowed really hard. It wasn't supposed to go like this. Not at all.

* * *

Sally went into Andi's room again and saw her lying there, eyes open. She sat down and looked at her. "You okay?" She took her hand and brushed some of her dark hair out of her eyes. Andi nodded. Her eyes filled with tears.

"I don't understand what happened… I'm so confused." She licked her dry lips and took a breath. "I feel like I've been picked up and dumped in another world. Where's my Mum? Why isn't Dad here?"

Sally didn't know what to say. Jo had always been really tight lipped about their families and where they came from. "Jo will be back soon. She has gone into town with Mr Robert. They should be home tomorrow, all being well." It was hard to be definite about these things. Unexpected things pop up.

"Home tomorrow? Where have they gone – to the moon? Why can't they come now? Who is Robert?" Andi's eyes looked flushed and anxious. Sally tried to soothe her.

"It's okay Andi. It's okay. We're going to work on a surprise for Jo. She doesn't even know you are really awake. She'll be *over* the moon to see you. And we're going to do even more things to show her. She'll be ecstatic, I know! Every night she comes in to talk with you about stuff. She's been here all the time. Really."

* * *

Jo got up again and limped to the window. She felt increasingly frustrated at being hobbled. The sky had greyed over with dull cloud and it started to drizzle. The humidity was thick and the dusty road seemed to steam as water misted down. Time was suspended. What would happen now? What *could* happen now? All the processing Jo had done the previous night suddenly became obsolete, as it sunk in that Mainstar was in danger of going financially under once again. Without the income from the wool clip, there may not be enough money to satisfy the mortgagees. Was this even any of her business? No probably not. But she felt for Sally and Billy and Molly and Robert and Charlie and Eunice. They were her friends, and friends were her business. They were all about to lose their home and their jobs.

Suddenly Jo realised that she could not change any external factors. She could not miraculously produce thousands of pounds to save Mainstar. Andi would say that God could, even if she couldn't. But perhaps whichever way

193

it went: either staying or moving on, she could be that orchid to brighten the moment. Would God save them like Andi would expect? Or was this just like a fork in the road that would take them in unexpected directions?

Jo clung to two things Andi had told her: that God always knows best... and He doesn't have to rely on ordinary ways to fulfil that best. Jo took a bible off the shelf in the border's lounge, and opened it up. Some words jumped off the page at her: "...*three things remain: faith, hope and love....*" Well, she didn't have much faith, not much at all... but she knew Andi said she didn't need *much*... and it still counted. She would have to go with that. And she had love for her friends in her heart. But hope? What was hope really? Was allowing for the possibility that saving Mainstar might not be in the plan, just a coward's way of letting everyone off the hook? Would poor business decisions and bad luck prevail just because they had to? She had no idea. It would be just as reasonable to become an entrepreneur like Sophie or expect the money to buy the whole lot herself to fall from the sky. Huh, she thought cynically. She didn't even know any grown-up she could talk to. Why did it always seem irresponsible to expect the impossible? Well, blow it - she was not going to give up hope! She was going to ask God for the impossible… because Andi would if she could… and right now she couldn't.

"Well God, Andi says you understand all sort of things we know nothing about… and I don't want to stick my little bit of faith in where it is not supposed to be… but I'm really worried about Sally and Billy and all the others at Mainstar. I'm asking you to save it God. Please. Don't let them have to sell… and lose their home and their jobs. Can't imagine what can be done now that the wool-clip is gone. I know I've even seen the letter in the basket about the foreclosure of the mortgage… but... huh… don't know what else to say. Except… please! Amen."

Jo sat down in the window seat and sighed. One day soon her foot will be better and she'll be able to go for a jog. The rain started to fall a little more steadily. There were puddles in ruts on the road where a sulky had recently gone past. Drops plopped heavily in water lying on the path to the house, and colourful geraniums bowed their flowers gratefully for the rain.

Robert rode up in the dull evening light. His heavy greased raincoat and felt-hat were dark from rain, matching the wet flanks on his horse. His stepped over the water on the path in one stride and stamped mud off his boots on the bootjack at the edge of the verandah before he stripped off his jacket and came inside.

Jo stood as he came in. She looked at him. Stress lines around his eyes showed deeper than ever. "I've just been to see Charlie. We went over to meet Betancourt. He has given us until the end of the month to come up with the money… he's not changing his timeline…" He sat down and swore. "We're done."

Jo raised her eyebrows. "Just like that?"

Robert looked at her as if he was seeing her for the first time. "Just like what?"

"Like that! Why are you so unwilling to fight for this? Surely Charlie does not feel the same way."

"You might have done accounting at school, Girl, but this is real business. It's over. Without the clip to see us through until Charlie's wedding… it's over."

"Did you talk to Eunice?"

"What about?"

"Getting married sooner – maybe, I don't know. She's the one with the money."

"Eunice?"

"Yeah. I reckon timid little Eunie has got a whole bag of surprises inside of her. Given half a chance, she'd do pretty much anything in her power to help Charlie. I know that."

"Power – Eunice." He laughed scornfully, "There's two interesting thoughts that hardly go together."

"Come on Robert. It's not like you are bursting with options. Eunice is an easy one… try her out at least.

"You seriously think that old Gossip would change any of her agenda to save us?"

"That's *Mrs* Glossop with an "L"… and I think you should at least ask. She's family isn't she?"

He smiled a wry smile. He deserved that. "Point taken. Eunice was with us this morning when I spoke to Charlie. Yes, you are right: she did offer to bring the wedding forward. But Mrs Glossop wouldn't hear of it. She was quite beside herself, finding out the truth of our affairs. She accused Charlie of criminal deception. It got quite ugly. Eunice was distraught in the end."

Robert ran his hands down his face and then back through his hair and down the back of his neck. He felt tension in every muscle. One thing he was grateful for. His father was not here to witness the indignity of this. How he would be shamed! All the scheming and planning and conniving he went through, right up until the last hours on his bed, all to protect his investment in his legacy; and now it was being systematically put down the gurgler. Robert knew it was mostly bad luck… if such a thing existed. Like the accident. Who could foresee such a disaster? There was not a more skilled and reliable Bullocky around than ol' Tom. He swore again. It was just awful bad luck.

He stood up suddenly. "I have to go home. I've got to tell Sally. You were right. She needs to know." The mention of home-and-Sally went hand in hand. It gave him something to focus on, and as dreadful as it was, it stirred his resolution. "I have arranged with Charlie to sign some final things at Aunt Millicent's in the morning. We'll leave straight after that." He went to his room and Jo could hear him organising and sorting stuff.

Jo sat back down on the window seat and looked out onto the street. Another wet buggy went by, slow and bedraggled in the rain. Jo could not help but wonder why everything seemed to cry when it rained. Somehow the world sensed the tragedy that had hit this family. And then, as if the clouds had read her thoughts and empathised with her pain, a long heavy rumble rolled across the low darkening sky. There was a slight pause as if the clouds were gathering their breath, and then the rain teemed down. The water gushed off the shingles over the window and curtained the gloomy scene before her. Water swept in rivers down the street, tracking along the wheel ruts and washing them deeper, so that the water ran brown, stained with liquid mud.

* * *

16.

The rain that followed was unlike anything that Jo had witnessed before. Once it started there were endless days of unrelenting rain, rain and more rain. For a couple of hours the cloud broke and blue sky peaked through, just long enough to turn every one's eyes to the sky and raise their spirits, then to drown them once again as the clouds regathered to pour more water on drenched and saturated land. Brown water and washed up debris lay everywhere. The creeks rose high above the culverts and bridges. They'd been cut off from going home for a more than a week and it seemed now they would be cut off from the other side of town as well. That's when Robert decided to move over to Aunt Millicent's. Besides, Mrs Hillary was run off her feet looking for places to put displaced people moving into town to beat rising waters.

They took their suitcases and covered as much as they could under canvas and heavy blankets. Their buggy moved slowly in the muddy quagmire that had been a street just a week before. Robert got down and led the horses by the harness when the wheels refused to turn and just dragged through the slosh. They passed drays piled high with tables, cane rocking chairs and other household articles that had been salvaged from submerging farmhouses and covered optimistically with canvas sheets and blankets.

Grimy children splashed exuberantly in muddy holes around the drays declaring war on each other by enthusiastically slinging handfuls of slop into their opponents' hair. Squeals of laughter and quivers of fake terror gave their position away as they cowered behind the wheels hiding from attacks. Jo watched them with delight. Funny how kids have a way of turning the most miserable circumstances into a fantastic game. She guessed that when they grow up, they will talk about the flood that turned their town into a refugee camp, and fondly remember playing in the mud under the stranded drays.

Never had one trip across town taken so long. They detoured around the main streets, in an effort to move on the firmer mud of less trafficked roads. Everything was degrees of sloshiness. Jo looked out over the Town Common that was community-grazing land for house cows and school ponies. All that could be seen was a brown inland lake that stretched far beyond the creek. Just a few big old gums and she-oaks poked their branches up like drowning ladies calling for help.

They came to the final crossing to get to Aunt Millicent's side of town. Jo's heart sank when she saw the rush of brown swirling water that was creeping higher and higher up into the trees that lined the side of the road. Robert joined a gathering of onlookers. They were professional observers.

"Ya might make it..."

"Doubt you'll get a light trap like yours through."

"Struth... It'll wash ya to Timbuktu."

"Aww, I think ya missed it mate."

"Na. Your horses look good. You'll be right..."

"Don't remember it ever gettin' as high as this though…"

"No worries…" A man with a long soggy beard that dripped rain into his coat pocket made this last comment. He seemed the least convinced of all.

Robert quietly weighed the evidence. The water was still rising and his choices were limited because they had already relinquished their room at the boarding house. He could camp damp in a wet buggy and be rained on for an indefinite period, or make a go of it, and have some of Aunt Millie's famous Porterhouse stew for tea. The porterhouse won. Hands down.

He turned the horses around and drove back up the street. He unharnessed the buggy and strapped it to a sturdy box tree with a long hemp rope. He let one horse go and sprang up onto the other horse's bare back and helped Jo up behind him. He grunted to the crowd. "We're going through fella's. Hang on tight," he instructed Jo, as he plunged into the swollen waters spurring his horse on with muddy boots so it didn't have time to get spooked by the murky whirlpools swirling in front of them.

The horse raised his head and flared its nostrils, snorting rapidly as it fought the weight of the water churning around its legs. The crossing was wide and peppered across the water were various trees submerged at different levels. Robert was ruthless in his determination, urging his horse forward. Suddenly the bottom gave way. They were plunged deep into the muddy torrent. Jo clung onto Robert and wrapped her legs tightly around the horse's belly as the water swirled around them tugging at them viciously. Jo couldn't look. She closed her eyes and screamed a prayer. Robert hadn't given her time to absorb what was going on. She hadn't really understood the insanity of riding a harness-less horse through surging floodwater.

The horse pulled hard against the current; head stretched forward, the whites of his eyes showing in fear as it struggled to regain its footing. Jo could feel his muscles straining as its legs thrashed forward. For all their motion, they were momentarily stationary. Water roared in their ears. Then, slowly, slowly they were making progress. Closer, closer… they struggled to get nearer to the other side. Spectators watched them progressively edge downstream toward the opposite bank.

Above the roar of the water Jo could hear the cheers and enthusiastic screams of the onlooking crowd. It gave her a warm sense of knowing that these strangers were cheering them on. Immediately she felt the horse find traction and gain its footing. She breathed with relief. They were winning! Confidently it moved up out of the water, its flanks trembling in fatigue. Jo turned around to wave thanks to the cheer squad they were leaving behind.

She gasped. Dipping and rolling directly toward them was the huge stump of a fallen tree! Massive roots still entangled the muddy soil that once rooted it to the ground. It sailed toward them like a child's matchstick boat, racing in a street gutter. Jo screamed and pulled at Robert's shoulder. She heard him swear. He spurred his horse on. The water was too heavy. He swore again under his breath. The monstrous log snagged momentarily on some branches that bent and swayed like delicate reeds. It rolled effortlessly over the top, submerged and then bounced to the surface, still rushing at them.

"Quick," yelled Robert. "Grab the tree!" He hoisted her up into the arms of a thick wild box tree and turned the horse downstream, it's only chance of survival. He jumped onto its back, lifted his body off onto the large branch where Jo was clinging. He swung his heavy waterlogged boot and spurred his horse away. Now free from his riders, the shove in his ribs sent him rushing with the floodwater downstream. Jo watched in horror as the horse's bay head bobbed and dipped its way down stream, fatigue taking any hope of control away.

Suddenly the tree jolted. Whole branches shuddered with the impact as the log smashed against the trunk. Jo hung on grimly to the rough bark. She closed her eyes again. It was too horrible to contemplate what would happen next. Just now she needed to hang on. It was like a battering ram. The water kept pushing the log against the tree, pounding its trunk. The flooded torrent was unrelenting in its swirling and roaring, demanding that the log be kept moving. Eventually it broke free and tilted back into the main surge of water.

As Jo felt it scrape passed, she opened her eyes and scanned for the horse. And far down the edges of the swollen water she could see the limp brown form of the horse moving through the shallow waters and trees. Some onlookers, who had watched the scenario with panicked interest, had followed it down and were gently leading it back by its halter.

"Jo," Robert reached out to help her. "We have to move up." The churning water was rising. They scrambled higher into the branches watching as each knot on the trunk disappeared into the murky brown river. This huge tree was now was a shrinking island in the middle of the torrent, and both banks were receding further away.

What is it with trees? The Gully... now this? Jo closed her eyes again. All she could hear was the constant roar of water in her ears. She looked at Robert. His lips were moving in prayer. It hardly seemed the kind of thing he was used to doing. *Oh boy*, thought Jo, *I guess that means we are in a very deep predicament!*

Robert opened his eyes and looked at her. Did it take hoisting him up a granddaddy box tree in a raging flood to get his undivided attention? Was it too late now to find where his priorities should be? Why is the light clearest when everything is blackest? A face appeared in his mind. But it wasn't Sally he saw, as he might have expected: it was her father.

As a lad, he would go fencing with Will McBride. This was before Will worked at the timber-mill. Mainstar joined the trend to put boundary fences all the way around the station. Gangs of men would be working away for weeks. He remembered overhearing McBride urging his old man to let him go with him. He had felt a rush of pride that his company had meant so much to Will. They camped out under the stars, sitting by the fire, eating damper and syrup, roasting a rabbit they had trapped, singing ballads by the firelight. Will would pull out his mouth organ and hand it over to Robert to play a tune. Why would this be the thing he would remember now?

They talked about stuff while Will showed him how to rub a bushman's concoction onto his hands to toughen them up. Robert's theory was that it stung more than the blisters across his palms and was intended to make them seem trivial. He would bite his lip hard and pretend it was okay by talking tough. Sally's father never let-on that he noticed anything, and didn't berate the schoolroom softness of his hands.

Sometimes they would talk about God. Will showed him his threadbare testament he carried in his breast pocket, and asked Robert to read passages to him. Then he'd rehearse a ballad he was going to read in church. He would tell Robert what prompted him to write it and why it meant so much to him. Robert could never fault his thinking. Sometimes he'd ask Will about the next poem he was working on… and always the poet would pull out a sheet of paper and ask what he thought. He was impressed that Will would even ask his opinion. It made Robert feel he had special status.

Sometimes Will asked him to think up questions people might struggle with, or how they might react to what he wrote, and he would respond to each one. Will said he was helping him prepare. Robert went to church with the family one Sunday. He almost expected the place to erupt in volatile controversy as he read each line. He was surprised by the captivated hush that fell over the congregation.

When he asked Will about it, he said simply, "God helped me prepare my heart… and he prepared theirs as well. That's the key, my boy… preparing the heart." Will was so confident in the humble way he related to God. He continued, "You know, I did it once without preparing. Might as well have gone and spoke to the trees, for all the good it did. Nothing bad mind you… no one walked out… but it just didn't touch their souls. It was a good poem too, but it just didn't touch anything. Swore I'd never do that again without preparin' – if it be in my power to do so." And he grabbed Robert's shoulder warmly and said, "Thank ya for helping me prepare, son."

One night by the campfire Will pulled out a wad of papers stacked in a thick leather wallet. He passed them all over to Robert, and said "Rob, I want you to have these. They are as much yours as mine, because you've invested in them by bein' interested. God might choose to continue to prepare people's hearts with them. You never know."

Robert shifted his weight on the wet branch and wished with all his might that he could grab Will's hand in return and say, "Thank you for preparing my heart too, Will McBride."

Robert looked at the swirling water creeping up the bark of the trunk and felt the Spirit of God tugging his heart. He knew what McBride would have said, "If you know your engineer, Rob, he can adjust you according to the master-plan; that way you won't ever be out of sync. Don't forget that."

Robert closed his eyes against the rain that plastered his hair flat against his head. Thoughts churned through his mind restlessly: farmer's soil, farmer's machinery... farmer's heart. He sighed and gave in. "For you then God. This farmer is yours; Mainstar is yours. If we get out of here… if You see fit to give me another go, then show me how to make the machinery of my life run smooth... just like Will McBride."

It had been long time since Will led him in prayer by a campfire. He had promised to get to know the Master Designer. But life happened, and so did his father. Madegan Senior flew into a rage when he found out Will McBride was infecting his son with religion. The fencing trips were cancelled. Sheep farming became the only focus. He was sent to boarding school… in the tradition of the Motherland. And as he grew older, he came to admit he had just been a kid under the influence of a remarkable man who shared ballads by firelight.

As he looked at the swirling water again, he realised it was not long after that last fencing trip together that Will McBride went to work at the mill. Robert's mother got sick first, and he was brought back from boarding school. Then his father became ill, but because Sally was so needed at the homestead, the family stayed in the worker's cottage rather than moving on. Things were definitely cool between the stationmaster and the tenant in the cottage by The Gully. He hardly saw Will McBride after that, but Robert was determined to protect his growing friendship with Sally. It became their secret; something only he and Sally shared.

His father had aggressively obsessed about an inheritance for his sons. Yet for Robert, it seemed that for all his ranting and plotting, it lacked something very basic. "You know God, if I have to choose a legacy to follow, I prefer the heritage of the poet-parson, teaching life by the fireside." And it seemed to Robert that it was the easiest choice to make, out of love and respect for a simple man who lived as he spoke.

* * *

17.

They moved up the tree again. Any hope of aid seemed to be fading with the light. Robert watched Jo and kept prodding her as she dozed like a koala in a fork of the tree. "You can't sleep Jo. You mustn't. There's no way I'll be able to hold you. Hang in there. You can. I know you can."

"Yeah, but do I want to?" muttered Jo groggily. She was so tired. Her arms and legs had lost sensation long ago. Everything ached. Her head throbbed and it dropped down every now and then, when it was too heavy to hold up any longer, bumping hard against a branch. Pain would shoot through her brow and start her back into wakefulness a little longer. She was so thirsty. How long since she had had a drink? There was so much water everywhere; how could she be thirsty? She longed to cry, but her eyes were dry, like gritty sand and no tears would come. And all the while the water below them roared and growled waiting for someone to slip in their resolution.

"We'll keep each other awake. It seems a long time since we were so close to Aunt Millie's porterhouse stew."

"Great," said Jo, "Don't start talking about food! That's all I need – to notice how hungry I am as well as everything else!"

"We gotta talk about something…"

Jo groaned. "Why?" She just wanted to sleep and if she couldn't sleep, she almost wanted to give up. Almost.

"Because…"

"Just 'because' doesn't count…" her voice trailed. He was beginning to sound like a dripping tap, persistent and annoying. More water.

"Okay then. What about this? I believe God has got some good things ahead. I've resolved that if I don't fight for it – I'll never know."

"Did you say 'God'?" Now Jo opened her eyes. Now Robert too? Was the whole world religious? She had forgotten her own pleading prayer and was unconvinced any other tragedy could befall this family. She had no concept that those looking on from the bank felt that Madegan's family would have another tragedy to deal with come morning.

"Yeah, I did."

"Where did that come from?"

"Sally's father. When I was a young fella… he prayed with me."

"You're a Believer? Like Andi?"

"You seemed shocked..." Robert smiled grimly. He didn't really want to talk about his personal faith…because it was... well, personal. But he could see this stirred Jo when all his other attempts at conversation had failed.

"I'm sorry I sounded surprised. I just didn't know," she said

"*Saved soul, but wasted life…*"

"Pardon?"

"It's something I heard someone say once. It sorta struck me at the time: that's me. I've got my name in the Book of Eternal Life: my soul's safe, but my life hasn't had much direction: its being wasted. I guess I had to be shoved up a tree in a flood to get my attention, so I don't waste another moment."

"Well, I'm glad you've finally got the message. I wonder if that automatically qualifies us for a Divine rescue?"

Robert looked at the fading evening sky, and the row of lanterns lining the bank of the swollen river, were getting brighter. Realistically hope was fading with the light.

Jo scowled. "We are in a serious spot here. If you're into Bible stories – we could do with Jonah's whale about now. He was tossed into a huge storm in the middle of the ocean without a lifeboat. It was a bit like being rescued before helicopters are invented. Our rescue will have to be a miracle… which I wouldn't mind happening sooner rather than later." Jo shocked herself by the matter of fact way she spoke about it. As the words came out of her mouth, it sounded like someone else speaking. Funny, she didn't know many bible stories, but that fish was pretty famous… and she'd been to a concert with Andi where someone had shared what that story meant to him in between sets. She was gunning for an impossible 'out' just now too.

"What do you mean by helicopter?" Robert looked through the leaves at her.

"Oh…" *Ooops* thought Jo. *Not this century.* "Ahhh, it's something I read that famous Italian guy, Leonardo De Vinci wanted to invent… a machine that flies… reminds me of a dragonfly… the way it just hovers around in the air, but the technology doesn't exist. It will one day – I guess," she said lamely. "Just thought it would be kinda handy just now - to get us out of here."

"Well that's it of course!" said Robert excitedly.

"You have a helicopter?" Jo asked. "Ludicrous".

"We can't go *on* the water – but we don't have to – we'll go *over* it!"

"Okay", said Jo dubiously, "that is about as plausible as a fish swallowing you whole." But even that worked once, so why not? "Is asking '*how*' too specific a detail to trouble you with at this time?" she asked cautiously.

"We need rope…" and he called out to the people on the bank, over the roar and rush of the water. Suddenly they were activated as if some strange chemical catalyst was poured over them. Solutions began to materialize as light on the horizon was quickly fading. Jo just closed her eyes and hoped that whatever he was planning was going to work - soon! Not much could happen in the complete dark. The idea of staying here in the night would really freak her out.

With a bushman's catapult, a lump of weighted bag, and a fairly substantial amount of prayer, after two or three misses, a missile tangled in the branches of their tree attached to a long rope. "Aunt Millie!" Robert called to the sky, "put the Porterhouse on, we're coming home!" He scaled up the tree and firmly anchored it to the trunk; those on the bank did the same, stringing out the rope like a clothes-line, pulling it tight so that water flicked off the rope as tension took up the slack.

Jo looked at him dazed. She knew instinctively what he was expecting her to do. Suddenly she wished a fish *could* swallow her whole. That seemed by far the more rational option than scraping along the surface of flood water, dangerously washing with debris. She shivered and her empty stomach felt sick. She dry-retched over the branch she was sitting on. When she opened her eyes, she was looking straight into the dark shadows of swirling water. She felt so tired. Her legs were like jelly, trembling from fatigue and fear. How could falling be anything but inevitable? There is no way she would have the strength to hold on. The lantern lights were so far away.

"Jo! We're running out of light."

She didn't move. She couldn't. "I can't do it," she whispered faintly.

"You can and you will. What's that thing Will McBride wrote about once? 'We can do all things because God gives us strength?' Just now I'm asking that God will do that for us... you can do this."

"I can't... there's just no way I could even if... it's impossible."

"Do you want to know something? Your life depends on it."

"I won't be able to hang on. I'm numb all over. I can't do it!"

"This is what we've got to work with... which is more than we had half an hour a go." For once Jo heard irritation in Robert's voice. He spat into the water and closed his eyes momentarily. He pulled her up to her feet and massaged her calf-muscles and arms... urging sensation to return. He took off his belt and strapped them to her wrists like handcuffs over the line. He removed one of his long leather boots that he slung over the rope. "Hang onto the boot – foot in one hand... that's it... and the top of the boot in the other. If you slip the belt will hold you. When you hit the water use the rope and pull yourself over to the bank." He paused. "Are you ready?"

"*No!*"

"Jo..."

She looked at him desperately. He wouldn't dare push her... would he? Just then something moved on the branch behind him. Her groggy eyes tried to focus in the dimness of the cloudy dusk. Suddenly the hairs on her arm stood up as she realised: a snake! Its forked tongue flicked in and out, its smooth brown body followed along the length of the branch; back into the leaves... it went on forever. "Robert," she whispered hoarsely, "there's a ...*snake* behind you!"

He looked into her wide-open pupils and did not move. He just whispered... "The flood water... everything will be crawling with 'em. Go quickly! I will follow. Quickly. Go!"

Jo launched out into the welcoming spaces in front of her. Her body tensed as she felt the rush of wind scream about her and the branches of trees flicked at her like whips as she hurled passed. She closed her eyes and realised the screams were hers. Her eyes opened to see the lanterns race closer.

Suddenly her feet touched the water and in panic she lifted them high... but the momentum plunged her into the water. She screamed and screamed, thrashing for her life as she felt the rough hands of men lift her out of the shallows onto the back of a wagon and wrap her in a blanket. An anonymous hand passed her a mug of warm soup. More comforters wiped at the scratches on her face and arms and applied a soothing lard-based balm. Then Robert was there; someone handed him a mug of sugary billy-tea. Never, he declared, had such a drop seemed like the nectar of heaven.

* * *

Robert sat back from the lace tablecloth and wiped the corners of his mouth on the napkin he retrieved from his lap. "Aunt Millie, if I didn't know for sure we weren't washed away in that creek, I would say I'd died and gone to heaven. That was the most delectable morsel my pallet has ever been privileged to experience!"

Aunt Millie sat looking at her nephew sitting at her table like a refugee in ill-fitting clothes she had salvaged from her cupboards. She squeezed her lips into a terse, uncomfortable smile.

"I trust your friend is settled, Robert?"

"I asked Ellie to check on her before I came down. She was asleep."

"Robert, I hear some very disturbing talk about town. Francine Glossop came to see me. It is a disgrace. What would Harold say if he were here?"

Robert looked at his aunt thoughtfully. Aunt Millie was his mother's sister. How he missed his mother's quiet gentleness. She had a softness about her, yet he remembered those times when she was as stubborn as mud. Millie had shades of his mother's unreasonableness and her sensitivity too. In fact, when it came to Millie, she could be very sensitive! Still, he loved her dearly. "I appreciate that you have always regarded my father well. But he had a few ideas that some would probably not expect."

"I know Harold had the highest sense of family. That is what I know! He was devoted to your mother."

Robert couldn't argue with that. "Yes, he was."

"And," Aunt Millie continued defiantly, "he was always so proud of you boys and your success."

He paused. Should he share his perspective on that? He decided to say nothing.

"And, I'm sure that a purely mercenary alliance, without any regard to the people involved, would be revolting to him." Aunt Millie's chin was high. This was an affront to her family's reputation.

"My father spoke with Mrs Glossop before he died. He said he admired Eunice greatly. He even said that he anticipated… romance."

"Poff and twiddle! How could he say that?"

Robert shrugged. "He did."

"He told me himself he thought it a shame the poor girl didn't have more spunk! Why would he want Charlie to marry someone he considered a limp rag?"

Robert let the words speak for themselves and lifted his brewed coffee and smelt the aroma like a bee hovering over a flower. "It's not as bad as you think. Eunice loves Charlie very much… and I have reason to believe Charlie returns her affections…" (*somewhat…*) he qualified silently under his breath.

"Well, we'll see about that. I've never seen Francine Glossop in such a state. She said as soon as she could get to her lawyer she was going to cut Eunice out of the Estate – if she persisted in marrying him. So, I suspect it will come to nothing now. Two paupers don't marry and make a decent life together! Unless it is all just a storm in a tea-cup? All that trouble… surely you have sorted it out?"

"I received this letter before we left the boarding house." He pulled a damp envelope from his vest pocket and laid it on the table. He looked at it warily as if it was filled with crawling red-back spiders… and he wanted to squish them violently to a pulp. "If it is – as you say, a storm in a teacup: the storm is cyclone-rated and the teacup is the size of… Mainstar."

Aunt Millie sat still, looking like someone had just slogged her forehead with the backside of a fencing shovel. She could see the Financier's insignia on the top corner of the envelope. "Then Robert, if there is so much at stake, why are you going around town with that girl?" said Millie, pointing her chin upstairs towards the bedroom where Jo was asleep.

"What are you suggesting Aunt Millie?"

"I am merely suggesting that there are plenty of eligible girls who would be delighted to keep company with you… those who are ladies of means."

Robert laughed. "Aunt Millie? I am shocked! Would you also suggest mercenary alliances… in concurrence with my father's posthumous petition?"

"Not at all!" she looked horrified at the thought. "It is just that, well in the light of *all* the circumstances, if there have to be girls… it wouldn't hurt to be a little… discerning."

"Which is exactly what my father was thinking. He was ahead of us all… as usual. It's just unfortunate I don't agree with him."

Aunt Millie looked distressed. "Now Robert, I know your father was not a religious man… but he held very high morals. Honouring your parents is a Biblical principle that it beholds us all to attend to regardless of our faith."

"I don't think I have been dishonouring."

"But you just said…"

"I said I didn't agree with him. It's not the same thing."

"You should follow Charlie's example… he has not argued with your father."

"Charlie followed Dad's instructions to a tee because it suited him. If it didn't, he would not blink an eye at doing something else."

"You seem very sure of that."

"He is my brother…" Robert put down his cup and sighed. Why did everything have to be contentious?

"Twin-brother Robert… exactly!"

"I have lived with our similarities and differences all our life. I know them."

Aunt Millie found she was not gaining any ground. She changed tack. "But we don't know anything about this Josephine-girl. She could be a liability! A millstone for your future. Robert, be sensible."

"Aunt Millie, relax. She won't marry me."

"Marry you! Robert – have you given leave to your senses? You didn't even consider such a proposal surely!" Millicent gasped. The scandal that implied was almost too much for Millicent Fillips to contemplate. "I always thought Harold… bless his soul… would do all he could, to protect Mainstar."

"Aunt Millie – what it comes down to is that I cannot marry at all. My father has seen to that. I had hoped that Charlie would be happy…

have an heir and all. But even that seems to be doomed. It's ironic don't you think – that the very thing that Father sought to protect Mainstar with, has been a factor in its demise?"

Millicent rose from her chair. "I know you mean well Robert. But sometimes I think it would be a little bit more appropriate for you to take a leaf or two out of your father's book!"

Robert sighed again. But sometimes Aunt Millie's persistent and stubborn naivety was beyond comprehension. She was not a stupid woman, and even his mother had seen the glaring faults of Harold Madegan, as well as his powerful strengths. He looked after her as she left the room. Aunt Millie only ever saw Harry as the doting husband to her sister; her civilized, successful brother-in-law. He was everything her gentle, easy-going Herbert was not. She only ever allowed the slander she heard about Harold Madegan was based on jealousy. In her eyes he was some sort of misunderstood saint that rightly should be canonised.

For Robert the reverse was true. He had to doggedly remind himself that his father was not a villain whose dark heart was riddled with evil intent. He was just a man with fallible faults

– human and mortal. Robert found that carrying responsibility of Mainstar made some of his father's decisions more comprehensible. Still, there were some things that he wished he could step inside his father's mind and crawl around to find the reasons behind them. There simmered a faint glow of hope that perhaps his father's driving motivation was not just to make his life unbearably miserable.

A warm, wet nose nuzzled his hand. "Hey Carey-girl… grown web feet yet?" Robert rubbed her black coat and scuffed her ears into knots. She sat her broad back end heavily on his freshly polished boots and drooled geriatric affection in his lap. Oh, for the uncomplicated life of being a dog. Devoted. In a dog's eyes, no one can do wrong… no one can fail… no one can *not* measure up because the only measure used, was love.

He grimaced as he thought about his clumsy Carey-dog comment about Sally. Jo had really fired up over that. How could she understand that this dog was his best friend? His brother had abandoned him for sporting friends, and influential names. When they had stayed here on the way to and from boarding school,

Charlie would disappear into town, and him and Carey would go down to the creek together: fish, chase ducks, dangle craybob traps, and sling-shot anything that stayed still long enough to get your eye in. It was that soul-mate dimension he referred to in Sally… being himself without having to measure up to lofty expectations.

Robert sighed… and pulled out his pipe. He looked at it slowly and then tucked it back in his pocket. He didn't enjoy it anyway. It was just a thing gentlemen station-owners did. So, Robert carried a pipe because it seemed another way of measuring up, and fitting in. It was hard to live in a "measure-up" family: especially if Charlie was your brother. Charlie was smarter, quicker, more decisive and got things done. Those things appealed to the businessmen in town, and on the land: a boy after his father's own heart. Robert on the other hand, was dreamy, lazy, indolent and slow… or so he was often told. Those things could not be tolerated. Those things had been the focus of his father's mission in life: to work them out of this second son, so he could secure Mainstar as his legacy for future Madegans.

Robert stood up and went over to the upright piano and traced an intricate swirl on the walnut veneer with his brown work-calloused finger. He lifted the lid and sat down, and gently played a melancholy impromptu composition. He realised that this was just another point of not fitting in. Music was for girls, not men who ran sheep stations. If there needed to be entertainment, the women could do it. He smiled wistfully as he realised he was never taught the piano, he just knew. How accomplished could he have become with some training, he wondered. Playing the piano was one of those things that Aunt Millie let him do because she enjoyed the evening concerts while she did her embroidery work. It never occurred to her that Harold would not approve, and Herbert never enlightened her.

* * *

18.

Charlie borrowed a horse and went back to Mainstar as soon as he could get through the cut roads and creeks. When the water receded, Robert retrieved the buggy from its riverside anchor. It had been only partially submerged and a solid scrubbing with a fair bit a grease around the wheel-hubs brought it back to useable. Jo sat beside Robert in the buggy but they had no supplies to take back. The pantry shelves in town had been eaten bare. The town was moving ever so slowly again. Families repacked their things and started to return to see how their homes had faired. The evacuated houses on the low side of town were now being mopped and scrubbed to make them liveable again. The locals declared it had been the worst flood in living memory.

Everything smelt. Their clothes were musty from the damp. The whole world seemed to be coated in putrid silty mud. Rotting heaps of grass and washed up animals entangled in masses of debris were rotting along broken fences in a warm steamy wetness. The state of the road made progress slow. Repair gangs were out with carts, picks and shovels, patching up obvious damages to get the flow of life happening once more.

Robert speculated out loud about Mainstar. They knew the water level from the flood of '64. They knew which paddocks would give the stock the best chance of staying out of water. But they also knew nature was unpredictable. And to top it off, their father's number-one management policy had been broken. They had grown up calling it the *real* golden rule. It required that someone *always* stay at the property so that decision making was never left to workers - even workers with a long history of loyalty and reliability. One weekend for his brother's engagement party did not seem such a big deal. How typical, thought Robert... bend the rules, and you could guarantee you'll be caught out. But being caught out so severely even took Robert by surprise. The shock was seeping into his bones.

What would they find at home? The homestead had never been washed before. Was it inundated this time? The slab hut would have gone under... the question was by how much or was it gone completely? Was everyone safe? How much stock did they lose? Did it matter?

Was another nail in the coffin any more of a problem then the ones already there?

A little whisper in the recesses of his mind said: "Hope is an anchor for the soul... I will order your steps." And Robert resisted the desire to scoff that 'hope' hardly seemed a sufficient anchor for a disaster of this scale. But he had nothing better to offer and no other solutions to cling to. He recalled the things he had thought about in the box tree, the tree that had gradually been swallowed by rising floodwaters. His hands started to tremble as he remembered watching the branches where they sat go under... just before the waters peaked. They did not get out of that tree a moment too soon.

It took them three days to get to the entrance of Mainstar. They bogged twice and many times they had to stop and repair sections of washed track before they could progress. At night they had a basic snack of salted beef and damper before they made camp under the stars. Jo slept cramped and fitfully on the bench seat with a blanket covering her to keep the myriad of mosquitoes at bay. Robert rolled his swag out on the tail gate of the wagon, and made a smoky fire fuelled by cow dung and damp leaves in an attempt to keep the insects at bay.

Finally, they turned into Mainstar. Their road was also washed and gutted. Someone had already made a meagre attempt to fill in the big ruts with old branches and gravel, which allowed the buggy to get through, and meant that they did not have to stop and do the repairs themselves. This mutilated trail home suddenly seemed like a highway. They could see debris caught high in the branches of trees that lined the track. How Jo longed to know if everyone was okay.

When the horses turned the last bend over the culvert, and as they made their way up the rise toward the homestead, Jo could feel her chest filling with relief, brimming up towards her eyes. They could see the shingle roof. At last, there was a remanent untouched by the monster deluge, whose tentacles had reached into every crevice of the world they knew. Even the horses sensed the excitement and hurried up the road to the house-yard gate. But before the horses even properly stopped, they bounded out of the buggy like children anxious to be home after a long school excursion. Robert coolly jumped the fence and Jo, entangled in respectable skirts, fumbled with the gate. When she looked up, she screamed with delight as her eyes met Andi's narrow frame standing on the verandah! She pushed through the gate, respectable or not, and hurriedly scrambled up the stairs to her friend.

"Oh Andi! Oh Andi!" she said over and over. Tears of pure relief washed Jo's face as she wrapped her arms around her friend! "Oh Andi, you're okay – you're okay! Oh, thank God! Thank God!" She laughed and squealed her prayer without even thinking. "Sally! Sally! Andi is up! She's okay! She's really okay!" she excitedly announced, dancing about as if Sally had not yet caught up with this news! She looked up to see her standing in the doorway enjoying the thrill of witnessing the miracle afresh!

Robert was standing behind Jo, delight dancing around his eyes… and his wriggly moustache had started to twitch happily again. Jo was so ecstatic! Sally could see something had changed in Robert. Amazing what coming home can do, she thought. Even coming home to a disaster zone. She wanted to bottle this moment – bottle it and preserve it forever… because she sensed this was a precious rare moment that was not going to last for very long.

19.

The hardest thing is coming in to land after you have been able to soar above the clouds. There had been so many clouds lately that the joy of sunshine seemed to surpass any other pleasure. Andi retired to her room for a rest while Robert and Jo sat down at Molly's kitchen table. Sally poured them a cup of tea and Molly found some biscuits in her barrel of treats. Once, such a thing would have set the whole kitchen into a spin, but today, it seemed like the most natural thing that Robert would sit and join them.

They sat together, going over what had transpired while they were away. Charlie was out in the back paddocks with some of the shepherds and station-hands taking stock of the extent of their losses and damage. Billy was down at the shearing shed helping the men clear up the yards. The shed itself did not go under but it was an island for many days surrounded by water that lapped through the slated floor. When the rain started Sally said she knew it was going to flood. She had got the cart, and together Billy and her salvaged as much stuff out of their hut as they could. They stored it in the shearing shed up on wool classing tables pushed together. She called the workers together down at the shed and mapped out what needed to be done in the absence of the bosses, because when they didn't *get* home it was obvious they couldn't. Single-handedly she allocated men to take charge of moving sheep. For days no one slept, but snatched naps so they could work around the clock. Molly had food constantly on the table and the men would come in at any time to dry off, have some tea and refuel before they went back out. And then there was nothing to do but wait. And the waiting was hardest of all.

Sally had stepped well outside her allocated jurisdiction, she knew that, but she could not stand by and see her loved home wash down the creek. Sally said it seemed strange but she remembered the games she and Robert had played as kids when they would plan what to do when disasters struck. Back then it had not been a case of "if", but "when". They had covered every scenario, bush-fires, drought, even cyclones and earthquakes... and she tried to relive those games of strategy.

She told them that for years, old Mr Madegan had consulted his sons, his overseers, his managers and agents as if she was invisible.

She *had* been invisible. His nurse was not *really* there. Just an indispensable extension needed to get a drink, an elixir or give a foot massage, as he needed it. It never occurred to Harold Madegan that Sally was tutoring herself in Station Management. She would play games to amuse herself and try to stay one step ahead, anticipating answers to questions, instructions, and solutions to problems. If she disagreed with Mr Madegan's strategies she would make herself give three reasons why her way was an acceptable option, or a better alternative. Sometimes she just had to admit that old Madegan was right.

It seemed that no one wanted to argue with the young housekeeper as she directed men to take charge of specific areas of responsibility. She could do no more and hoped it would be enough.

Then as the quarters flooded in, the homestead became a boarding house. Like never before she ruled with an iron rod. To start with, the exhausted men slept for days, recovering from their huge and tireless efforts. Then they played cards and two-up without betting money, using matchsticks as currency. They probably had every intention of redeeming these sticks when they had access to full money pins again.

The water continued to rise even after the rain stopped. It peaked just at the butts of the gum trees that stood guard like Roman centurions outside the fenced homestead yard. And then the water was gone, leaving the mess and the smell and the clean-up. Everyone was restless when the urgency of crisis was over. It was such a relief to see Charlie ride through the murky brown water washing over the culvert. She easily stepped back into the shadows and went back to washing bed sheets and cleaning floors.

Jo looked at her amazed. "You did all this! Sally you are incredible! And you told me you wouldn't want to do this!"

Sally smiled. She knew something had changed in her. She could not deny it. Something had been released and no amount of social putdowns could shove it back down again. "I've thought about it a lot. This is what I do every day only on a bigger scale. Managing a house requires the same processes, but the scale of this was much more exciting. And to see it work! I fully expected Charlie to reprimand me.

But he didn't. He said nothing except a simple "thank-you". It was the single most powerful thing I've ever heard him say!" She stood up and refilled the teacups.

Robert had said little except for asking a few clarifying questions now and then. He didn't seem shocked at all. He already knew what was in her. He sculled the freshly poured cup and stood up. "I'm going down to the shed to check what's happening there…. and have a look around. I'll send Billy up to help you here." He paused and looked quietly at Sally. "Don't forget our date," he said as he strode out the door.

Jo stared after him as he shortly reappeared riding bareback down the track – the hooves kicking up clods of mud and flicking them out as they went. He was too anxious to see what was happening to be bothered saddling his horse. Jo turned to look at Sally, her deep blue eyes still staring thoughtfully after him. "Did he say "date"?" said Jo. Sally nodded, but she didn't look as pleased or excited as Jo expected. "But that's good – isn't it?"

"I think so. I'm not sure. Something's happened… and I don't understand it yet. I guess that's what he wants to talk about. It's good he finally wants to talk again. It's been a long time." Then Jo understood her reserve. Everything was changing. She was catching up with all the changes: the changes in her, in him, for Mainstar.

Sally had wanted to stall the changes, make them stop and go away. But she realised, as she cared for Andi, that change could be good. Small changes in Andi's health made her excited and showed her change can be positive: progress. And much more – that dramatic change can be a miracle and not a catastrophe at all. Sally smiled pensively. It was strange that God would make her aware of 'change' right before the flood. And now something was changing with Robert as well. "Keep showing me; *please* keep showing me. It's getting rather interesting… seeing things from Your point of view," Sally prayed. And suddenly she realised something: she was not afraid! The fear had gone. The fear of being homeless; the fear of stepping out of line; the fear of failure; the fear of being buried and life passing her by. God knew. He would see that it would work out. All she had to do was what he set in her hand each day. Last week had extended her beyond what she had ever imagined. She had prayed through every discussion, every decision; and she had seen provision after provision, even in the face of disaster and destruction.

* * *

Jo went in and sat by Andi's bed. She just looked at her friend for a long time. She stared at Andi's tired drawn face, resting in a natural sleep and was so grateful.

Andi stirred and opened her eyes. She smiled at Jo sitting there misty eyed. "You don't know how good it is to see you," she said quietly.

"Oh, I might have an inkling!"

"I've been so confused. I couldn't understand where I was. I want my Dad and Mum so much!"

"Do you understand now? Where we are, I mean?"

"I think so. For a long time, I thought it was a dream… about the basket. And one day I went looking for it. I had to find the basket… I had to know that it wasn't a dream… and I couldn't find it… I thought I was going mad. Sally found me rummaging hysterically through the chest of drawers." Andi looked at the tallboy cabinet standing by the bed. "Sally is so kind. She didn't say I was crazy. She just gave me a hug. She said you'd taken the basket to put your things in because that was all we had when we got here. She told me how Billy found us at the hut…"

"That seems like forever ago…"

"It seems like a dream… but when Sally was telling me my part of that dream, I started to believe it. I remember Billy hitting us because he got so scared. Billy comes to visit me every day. He brings me little things he finds. He said that I had promised to be his friend before I got sick and that he was my friend always. I remembered something about Goldilocks. He said you tell him stories every night."

"Billy's a cool kid. You made me see that…"

"I did?"

"Yeah, you did that disgusting thing of spitting in your hand and then shaking with it, just to let him know you were not mad at him. I know how much you hate mucky stuff. That was the noblest thing I've ever seen you do! Very impressive! Mind you – at the time I thought you'd lost your mind!"

"I… I don't remember doing that. What I want to know is if you are just a dream, and all the stuff in that other place…. is that real?"

Jo looked at the intensity in Andi's eyes. A worried, frightened, lost look clouded in. "You mean home?"

Andi nodded. She wanted to believe it all, but she couldn't quite bring herself to say it out loud, in case she really was teetering on the edge of unreality and insanity. Jo wanted to reassure her, but she didn't want to make it seem too heavy and bizarre… which was kind of impossible considering. The pause made Andi panic… an irrational scary feeling started to swing in and out and around her. Perhaps it really was just a weird, extraordinary nightmare after all.

Jo saw her panic rising. "Hang on there… which part don't you get? The bit about the cars or the trucks or the aeroplanes or televisions or ipods or computers or mobile-phones or satellites or microwave ovens or automatic washing machines or flushing toilets or space-travel… or the school-work… that's it… algebra! No hang on… *I* don't get the algebra, and you do!"

Andi stared at her wide-eyed! Jo blinked back at her – as if what she had just said was the most normal, ordinary thing in the whole world! And they burst out laughing. Andi was not yet convinced that this was not a dream… but at least in the dream she had her friend back, and her friend had the same irrational memories, of the same fantastical science-fiction world that used to be home. Just talking about it gave Andi a warm sense of familiarity and homeliness. She could trust that feeling, if nothing else.

Jo was on a roll. "In fact, I don't miss those things so much…" she said rather reflectively… "But I do miss my jeans and long hot showers and *my* Dacron filled pillow with all the bumps that match *my* head, and my dog Boof, and my Mum's chicken satay. It just goes on and on!"

Andi caught the connection. "Oh I miss my clothes – especially my own nickers, and pop-corn at the movies and sun-glasses and real shampoo that isn't used for washing sheets as well, and the radio and my music and emails and being able to read a million books...especially my Bible without the *'thees'* and *'thous'*…"

They both laughed at the ridiculous list of things that they missed. "I think I've missed laughing with my friend most of all…" When it subsided, they gave each other a hug, warm and full of gratitude, knowing that good things were always just a friendship hug away.

"How wonderful to have my friend back," thought Jo.

* * *

20.

Robert spent the rest of the day working down at the shed, and they seemed to barely scratch the surface in what needed to be done. They seemed to have fared far better than some of the places around, judging from stories that the men were telling. He promised to come home while it was still light enough, so he could walk Sally to the hut to see what damage had been done. She knew it had gone under, but she had not had time or courage to see the extent of it, or if it was still even there. She was relieved that Robert suggested he go with her. Robert had another motive. He wanted to talk to her alone.

Sally went through her chores with exceptional speed. She sensed change, and she desperately wanted to know what it involved. She dared not guess or hope too much. That was not safe ground to travel. "Best wait and see what is really happening," she told herself over and over. Oh, she had missed her friendship with Robert so much.

She met him at the gate in a fresh dress and polished boots. She felt a bit silly but he had dared to call it a date, and she felt bold enough to call his bluff. Robert looked at his silt-coated trousers, grimy work shirt and roughly washed forearms still coated in residue mud. He didn't look shocked at her presumption. He just quietly apologised for tardiness and said, "I'd really like to bathe… if you give me ten minutes I will return - more respectable company. I am starving though… could eat a horse. If you could catch me one – I'd appreciate it." Before she could reply he bounded inside. Sally went into the kitchen and put together a picnic tea in a basket. She put in lots of heavy bread thickly buttered and sustaining salted mutton, some of Molly's sweet honey bread, raisin biscuits and some lemon-syrup water and cups. She grabbed an old blanket from the cupboard. Now it really did feel like a date… and a nervous twinge fluttered in her tummy. Molly watched her preparations without a word. Sally had simply told her she was going to check the damage at the hut. As she went to slip outside once more, Molly opened the door for her, "Good luck sweetheart…" Sally took a deep breath and squared her shoulders. She knew very well Molly was not talking about floods washing away bungalow slab-huts.

Robert was already at the gate. Sally smiled at the break-neck speed that required him to be standing casually leaning on the fence in clean clothes and boots. He tipped his hat gallantly and took the basket from her hand. He offered Sally his arm and they walked around a mud puddle, down towards The Gully.

They said nothing for a long while… and then in the quietness Robert spoke, "Have you any idea what you might find?"

"At the hut or in the rest of my life?"

He turned and looked at her. "What would you like?"

"Both - of course. Sometimes not knowing is the hardest thing of all."

"What advantage would Faith afford us, if everything was mapped out?"

"Oh Robert!" Sally didn't want to be annoyed… but sometimes – really! "I don't want it all mapped out. Just an assurance that…"

"What?"

"Never mind…" It is much more difficult to share what's on your mind when there are other things at stake. They walked on in silence. Sally's thoughts began to spin. What if his offer to come was just prompted by a humane reaction to trauma? What if he was doing an honourable, but meaningless, employer-employee thing? She had hoped for so much more. When he first came home this morning… that look… she felt for sure it was just for her…or was it truly just a fantasy developed in her mind generated by the changes the past days had wrought? The silence seemed to get very loud.

"Is it just me… but you seem nervous?" Robert was always so cool.

"My home may have been washed away. Does that seem so unreasonable?" Sally's tone was clipped.

Robert was fishing; fishing for signs that the hope he was investing in was not in vain. But she sounded so irritated. Perhaps he had read her wrong. Perhaps he was just persisting in living a childhood delusion.

"No, I guess not." Why was he so tongue-tied? This was ridiculous! He needed to tell her what was on his heart before they got to the hut. Once they got absorbed in the outcomes of flood damage, the moment would be lost. "Sally?"

"Yes?"

"Would you mind if we stopped here to eat. I'm really very hungry."

"Sure." She looked around for a less muddy patch of grass. The sun had dried the surface, but everything was still squelchy underneath. Eventually they found a log. Not quite the picnic she had pictured. Still, being practical was never far away from Sally. She draped the rug over the log and wished she had put on a more sensible dress. Maybe she expected too much. Still, something was bugging him. She needed to love him enough to allow him the freedom to talk. "Mr Robert – your meal is served," She curtsied in a very maidly way, uncorked the bottle and poured the lemon drink into a mug.

Robert had a mouthful of bread and beef… half chewed, when he spluttered and choked, spitting sandwich all over the rug. "*Mr* Robert?"

Suddenly Sally realised she had the upper hand. "Certainly – *Mr* Robert, did you want your drink now or with your sweets?"

"Oh Sal, give me a break." She shook her head uncomprehendingly and shrugged. No way was she going to make it easy. This was as much his doing as hers! "The Mr Robert thing. When did that start?"

"Well, let me see… I believe it happened around a quarter past four, the afternoon of your father's funeral. My - I surprise myself – I have such a wonderful memory!" Now she was annoyed. Why would he pretend to have only just noticed? That happened over two years ago!

"Humph, of course I remember!" He went back to his bread, to gather his thoughts. Maybe Sal just liked the security of being an employee. Maybe she… oh he could speculate forever. There was nothing for it but stripping himself bare… showing the ugliness of his weakness and allowing her to respond to whatever she saw. He knew she didn't have a malicious bone in her body. Of that he was confident. "Sal, sit down please. Here. Beside me." She sat… on the far corner of the rug. He looked at her perching there. "Fair enough. Sal, since you brought it up… I need to talk to you about my father's funeral."

"Really – it was such a long time ago. The Bible says to let the dead bury the dead. Sounds like good advice to me."

"Not so long that it hasn't lost its sting. I need to. Please."

She nodded reluctantly. She didn't want to go through that pain… not now… not when things seemed to be getting better.

Robert took the mug of lemonade from her hand that she clung to securely and gulped the sweet syrup. He would have preferred a beer, considering how he was feeling. He poured her a drink and handed it back to her. "After the funeral, our attorney read my father's last will and testament. It was a bit of a marathon. Knowing my father's particular delight in attending to details, I guess that is no surprise. It was after the reading that I saw you… and I said some things. I was very angry but not with you. I wanted to say sorry."

Sally looked up into a tree and saw grass and bark caught high in its branches. A week ago, she would have been drowning. Why did it feel like she was drowning now? Tears glistened in her eyes. She had tried for so long to cover the hurt. What could justify what he said? She thought he didn't even like his father that much. How wrong people can be. "I understand you were upset. I felt the same when my father died. We say things we don't mean. I forgive you."

Robert shook his head. "No, you don't understand. I wasn't angry at losing my father – I was angry *with* him. He had so many expectations, like not getting familiar with employees. I know I am supposed to forgive him for what he did… I'm working through it. It's the hardest thing. I'm sorry for making you a victim of my anger."

"Victim?" Sally bristled her dark eyebrows arched in a fine line. "I am not a *victim*! Your ignorance is your own burden of folly to carry. I still live and work here, but not as any one's 'victim'!"

Robert allowed himself a pained smile. "If I didn't know better, I'd say you and Jo are tarred with the same brush."

Jo. There she was again... invading her moments. "You invited her to go to town with you." Try as she might Sally could not keep the hurt from her voice.

Robert stared at ground where clumps of washed debris entangled itself around small saplings. Had it mattered to her so much? "Yes, I did. I confess I wanted to be distracted... to forget. But all she did was talk about you... all the time! That part was... not a success... not at all."

"What do you want to forget Robert?" She looked away. Me?

"A whole lot of things... mistakes, wounds, history. I look at you Sal, and I admit that you probably have come out of this thing with the least scars... and I wonder how. Oh, that God would give me that grace."

Sally calmed as she looked into his hazel eyes. "I guess He has." Grace had made its mark.

"I don't want to labour it – but I want you to understand. After the funeral... I... I had planned... to let you know how I feel... how I..." Robert paused and took a deep breath. Well what for it? Here goes nothing. "I wanted to let you know I ... I wanted to ask you to consider ... being my wife." He looked over at Sally... she had stopped nibbling on a piece of beef. It was her turn to choke. She almost said something, but she stopped herself short. "But after the reading... it did not seem possible."

"Not possible?" She stared at him, the emotion rubbing raw on his face. "How could you hide such a thing so well?"

"I had to…"

Sally shook her head to clear her thoughts – she was missing something here.

Robert took a breath. "My father knew Mainstar had some residual problems. He sought to put in place factors that would help stabilize its future."

Sally looked at him suspiciously. He was getting off the track. Why did he have to change the subject and talk about the station when things came close to personal?

Robert continued. "One way of doing that is an independent injection of capital." How could he say this without making it sound tacky? He couldn't. After all that's exactly what it was. "I took the clause in his will for other legal opinions." He looked sideways at Sally. She was completely nonplussed. He pushed through. "They all said it would stand up to a costly legal contention. It baffles me still…"

"Well, that makes two of us. What did he put in the will… need I ask?" Sally knew what the essence of the document would have said. She nursed Mr Madegan for years. She had listened to his most personal rantings and his grumblings and his nit-picking with buyers and sellers and agents and neighbours. No one was exempt. But she needed to hear it from Robert.

"He put in the will, that if we were to retain our allotted share in the partnership, we had to ensure our prospective spouses had a defined amount of dowry."

Sally finally understood. "So, you had no choice."

"Oh, I had choices. I had to choose to tell you or not to tell you; to uproot you and Billy or to let you stay without obligation. That I couldn't choose. I'm sorry. I thought it would be okay… that things would go on the same. But I guess if I have learnt one thing… it is that things *never* stay static."

Sally sat stock still on the edge of the rug. She closed her eyes. They filled with tears and fell onto her dress unheeded. "Oh my. Robert, I am… shocked. You are saying the choice was not the station *or* me, but how to keep the station for all of us – for Billy and me as well? Oh Robert. Oh Robert!" She gripped the mug in her hand so tightly that her knuckles went white. "You absolute moron!" Sally turned on him with a tear-stained face and tipped the lemon syrup in her cup all over his head! She got up and left him sitting there stunned. She ran. She just wanted to be alone! For two years she had wondered what she had done wrong. For two years her heart had been torn apart by every whimsical imagination that a girl could devise. Every day as she saw him, or didn't see him, she had tried to work it out… and she had been so wrong! So completely wrong!

Robert licked the syrup off his lips and wiped his face on his sleeve. "Well, for the average Irish lass, I would say that went reasonably well."

* * *

21.

Work stretched out before them like an unending road. Robert was consumed by project after project. He left before dawn and came home after dark every day.

Jo took buckets, mops and brushes over to the hut and helped Sally scrub the silted walls down. Her ankle was better and only ached when she was very tired, which still seemed more often than not, these days. The verandah sagged in one corner but Robert had workmen come and repair the damage.

As if by some ultimate miracle of survival, the climbing rose, shredded and limp had stayed in the ground… and Billy gardened around it, nursing it back to health. Healing must be a family thing, thought Jo.

Inside, the news-print wallpaper was mud stained and peeling off in revolting lumps. They scraped it back and proceeded to do some redecorating with fresh newspapers and wheat-flour paste. Andi sat at the table to help them with this project. She smoothed out flat individual sheets and smeared paste onto the back. She trimmed old discarded Christmas cards that Sally had salvaged from the homestead, and suggested ways of arranging them to add colour to the black and white walls. Andi stencilled a bright floral pattern across the top of fresh hessian using crimson cochineal dye. They helped tack it to a beam to make a divider between the sleeping area and the living room. Billy moved their stuff back in and they helped restack the shelves with their few personal belongings.

They stood back to admire their work. The room had a fresh airy feel, but instead of feeling exhilarated at having a job well done, the girls were grim. They knew now that they would have to say good-bye. Mainstar was officially on the market. No miracle had zapped from the sky. Their hard work was gradually restoring flood damage… but that was just going back to square one.

Mr Betancourt appeared on the homestead verandah, the first day of the new month with his young, pimply-faced clerk holding the official documents in his hand. He loudly sympathised with the plight of the brothers who had to be brought in from the paddock to sign the papers he required.

Even Charlie said nothing now – there was nothing left to be said. The humiliation was tearing his soul. He wrote a letter to Eunice and filed it in his desk for the time to send it. It was cold and official and resigned. Gentle Eunice, he thought softly… you deserve much better. How he wished it had worked.

He hadn't realised how much he had really wanted it to turn out well between them. The fight she had put up to hold on to their engagement… to bring forward their wedding had surprised him. He saw something underneath the compliant exterior that stirred his interest. How could he have courted her for the respectable twelve months and not seen that? What else was there hiding, waiting to be discovered? He desired to see her blossom and grow out from underneath the mountain that was her mother. Would she be left to some other mercenary who would tell her lies to get hold of her inheritance?

A protectiveness rose up within him. And then he remembered the shame of his own behaviour, carried out under the letter of etiquette. He even waited the twelve months of mourning after his father's funeral to make contact with Eunice. He reviewed his calculated and emotionless strategies and it burned a hole in his heart. How could he? He had despised Robert because of his peculiar fickle morality. He humoured him only because he was his brother. Now he wished that he could say to Eunice that his motives were sincere: that he had not been playing a desperate game of economics with her emotional timidity.

He wanted to believe that this candid evaluation was not just an outcome of being caught out, but he had to admit that it probably was. For the first time in his life he was looking down a tunnel of no money, no work and nothing in place to fill up the vacuum it left. He had to honestly take stock of what it was showing him and he thanked Robert's God for not letting him get away with it. He felt he didn't deserve anything better.

* * *

Sally wavered between the elation of knowing Robert really did love her and the devastation of moving out of the familiar life that she had always known. Again, and again she marvelled at the complete peace she felt in her heart. It was sad and scary and unknown, but it didn't matter. God would make a way where there was no way. She was confident of finding another position. She no longer looked on Billy as a liability. He was willing and helpful and easy to get along with. There were many more gifted men who were not as useful around a property. They would definitely go somewhere else. The thought of working for new owners at Mainstar was unbearable.

One night, Sally, Billy, Jo, and Andi were walking back to the hut under the gentle light of a half moon and a myriad of stars. They were talking about some of the possible opportunities before them. They met Robert walking across from the shearing shed. Sally stopped to pass on a few messages and to tell him that Molly had already retired and his meal was in the warming oven. Jo grabbed Andi's hand and quietly manoeuvred Billy ahead. "We'll start supper," she whispered in his ear. Sally looked like she was being ambushed.

Robert leaned on a post and took off his hat. He ran his hand through his dark hair and sighed. Fatigue was seeping out of every muscle. "Was wondering if you could walk with me a moment, Sal?"

"I don't know Robert. I am pretty tired… and you look ready to collapse."

"I am.   But something is far more pressing…"

She looked at him in the dim light. She suspected what was so pressing. "Very well then." She stood stock-still.

"Will you walk?" Robert craved motion, in case he seized up and lost the flow of his thoughts. This had been on his mind constantly, but no opportunity had arisen…until now.

"Here will do."

"You are determined to make it hard."

She ignored that. "What is on your mind?"

"You are. Constantly. Sal, you know I love you. I want to know if you return my affection. I want you to be my wife. Will you marry me?" There. He said it.

Sally said nothing. She had longed all her life to hear him say those very words and now he had. Tears filled her eyes as she looked up at the moon and saw the silhouette of some late settling birds land on trees along The Gully. This was also late. "I don't know Robert."

"Don't know – what? That I mean it? You know I mean it!"

"Your timing is a bit… well, suspicious."

Robert stood stunned, glued to the spot. Did she really say that? Or was tiredness warping his senses? "Suspicious? What do you mean?"

"I don't want to be second best… not for you. Not for anyone."

Surely, she could not be serious? He swallowed. This was not what he had anticipated. "Second best? Sal – you are not second best. There has *never* been anyone else."

Sally shook her head, and strands of her hair fell in about her face. How could he not know what she meant? "Think about it, Robert. We are best friends. Then one day your father dies. Suddenly I am… a stranger… no worse! I am just your maid, an employee. I see you every day, and for two years you say only polite words or make only courteous enquiries. You make no attempt to explain or acknowledge what I did or what happened. Now I find out it was because you would lose your share in the station if you marry me…"

"But I explained that…"

"… and at that same time, I find out you really *do* love me… but now you will lose the property anyway… so well, it seems, you think: why not marry the servant girl after all?! I don't think so! I am not leftovers from yesterday's menu." By the time she finished saying it, she felt hot and cheated. Why couldn't he have just told her what happened? Is there no way he could not see that it made all the difference in the world?

Robert closed his eyes. God! How could I have been so daft? Help me! Don't let her go! Not now. Not now. "Sal, look at me. Do you really believe that? Do you really think that I said nothing because I wanted Mainstar?" She turned her face toward him and sniffed. "Sal, this place is nothing without you. I know how much you love being here… and how Billy loves being here. I made an error. My judgement was wrong. I'm sorry."

"What I don't understand most of all… is how you could not trust me! How can you seal yourself off from a friend just because you don't have all the answers? That is no way to live with a wife. I don't want you retreating inside yourself for years because you don't have an answer Robert. It is so basic… to me, to us! It is how we are! Not having the answer is *not* the problem! But you *do* have control over whether we talk about it. That sort of *sharing* is the part of this that I don't want to relinquish. It is the difference between being your wife and your housekeeper. I am already your housekeeper Robert. I want so much more… and it has nothing to do with money or owning farms. You know that!"

Robert looked at her standing there, her eyes flashing like sapphires under moonlight… and he couldn't help himself – he had to smile! Only God could retrieve this mess. Oh, she was class. Principle and spirit and ability, topped with beauty as well. His heart ached over mistake after mistake. She was too good to be true. She saw him watching her, and she suddenly became very self-conscious. She paused and blushed. "What?"

"I was just thinking. Perhaps it goes both ways. Though you deny it, your refusal *could* have something to do with the property. I am no longer a man of means. What you see is what you get. I will work hard… I will do everything within my power to provide for you and Billy. But… perhaps that is not enough… perhaps your ambitions rise higher?"

"Oh, that is disgusting! How could you suggest it?"

"No more sordid than you suggesting that I was holding you like an Ace card… to pull out of my sleeve when it seems the game is lost. If you know me at all, you would know in your heart that is not the truth."

She paused and said nothing for a long time. "Robert?"

"Hmm?"

"Will you walk with me?"

"Hmm." He put out his arm and she took it. Then they walked up the track to the homestead. He washed up as she took his meal out and restoked the fire to put the kettle on to boil. They sat down at the kitchen table as Robert wearily chewed mouthful after mouthful. He looked at her sitting across from him. "I like you being here. I want you to be here always." He took another mouthful and swallowed slowly. "You didn't answer me Sally. Please. Will you marry me?"

* * *

<h1 style="text-align:center">22.</h1>

Every couple of days, a new party came to view the property. There were tours of the homestead, tours of the shearing shed… tours of the paddocks and water holes, and stock. Inventories were made of the contents of sheds. The property that *was* worthless and in debt, now had a bright and rosy future – if you believed the talk that was exchanged. Suddenly it emerged as a dependable business opportunity that was going begging. Already the paddocks were lush and fertile after the flood. No wonder Mainstar had a prosperous look to it for prospective investors.

It made no sense to Andi and Jo. How could it be so great an investment, knowing the present situation? It was just sales' talk… lies covering a sticky quagmire of debt. Sally said she thought it *was* a good investment. Mainstar had hit a string of hard situations as most on the land do: their's just seemed to last longer. They were picking themselves up from drought and bushfires, when they lost the clip and were hit by a flood… but given all that, they were still viable, and the future did not seem so bleak to her. She said that if they had a more flexible creditor, in a few years they could be back to where they were when the sheep boom started.

Sally sighted figures to Andi when they sat out on the hut-verandah at night. What Sally said seemed totally logical. It was very disappointing that they could not take advantage of this opportunity. "Perhaps it is someone else's turn," said Andi graciously.

Sally shook her head. The reality and the vision did not match. She couldn't understand why she was being so stubborn about this, but the vision would not die. She even cried before God – lifting this vivid dream up like a sacrifice, asking Him to kill it, to ease the ache. But everything around her seemed to bring it to life again and again. Sally went about her work in a haze of grieving, knowing that each moment, the possibility of ever seeing it become a reality was slipping further and further out of sight.

The one spot of joy was Sally's engagement. The friends made a pact not to publicise the occasion until well after the upcoming auction. Instead they planned to surprise Sally with their own private party.

Robert particularly did not want to flaunt his engagement in the face of his brother's officially broken ties with Eunice. He did not know if Charles' depression was despondency brought on by the failure of their management, or the rejection of his future mother-in-law's backing. More likely it was a combination of factors swirling around like minestrone-soup in his head, but it seemed that he was slipping deeper and deeper into an emotional crevice and was becoming harder to reach.

One evening Robert and Molly came to the hut, bearing a cake topped with separated cream whipped into peaks, a couple of tall bottles of home brewed ginger beer and glasses in a basket. Earlier the girls had conspired with Billy to take Sally on an investigation trip of the gorge to see what flowers were reviving after the flood. They suggested to Sally that she needed some quiet time alone with Billy to explain the various changes about to happen – especially the big one about her engagement to Robert.

While they were away, they strung up ivy and mistletoe around the hut. They pulled out the table and covered it with a cloth borrowed from the Homestead dining room and put six glasses around the cake. Robert piled three large packages on a stool. Only one box had a slight watermark stain on the side. Jo thought *that* was the most remarkable miracle of all. Andi had been working on a special present for Billy and tonight was the perfect time to give it to him. She placed it wrapped, right on top of Robert's parcels.

Jo retrieved the contents of her gift basket she had collected for Sally in her spending spree at Mrs Cavanaugh's shop. She told Andi of the shopping rules that prevailed against all familiar shopping common sense!
Andi helped her to arrange the basket. "Will we tell her that I would've torched and burnt this basket, if I could have got Mum to buy me a new one! It almost looks stylish now!" declared Andi, as she arranged the lace-trimmed doilies and folded the face cloth around soaps and jars.

"Boy, you make that look so easy! I could have done with some of your artistic arranging skills numerous times while you were sick," said Jo with a grimace as she retold the adventure of her flower hunt.

Andi had made a centrepiece out of a half-open twisted piece of driftwood; placing a couple of candleholders she had made out of small tins. She decorated them with gumnuts, leaves and silver lichen. Then she stood the candles Jo had bought in the display. "Sounds like I missed out on a lot of fun..." said Andi as she adjusted her arrangement for one last time. She looked around the hut and said matter-of-factly... "I know what I would do for my catering assessment – if I ever get the chance: 'Colonial-to-die-for'! This is just wonderful! It is so completely inspired Jo. It's right that this basket should be given back to Mainstar... even for a few weeks, before A-day!" The reference to the 'Auction' had become something of a dirty word. They now all referred to it as "A-day".

The girls blew out the kerosene lamp and sat Robert and Molly in the evening dark, while they rocked on the bush twin swing hanging from the verandah rafters, faking normal conversation as they watched for Billy to emerge with his sister from The Gully. Eventually a lamp swung up the track. They were laughing and having fun. They stopped short when they saw Jo and Andi on the verandah chatting. "What's wrong? I thought you might have started supper." Sally sighed. Another late night... well then, so be it.

"Just looking at the sun-set. Only comes once a day..." observed Andi.

"Every day… pretty much the same time too."

"Oh, you're losing appreciation for natural beauty Sally. All sorts of special things can be seen in ordinary stuff." Jo shook her finger in a mock scolding.

Sally smiled. Nothing would faze her tonight. How could it? Her little brother, in his tall, grown-up way had not been at all surprised about her engagement. A little bit edgy perhaps. Considering the changes happening, that was not too bad. As Sally pushed open the door and held up the lantern to hang it, the whole room was revealed in its arrayed bush decoration! "Surprise!"

Billy jumped up and down. "I kept the secret! I kept the secret!" And he bowled over to give Robert a hug! He warmly returned it.

Robert took his hand and said, "You know Billy, you will not only be Sally's brother now, but my brother too."

Billy looked him in the eye and seriously held his hand. "We will be a good family together…" he said.

Robert was touched. "Billy, I think that is something your Pa would have said. Thank you."

They then laughed about their conspiracy as they cut the cake and enjoyed pouring the ginger ale into glasses as if it was fine champagne.

With delight, Sally savoured every detail that had transformed their little cottage. Then they presented their gifts. Sally's eyes misted over as she saw the basket with every possible little luxury tucked inside. "Oh Jo, I don't deserve this. I was so grumpy about your money, and you've spent it on me!"

Jo looked guilty… "Well, no… not really. I also bought chocolate… but I ate that. We were stranded for so long!"

Andi looked shocked. "Jo!"

"The rain was just wrecking it anyway!" she answered defensively.

Molly stepped up with smile. "Now, now girls, Molly's turn." She presented Sally and Robert with box each. Sally opened hers to find a batch of homemade fudge… caramel smooth and creamy. Robert had an array of assorted crystallised peel and glace fruits.

Robert stepped forward to propose a toast to his bride-to-be. He presented her with his parcels and apologised sheepishly that there was no ring for her finger.

"Robert, if you wouldn't mind, I would dearly love to wear my mother's ring. Pa had it made especially for her with a sapphire he found. It would mean so much to me to wear this ring for our engagement. It would be like a gift from my parents…" She went behind the hessian and returned with a tiny little wooden box. She passed it to Robert to open. He took out the ring and held it high up to the light. The blue colours flashed boldly in the lamplight. He slipped it on her finger and pressed his lips to her forehead. "I would be honoured to follow your father's legacy."

Then she opened her parcels from Robert and looked in stunned amazement at the extravagant layers of fabric and lace as the dress fell to the floor. She looked very hesitant. "Don't you like it?" Robert asked with concern.

"Well, it's so beautiful. I've never had such a dress… it is magnificent! It's just not very practical though…" Sally didn't seem to know what to do with it. Robert looked over at Jo with a 'I-told-you-so' look. Jo shook her head back at him. He was completely mistaken, and since he was not female. She knew what would work.

Robert took the cue. "Well, who needs practical? You have skirts and aprons to be practical."

She looked up at him in amazement. "Really? Oh Robert!" And she gave him an enormous hug. Jo nudged Andi and raised her eyebrows at him in that 'who-told-who' look. With enthusiasm she opened up the boxes to reveal matching hat and gloves, and a new pair of boots. She slid behind the curtain to model her new wares.

While she was changing, Andi picked up the last parcel. "This one is for you Billy… because you are getting a new family and that is something to celebrate!" She passed it to him and he ripped open the wrapping with enthusiasm. He held high a brand-new homemade teddy made out of flour sacks, with bright blue button eyes.

"The Goldilocks' bear!" he laughed with delight.

"You will always remember us when you tuck him into bed at night," said Andi with a smile as she was crushed in a bear-hug embrace.

"Always and always," he declared.

* * *

When the Robert and Molly left, the girls went straight to bed. Sally sat in the swing seat and gently rocked alone, revisiting the special events of the day. How wonderful life was – how blessed. The only grey cloud was the looming A-day. "God, would they ever pass-in a mortgage repossession auction? Lord I want to believe that You will keep it for us… but I cannot see how. I guess I don't have to really understand "how", but I can't help thinking that this might be You telling me this instead me suffering the insecurity of going away and trying something new. Why won't I let go of this? Oh God, it is like You keep bringing it up.   At the moment I want to relinquish it completely just for a little peace."

Sally opened her eyes and saw Billy standing by the verandah post. "Hi big-boy. How long have you been standing there? You'd better go to bed soon. It's getting really late."

Billy just stood there, sheepish and quiet. He moved into the lantern light where moths fluttered precariously around the glow.   His clothes were muddy. "Oh, Billy what happened? It is so late for you to have another bath… where have you been?"

"Sally?"

"Yes Billy," Sally tried to keep the impatience out of her voice.

"All the other people had gifts…"

"Andi and Jo gave you a lovely bear Billy…"

"But I never did give anything. And I had it all planned… but I never had any time because of the secret… and I wanted to give it to you really… 'cause you are my bestest sister… and I want you to have something really special."

"Oh Billy, you are the sweetest! I never expected you to have to bother about a gift for us!"

"But why? I is your brother. Pa said I should treat you real nice 'cause I is the only family you'se has. Getting 'gaged is very important."

"Yes Billy, our engagement is very important. I'm sure you will find something that is very special to commemorate our engagement."

"Cu-men-erate?"

"It means something to help us remember it as a very special time. That's one of the reasons people give gifts… and to say that they wish us well."

"I's wish you well… and Mr Robert."

"I know. Just take some time to think about it and I'm sure you…"

"Oh, but I has! I has a gift already. I just never has time to fix it up pretty. I had to helps with the surprise," he added importantly.

"You were very good at the surprise Billy. I had no idea what you all were up to! Clever thing."

He stepped closer to his sister and shoved a large heavy biscuit tin into her lap. It was caked with mud and weighed a ton. "Happy 'gagement Sally," he said shyly.

Sally closed her eyes. Oh, Billy Bowerbird! There was mud everywhere. He meant it all so sincerely. Give me patience! This isn't his fault. His heart is right. She carefully opened the lid and then quickly shut it again. "It's not full of live things is it Billy?" she joked with him. "I don't like creepy crawly things."

"No Sal. I don't get crawly things for you… ever. You don't like them."

"Just checking…" she said carefully. She went to open the lid again and quickly shut it once more. "It's not something that will smell awful… like a dead possum tail or something?" she asked with fake worry coating her voice.

"No Sal. You didn't like the possum tail I got you last time… I wouldn't get you another one for something important like a 'gagement."

"Just checking," said Sally cautiously. Billy laughed. He liked it when Sally played games.

"Com'on, Sal. Open it up."

She lifted the lid in the dull yellow light of the lantern. It was full of rocks. Small rocks and big… gravel and sand. 'God, help me to react in just the right way. This is important to him.'

"Are these some of your treasures Billy? Some special rocks you found when you go exploring?"

Billy was exhilarated. She had got it in one! "Yes, Sally, they are! How did you know? I only kept the good ones for you. I's got lots and lots of tins with not so good ones."

"Well there are lots here. How long have you been collecting these?"

"Oh, forever and ever. I do it every day… in my exploring time. I like it… it reminds me of Pa. He liked rocks too."

"Yes, he did." And she smiled fondly as she rubbed the ring on her finger.

"Well, its bedtime mate. Just wash your feet off and change your clothes. Don't worry about a whole bath now. It's really late."

He smiled at his success. Sally was really pleased. He had made her happy. "Happy 'gagement Sally. It will be wonderful to have a whole family again."

"Thank you, Billy. You are the best brother in the whole world. I love you. Good night." Sally yawned. She was tired and the quietness had a peace about it. In a way she wished this day would never end. If it stayed today forever, A-day would never come.

She looked down at the muddy tin that Billy had dumped in her lap. It was a tin jammed packed full of love. "God how precious that is. Thank you so much." She picked up one of the stones… jagged and rough. She almost expected Billy to collect river stones, smooth and coloured with patterns. He was always full of surprises. She looked at it smiling. Rocks. Isn't it amazing, she thought, that a bucket full of rocks is a perfect gift when given with love?

She looked at it sleepily, trying to see what qualified it in Billy's mind worth being a "collectable". He constantly had collections he was adding to all the time. He had his dead insect collection, an egg-shell collection, his seedpod collection, his feather collection, a bone collection. He started a dung collection once, but Sally canned that one.

She turned the rock over in her hand and a seam, dark and glassy caught the light. She looked at it curiously. Sally straightened her head and focused on it, lifting it up to the light, her brow furrowed… the pupil in her dark eyes widening more. She traced the coldness of it with her finger. She chose another rock, rotating it carefully under the lantern light hanging on the verandah.

She quickly got up and went inside and put the tin on the table. She took the lantern down and sat it on the table, turning the flame up high. One by one she went through the tin. One by one, she sat some rocks to the side and others to the left; small ones in a third pile. Finally, she came to the last one.

She sat there for a long time, tears streaming down her face. And that was how the girls found her when they woke up the next morning.

* * *

23.

"Robert, I want you to understand that it is not because I don't trust you, that prompts me to ask this." Sally stood before him at his desk while he worked on some figures. "You would never do anything to jeopardise Billy's sense of security. He is family to you now."

"He has been for a long time, Sal."

"But other people don't see him like that. They think that because he is simple, that he should not be allowed to follow his heart. Collecting things has always been a part of him: you know that. I don't want them to steal away his collections because they see them differently to how he does."

Robert looked up at her perplexed. Sally had dark circles rimming her eyes. Surely, she's not losing sleep over this? Her protectiveness to Billy sometimes seemed more than what was warranted. But he sensed her anxiety, and he felt obliged to follow it through. "Well, what do you want me to do?"

"I just want it formally recognised that what Billy has, or has found, is his... and not part of Mainstar and not belonging to the creditors."

"Well, of course they are his! You are not being very rational Sally. Why would they want to take his bones or his eggshells?"

"What if they told us we couldn't take anything away? Billy would be devastated."

"A letter – is that what you want?"

"A letter or a document, signed by yourself and the principle mortgagees, giving Billy scavenging, fossicking and mining rights… that would leave no room for doubt."

He sighed. "Very well." He needed more work like he needed a hole in the head, especially something vague, unnecessary and over the top.

"And Robert, I'm sorry to press you, but I would really like to have the letter today so I can file it with the proper permit and Pa's documents, when I go to town later. Could you do that?"

"Sorry?"

"I'm going into town today and I would like to take it with me." She could have been telling him the cabbages had just gone to seed. Sally had never gone to town by herself… ever! And yet she seemed so normal about it.

"Sally, are you okay? I know this is a very stressful time…"

She smiled. Oh, she was fine! She almost thought about giving this delightful man a big kiss, but she turned to see Charlie walking past the door, and quietly resumed her composure. She just looked him in the eye and said, "Robert Madegan, this lady has never been more right in her life!"

"Got to try out the dress, hmmm?"

"Maybe." She smiled.

"There should be people arriving soon. I'll see what I can do. You'll get your letter."

However, when Robert presented Horace Betancourt with a draft letter, giving Billy those rights, he just laughed. "The simpleton has no such rights. You're a simpleton yourself if you think so! He's probably been pilfering stuff all his life and declares he's just been scavenging!"

"Horace, the kid is harmless. His sister is just concerned that what when he leaves, he will be able to keep the things he considers precious. Guess she's got to live with him. He collects junk … nature's curiosities… snake-skins, bird's nests, bones – that sort of thing. He is as honest as they come. More so probably… the burden of an unsullied and simple mind."

"You're a soft touch Madegan. No wonder you are in the mess where you are." Robert let the line pass by without comment. A few more weeks and he was leaving this chapter behind him. Better to be a soft touch, he thought, than a cock-fighting crook. "Well, okay then," Betancourt conceded with magnanimous generosity when Robert did not give him any mileage from his verbal bait, "but I'll get my clerk to add a clause: anything man-made, anything pertaining to the machinery working on the property stays. Don't want him sabotaging our outfit by stealing a cog and calling it scavenging. Never know with these types, especially if they think they are hardly done by, or feel displaced. They get malicious. You can't be too careful."

When he handed the letter over, Betancourt waved it in front of some prospective buyers. "That's how we work here: make every effort to accommodate the wishes of both parties. This letter here: looking after the interests of the village idiot. Simple man, bowerbird by nature… says he can keep his stuff. Here," he said proudly, "You are my witnesses. Actually – would you mind now? Need to make this all legal… doing it properly… as always! Sir, if you could sign and date here, under my name at the bottom…"

The man quickly scanned the letter, and added his name to the document, nodding in approval. "Most generous of you sir. Many businessmen would not do this for a dimwit."

"That's not my style, as you can see. Everyone is important to Horace J. Betancourt. As they say, *'Need a deal to be done? Betancourt is your son-of-a gun.'*" The man and his wife laughed at his slogan. They were obviously impressed. Such an honourable man, with a sense of humour as well! The best sort to do business with. Carefully, he fed them a line about easy finance being available if they wanted to step into his temporary office set up in the homestead dining room. They followed him like sheep.

* * *

Sally and the girls took Billy with them into town. They made good time and Jo was pressing Sally for an outline of her plans. But she was processing details in her mind and was a million miles away. They took a room at Mrs Hillary's boarding house again. Sally laid out on the bed the stones that Billy had found, now washed and clean.

Jo picked up one of the stones and held it up. The blue crystals were glassy even in their raw uncut state. "Billy, how did you know? These are so beautiful…" They were trying very hard to play down the significance of what Billy had achieved in case he got scared and started talking.

"I just did what Pa showed me to do. He showed me how to dig with my pick and shovel… and use his sieve and stuff. He told me I was a pick-and-shovel man. I just did it… every day. I found one every day. That's what Pa said… even if it was the tiniest one, he wanted to find something. I am very good at seeing the little ones too. And I kept it secret. I am very good at secrets."

"Billy it was *such* a good secret! We want to keep it our secret for a little longer. It is nice to make secrets last," said Andi as sat on a chair, staring in quiet amazement at what was laid out before her. She had never seen so many gems in one spot. Sapphires – they were all sapphires! A few were yellow and orange, some were mauve and others almost rose-pink… but her favourites were the rich, dark blue ones.

Sally changed into her new dress. Jo got into hers. Andi was staying with Billy to look after the stones. Sally could not risk leaving them alone. They had to be so careful. She took a linen handkerchief and wrapped up a selection of small specimens. She picked some quality samples and one or two quite flawed ones. She was amazed about what she had remembered her Pa telling her about how to pick a stone. Little droplets of conversations seemed to fall into her mind unexpectedly. The small collection of stones that her father had accumulated needed to be sold after his accident to cover medical costs. Sally refused to sell the last one – her mother's ring. It had taken a while to rid herself of those debts. She smiled again as she looked at her finger. It had been worth the sacrifice.

They walked down the street. Across from Mrs Cavanaugh's drapery stood a jewellery shop, small and unimpressive. Sally opened the door and a bell tinkled happily.

"Good afternoon, Ma'am, how can I help you?"

"I have some stones I would like to have valued. Who would I need to speak too?"

"That'd be Mr Holder, Madam." They were led out the back and behind a large low workbench by the window sat Mr Holder. He had a balding head and thick pudgy eyelids. There were backs off pocket-watches in various stages of repair, rings and brooches scattered around his working mat. Fine tools and little bits of left-over wire and cogs littered the table. Sally's confidence did not wane.

"Sir, my name is Sally McBride. I have some stones I would like you to value."

He looked up and put down his monocle. "Oh yes. McBride. I remember you. Found some more of your father's stones?"

She nodded and pulled out her pouch and opened up the handkerchief in her hand. She deliberately chose a flawless one. He took it without interest and turned it over between his fingers carelessly. He picked up his monocle again, placed it under his thick brow. It made his eye look enormous as he glanced at the stone. She passed him another of good quality. He seemed even less inclined to look closely.

"Well, Mr Holder, what do you think?" she asked hopefully.

He looked at Sally carefully and said nothing for a while. He took his eyeglass off slowly and coughed apologetically. "Miss, I can see you have your hopes up. But it seems obvious your father put these aside because they are not of the quality of the other ones. These are very poor specimens. I have seen much better this week, many, many times. I'm sorry," and he stated his price that was much less than Sally had hoped for.

"That's all? What's the problem with them?"

"Well, Ma'am, if you knew your stones you would know flaws and fractures can be quite difficult to see without a trained eye…" He left the statement hanging and went back to working on the insides of a watch. Jo thought he looked like a kid doing a backyard biology experiment on the guts of a frog. She looked at Sally and saw her back straighten.

"Well, Mr Holder, it just so happens that I *do* know my stones. I know which are flawed and which are quality stones. I mixed them quite deliberately to see if you would do right by me! But it seems that we are quite wasting our time." She scooped up her stones… and he quickly placed his cold pudgy fingers on her wrist. She shook him off like a reptile had just crawled over her. "Do *not* touch me, sir!"

His eyes narrowed. "Now, now Miss McBride. I might have been a little hasty… I'm sure I could have another look… perhaps come to some acceptable pricing."

"Start with a genuine offer, or these stones walk out the door. I do not take lightly being treated with frivolity!" She purposely selected the best sapphire and popped it back in the pouch. "That just came off the market."

He swallowed and cleared his throat. It was not at all what he had anticipated. He made an offer; Sally countered it. He made another; Sally met him halfway. He puffed his way to the front counter and opened the till. He wrote out a purchase of goods receipt and Sally signed it. She tucked the money inside the pouch and nodded. "Good afternoon Mr Holder. Pleasure doing business with you."

The bell tinkled as they left the shop. Mr Holder took a small tin flask from his coat pocket and smugly unscrewed the lid. He took a swig and wiped his mouth on the back of his hand. He smiled a greasy smile to his assistant. "I just made more money in ten minutes than a month's worth of watch repairs… and the tart has no idea she should've got double." He was proud of his undetected cleverness.

Sally and Jo walked sedately down the street, smiling to passers-by with polite civility. "Scumbag!" said Sally with contempt under her breath. "He gave me much less than they were worth!"

"You didn't tell him about the rest."

"And I'm not going to. He just missed out on the business opportunity of a lifetime!"

"Now what? You need to sell more…"

"Not at his price. Bank-robbers have more integrity. I let him have those because I need money for a ticket. I'm going to Sydney. And while I'm gone, I want you and Andi to do some things for me."

* * *

They waited under the scant shade of an awning for the Cobb & Co. coach to arrive. Billy was torn between letting Sally go and being the man of responsibility at home. Andi held his hand reassuringly. "We will be so busy that we won't notice the time she is away visiting," she told him.

Sally clutched her father's leather pouch that held all his documents she had secured from their legal man. Inside was the address of a man Will McBride had said was a trustworthy friend. He traded in gold, silver, gems and pearls. To meet this man was Sally's mission. She wore plain, travel-practical clothes and had the stones in the bottom of her age-worn carpet travel bag, overlaid with other clothes on top. She took a deep breath. She felt so completely daunted by the task ahead. Still, nothing ventured, nothing gained.

The coach rolled up and dust swirled around as the passengers gathered their bags and said farewells. Sally handed Jo two letters. "This one is for Robert... and this one you know about already. Thank you."

Jo and Andi gave her a hug. "You'll do great!"

Sally turned and gave Billy a gentle squeeze. "You are my big, wonderful brother. Jo and Andi will be with you until I get back... so you help them for me, will you Billy? They don't understand Mainstar like you do." For a moment he glowed with the importance of having exclusive knowledge.

"Bye Sally," was all he could manage. He swallowed hard, his Adam's apple bouncing in his throat. He had never been away from Sally before. It was difficult to watch her roll away as the coach set off on its journey. He held Andi's hand very tightly.

As the coach turned out of sight Jo turned to Andi, "Well! We have some shopping to do with the money Sally gave us! I know this quaint little drapery shop, where you can buy all sorts of things without trying anything on first."

Andi laughed at her. She figured Jo was out for revenge. But if Jo was expecting an apoplexy from the shop assistant when she asked where Andi could try on her clothes, she was disappointed. "Yes Ma'am, if she could come this way." In no time Andi had the dress on, alterations attended to and dress bought. They took their parcels and left.

Jo grumbled all the way back to the boarding house. "You, Andi, have the most extraordinary gift. Everything goes smoothly for you. No one yelled at you for touching their gear."

Andi rolled her eyes. "Get over it, Jo. I don't provoke as much as you do either."

They sat down in their room. "We can tick the first item off our list. Now – we need to write to Eunice and invite ourselves to morning tea."

* * *

Sally looked out the window with interest. She had never been this far south before… well, not that she remembered. She took a deep breath, and she could smell the fragrance of freedom, of purpose and mission. How significant to be given a mission, she thought humbly. "God please make a way where there is no way. Please go before me. Please."

On and on, the rocking of the coach lulled her into a dozing state of hypnosis as she watched tree after tree pass by. A gentleman and his wife nodded off also, the former having long ago given up on his newspaper, his small reading glasses slipping to the end of his nose. Another lady sat reading fitfully, steadying her book by hanging onto the sides of the windowsill, while they lurched out of ruts in the road and bumped roughly over loose rocks.

Suddenly the horses hauled to a halt. The stage driver was yelling, and sharp instructions issued. Sally looked out the window dazed state of half sleepy awareness. There was a fallen tree across the track. The team of horses stamped and tossed their heads, their sides dark from the exertions of bearing their load. The gentleman started awake. He patted his wife and consoled her as she started snivelling in distress. But when shots rang out, echoing around the hills, the realisation of what could be happening started to register. The door of the coach yanked open and a rifle barrel poked in through the gaping hole. Now there was no doubt.

"Out! Everyone out!"

Bail-up. Ambush. Theft. The words spun around Sally mocking her like an elusive mosquito. Her hair had come loose and dangled in her face as she lined up with the other passengers. She looked down at the dusty ground and started to pray. Not now. Not after all the hope that she had.

"We got a poor lot here Busta…" he yelled disgruntled to his gang, as he walked up the line. He yanked a bracelet off the reader's arm, a chain with a small pearl pendant from around the snivelling woman's neck and a dull cameo broach. She gave up a couple of rings. The man volunteered his tarnished pocket watch and a rather thin money pin. He came to Sally. She kept her eyes averted and put her hands under her jacket hem. Her ring. Not her ring! Sally said nothing and tried to slip it off without him noticing. But he saw movement under her jacket and grabbed her hand. "You! What have you got?" His voice was rough and raspy. He pulled at her hand and ripped open her jacket. Sally's ring was in her clenched fist. He prised her fingers open and held up the sapphire ring like a trophy. He stuck it in his pocket. "Well, that's about it, fellas. Even the church mouse 'd turn his snout up at this lot. They got nothin'."

They threw down the bags off the luggage rack and ripped open a large trunk belonging to the couple. They tumbled through the clothes and pocketed a couple of silk scarves and a neat looking gentleman's vest. They kicked the rest about disgustedly and swore. Sally saw her ragged canvas bag roll under the front of the coach and closed her eyes. She dared not look at it.

The snivelling woman started to waver in the heat and the ordeal. Sally opened her eyes in time to see her wobble unsteadily. She grabbed the reader's book from her hand and fanned her face furiously. She loosened her high neck buttons and sat her down in the shade of the coach in the dust.

"Do you have a water flask?" she asked her husband quietly.

He reached into his inside jacket-pocket. The man rummaging through their luggage saw the movement. He pulled his rifle up short and lunged at him with the butt of the barrel. "You there! Stand!" he yelled as he hit him hard across the cheekbone. He staggered to his feet, blood pouring over his shirt. Sally cringed as the lady passed out completely.

"I asked him for a water-flask!" Sally stood and motioned to the reader. "Fan her…" She grabbed a shirt from the strewn contents of their trunk and folded it into a wad, and gently pressed it over his cheek. The man winced in pain and for a moment looked like he would join his wife in oblivion. Sally helped him down beside her. "You can see we have nothing. We are not wealthy. Please. Leave us. We just want to finish our journey. Please go…"

He hesitated and looked towards the leader hauling mail-bags over his saddle. He called his men back, and they mounted their horses. They fired shots in the air and rode wildly around the coach. The coach driver stood fuming where he was tied, his eyes flashing dangerously. He restrained himself sufficiently to say nothing. The rider with the rifle butt saw the challenge in his eyes and took it up. "You got a problem with us?" he said recklessly.

The driver said nothing, but he dared to look at him directly and not avert his gaze. Suddenly the horse rider pushed him with his boot in the stirrup. The driver staggered off balance as he was pushed again, and again until he sprawled in the dust. The bushranger jumped down and held his face in the dirt. "When one of the Black brothers say eat dust – ya don't argue… ya say "how much" – ya hear? This 'ere is our territory and when you ridin' it… ya pay dues!" He kicked him viciously in the side and sprang back onto his horse. Someone was whistling for him to come and he galloped up the side of the hill, out of sight.

Sally took the flask from the man's jacket and splashed a small amount on the lady's face. Her face was pale and clammy as a faint whimper passed her lips. Sally helped the driver to his feet, untied his arms and dampened his neckerchief so he could wipe his face. He flung around impotent with anger – hitting the side of the coach with his fists. Sally moved out of his way and picked up the scattered clothes to shake them out. She made a rough attempt to restack the trunk. Then Sally closed the bent and battered lid and sat on it wearily. Why was she always the one trying to fix things? Where was the person who would fix things for her? She started to cry out of relief and built up tension. The grief of losing her last tangible tie with her parents, the symbol of the new life she would have with Robert, bubbled to the surface. That was all she had, just one ring… and now that precious memory and priceless promise was in the grimy coat pocket of some rough barbarian who would hock it for next to nothing on the black market – pun intended.

Just then she saw her carpet bag, untouched and unopened under the wheel of the coach. "Oh, God. How thankless I am. You *have* fixed it for me. Thank you." She realised it could have gone a thousand different ways. Drying her eyes, she pulled the bag out from under the wheel and stacked it on top of the dinted trunk. Then she opened the door and helped the lady and her husband back inside. The reader stood and watched and resumed her seat without comment. The driver unhitched a horse and dragged the fallen tree off to the side of the road.

* * *

Billy drove their sulky up the sweeping driveway of the Glossop pseudo-manor. Andi and Jo were dressed in their new, best clothes, playing ladies visiting for morning tea. They gently tapped at the door and a maid dressed in serious black and white answered. "Miss Eunice is expecting you Ma'ams," and she led them into a sunny corner of the parlour. They waited uncomfortably on hard, stiffly upholstered settees.

Eunice came in a little flustered – the collar on her dress was crooked and her light brown hair was limp from where it was let out a few minutes ago. "Good morning Jo, and…Miss Andi. I got your card. I'm glad you're feeling better. It is nice of you to come to visit. I'm glad you felt you could come since..." she stopped. Why did everything relate to the context of her broken engagement: before the engagement or after the engagement. Didn't she ever have a life without Charlie? Well, she's got one now.

She picked up the teapot on the tray that they maid had delivered. She didn't mention the escalating tension between her and her mother. She sighed as she knocked the sugar spoon so that it showered brown crystals over tray and spilled on the floor. Eunice closed her eyes and sighed again. "Let's go onto the verandah."

They followed her out to the wide side verandah. It looked out over sloping lush, green paddocks of undulating cultivation. She sat down more relaxed on white cane furniture with puffy cushions. She pointed to the beginnings of some trellises in the cultivation paddock. "Dad's starting to plant a vineyard. He says it's a gentleman's crop. Don't know if they'll be able to keep the water up to it though, but he reckons he's got it all figured out."

The maid delivered the tea tray again and stayed to pour the drinks. The girls sipped their cups politely. Hot tea on a hot day didn't make a lot of sense to them. Still, that is what company does apparently. "I'll add an icy cold creaming-soda to the list of things I miss," Andi said to herself.

Eunice looked at them thoughtfully. "Mother has appointments with some committees in town today. She gives her apologies."

"Oh," Jo raised her eyebrows at Andi significantly.

"Please tell her we are sorry we missed her," said Andi politely.

"I'll do that," said Eunice as she nibbled a freshly baked wheatmeal biscuit and passed the plate. One of the biscuits slid off and cracked on the sandstone floor. A dog lying lazily by the posts roused itself and helped himself to the booty.

Jo wriggled. She hated this courteous hedging around. She just wanted to get to the point. She cleared her throat. "We have a letter from a friend of ours. She wanted us to deliver it to you. I don't think you've met her, but we can vouch for her." Jo lowered her voice. "She is secretly engaged to Robert… just like you were to Charlie before…" Andi glared at Jo, who whispered back. "I'd just thought it was neat how they could have been sisters-in-law."

Andi saw Eunice visibly wince, like a bandage was being lifted off a raw wound just to see how it was fairing.

Jo opened her purse and passed the envelope to Eunice. She took it and then politely put it on the tray. Jo stared at it in horror. "I know it is probably not usual to read mail in company, but I really think this letter should not, well, be… left.…"

Eunice raised her brows… and smiled. It was funny how Jo made everything an adventure. How could a letter be an adventure? But suddenly it was! She picked it up. "Please excuse my manners friends – you have made me quite curious." They waved her on, and she quickly read the essence of the note. She looked up at Jo and then read it again. She went through some of the sheets that were attached. "Would I be correct to assume you know the basic content of this letter?"

Andi nodded. "We helped Sally with some of the wording. She wanted it to sound right. We read through the other bits too, after Sally had it drawn up."

Eunice let out a breath and then put it down abruptly. "Impossible."

"Why?"

"Because it is. That's all."

"But it would be a way…"

"I can't..."

Jo did not like it when people said "can't". It was like a challenge, a dare for her to prove that it *could*. "I'm sure... if you thought it was a good *idea*... there would be some..."

"Well, do you like the proposal?" pressed Andi.

"I'll have to think about it..."

Silence hung around the air for a moment and then Andi rose to her feet. "Thank you so much for tea. I did enjoy meeting you Eunice. Jo told me..." she stopped. She didn't want to refer back to the broken engagement again. "Perhaps you could return the honour and come to visit us at Mainstar."

"To Mainstar? So close to... the sale?" She nearly said 'Charlie'.

"Especially before then. There will never be another opportunity. Please come."

Eunice paused. It made her think about all those plans, all those dreams. "Perhaps..." she relented. Perhaps just to visit - to say goodbye to the dream, and to Charlie. The other thing in the letter — that was impossible.

* * *

Sally looked with concern to the man and his wife. "Are you feeling alright, Sir? That was brutal, what he did." She looked at him. His eyeglasses were cracked and his cheek, swollen and bruised. Already around his eye, black-red puffiness hung about his lids.

"I appreciate your kindness, especially to my wife," the man said gently. "She had such a bad experience at our previous place. We are moving to the city now. I have an associate who has offered me a position." He sighed. Sadness hung around him like a myriad of poor choices were constantly appearing before his vision. "I used to work with a legal firm, doing accounts. I left that position to farm with my brother-in-law… but it hasn't worked. There are too many traumas. We lost everything in the flood. It has been too difficult for Ellen, with her delicate constitution."

"You obviously care for each other very much. That is to be admired."

"You are to be admired too Miss. You behaved so bravely. If there is anything I can help you with while you are in Sydney, anything at all, do look us up." He reached into his coat pocket and handed her a card with his name and address written on in ink.

Sally took the card politely: '*Mr Francis Spottnick ~ accountant / legal advisor*'. "It is a pleasure to meet you Mr Spottnick. It would have been nicer to make your acquaintance under more pleasant circumstances," and she filed the card in her father's leather pouch that laid undisturbed on the floor of the coach.

She doubted very much she would ever have need to take Mr Spottnick up on his offer, but she remembered her father saying, "Everyone is significant... maybe not to your plan, but you might be significant in their's, perhaps in unforeseen ways. If you look upon every encounter as an appointment from God, it will change the way you deal with people." Sally looked out the window as the memory of his voice echoed in her ear. "The Good Book says you could even entertain angels without knowing. Wouldn't want to give an angel the short shift, just because you're having a bad day..." She smiled as she remembered his laugh. It was hard, though, to think of that grimy little man in the jewellery shop as a God-ordained appointment. But why not? It would be just as easy for God to arrange a personable, reasonable tradesman. Or that horrible felon cruelly kicking the driver to the ground.

Maybe just fanning the lady's face was her significant moment for today. God said the little things done in His name counted. A thought flittered through her mind: "You have been faithful with the small things Sally; I will entrust you with much more."

* * *

Robert screwed up the letter and glared at Jo. "How could you let her go? This is insanity! The stress is affecting her mind."

Jo looked at Andi. They had fully expected him to support what Sally had done. "I thought that maybe the letter explained it," she suggested.

"Explains what? That she's lost her mind? Two weeks! It's the biggest blow we've been dealt in our entire life and she's gone on a *holiday*! To Sydney? In a few weeks she could be on holidays for the rest of her life!" He was fuming! Had she gone completely bonkers? What made her think that her engagement entitled her to ignore his wishes and take advantage of him? If he hadn't read it with his own eyes, he would not believe it possible. Her support in getting through this was more than just the presentation of the house. Or seeing the needs of the business contingent were being met; those who were constantly traversing his life. Everything about his private life was now public property. Everything that was, except Sally: he needed her here!

Andi and Jo backed out the door. "Maybe she needed to get away…" and they ducked as he picked up a sheet of ledger paper on his desk and wadded it into a missile. "We promised Sally that we would cover for her duties… we'll do *all* her work. And, ahh… we invited a friend to visit for just a little while… I hope that is okay."

Robert looked at them in complete incomprehension. They had not heard a single word he had just said! Suddenly his voice became very quiet. "Our life is not the same. It is never going to be the same. We are not in a position to entertain – get rid of them! Now!" and he threw the screwed up ball of Sally's letter in his hand at Jo, who nimbly caught it and ran!

"Oh dear," she puffed to Andi, "I have never seen him raise his voice before!"

"In case this helps – he didn't… he was too mad. Oh boy, I don't think that Sally…" Andi stopped still. "Jo, Sally didn't tell him. She said it was a *holiday*! Why wouldn't she tell him?"

Jo looked at her. "I don't know… but we follow Sally's cue. We say nothing… it may fail anyway."

"No – I don't want you to say that! Promise me Jo… promise me that we are going to support everything Sally hopes for - verbally and prayerfully… we can't do much… but we can do that."

* * *

Robert slammed the door to his office and strode around the side of the verandah. He bumped into Eunice, sending the folder she was carrying flying. "Oh! Miss Glossop! Excuse me. I am so sorry. Are you okay?" He bent over to pick up the papers that had spilt on the floor. Horses. They were all papers on horses. "I'm sorry. I was not looking where I was going."

She blushed from embarrassment. She felt the awkwardness of her being here. "Jo and Andi invited me to come. Perhaps it was a mistake, but they were very persuasive."

Eunice always seemed so fragile to him. It wasn't fair to be mad at her. He smiled at her. "Hmm. They're good at that. The timing's not good though. We won't be very good hosts."

Eunice could sense Robert's disapproval… and she felt sad. How different things could have been if only Mother had not… and she stopped herself short. This was her life. She was accountable to herself, her choices. "I am sorry too. Father had some work for me to do and I thought it was something I could do here without getting in the way…" Her eyes misted. To Robert they just looked constantly watery. "…and, I wanted to say goodbye. To Charlie. To be honest that is why I allowed them to talk me into it. We didn't have the opportunity. Everything happened so fast."

"Oh." How could anything get worse? All this emotion was not healthy. Couldn't she leave her goodbyes until later? Robert wasn't good at emotion; and his experience told him Charlie was less so. "Well, Charlie is down at the yards. He won't be in until this evening. Get Andi to show you around. She's still not up to doing much work." He strode off quickly before he said anything inappropriate.

Eunice sat down on a rough wooden bench. How different everything was here. The feel of the timber under her hands felt so real, so genuine. The honesty of Robert should have been a rebuke, but she found it comforting. It was like he trusted her enough to see the real him. She hated her life of masks. Only in the stables did she find the charades were lifted.

She looked out past the tall, pale trunks of the gum trees, down towards the shearing shed. No sloping vineyards here. No stately race-horses dancing in holding paddocks. But instead of saying farewell to the dream, the dream played around the fringes of her mind – like Prince Tyron in his exercising yard. They had plenty of permanent water here... that was paramount. She opened the file and took out the sheet with Prince Tyron's name at the top. Suddenly she didn't want to say good-bye. She wanted to see how far it could go. How far *could* she take the dream? Suddenly her visit changed from a listless, uncomfortable farewell, into a time-pressured undercover business assignment. She tried to prepare herself for the fact that Charlie might not even want to be part of it. Well, if it *was* about choices, she would choose to do it anyway.

* * *

24.

The day dawned like any other - kookaburras laughed and sang out their hilarious jokes. Robert rolled over and sat up on the edge of his bed. He had slept in. He could hear Charlie moving around. It had finally come. Release. After today he could take hold of freedom and say goodbye to Mainstar and start building a new life… with Sally. But he had not heard from her. He did not understand her dismissal of his needs… her blatant disregard for him. Was he doing what Jo had accused him of – focusing on his needs and ignoring hers?

Perhaps she really had lost the plot. Perhaps she was suffering much more than he acknowledged… perhaps she did not have the strength to face one more prospective face that could take Mainstar away forever. Was she running away? Her lectures on sharing their hearts seemed a little shallow in the light of her terse, uninformative letter. All she had said was she'd gone on a holiday and would be back the week before the auction. Yet the auction was today and still he had heard nothing. Today. Sally had signed her letter off with some worn little cliché about trust and being totally devoted.

Now he had reservations about that too. People only asked to be trustworthy if there was reason to doubt. Had he been duped? After all these years?

The only comforting memory that stood in his mind was when Sally presented him with her mother's ring, saying she wanted this family treasure to be the symbol of their life together. That ring was what held his hope, knowing what it represented was bigger than the doubts and questions that plagued his mind. Sally would never joke about that.

He worried about Charlie too. He was going through the motions but it seemed like he had no reserves to sustain him past today. Everything had been channelled towards today… the auction. Soon today would be over. Charlie had no one to build new visions with, except his brother. Robert wasn't sure Charlie would want to tag along. Charles had always been the leader – the ideas man and the force that pulled those ideas into being. Would he willingly become part of someone else's vision? Would he be motivated enough to generate another dream – alone?

The visit from Eunice had been a disaster. Charlie had spoken to her once… and then he refused to see her again. She hung around for a couple of days, spending most of her time with the girls pawing over sheets of paper. But any hope that they would part as friends was smashed. Charlie started banging things and yelling at workmen for irrationally trivial things. It would be a blessing when it was finally over. Just four hours to go.

Robert washed in the basin on the marble topped washstand and dressed in his town clothes. He pictured the offices of Betancourt Enterprises. The room upstairs would be set up with many chairs. On a little table near the door would sit the pimply clerk with a list of the upcoming properties for sale and other commercial propaganda. The feature property for this auction was Mainstar Station. It was likely that no other properties would be auctioned today. Just Mainstar.

Up front was the auctioneer's booth where the auctioneer would stand with his booming voice and eagle eye scanning the gathering for the indication of a bid. His family's heritage would be sold at the fall of the hammer. He had intended to go and watch, but as he shaved he decided there was no point. Why inflict himself unnecessarily with the burden? He had promised he would take the girls into town so they could look in on the auction… but now he didn't even want to do that.

The finality of it all, the unexplainable actions of Sally, and the dark mood that had settled over Charlie that had intensely blackened since Eunice's visit, were all adding up. He decided he would stay at Mainstar and wait out the day. He might even take a ride out the back and get some fresh air. The pressure of work had evaporated and he felt like he was struggling to breathe in the vacuum it left behind. The sale would bring some funds after the pay out of debts, for them to start again. But he knew the numbers; there would not be much left over.

Unaccountably Jo and Andi suddenly became interested in every detail of the farm. They seemed excited by the hype that surrounded the selling up process. He resented the delight they were taking in its demise. Billy could take the girls into town to meet Sally. That would do.

* * *

The room started to fill. Gentlemen stood around in their best Sunday shirts, holding briefcases and wads of paper. Occasionally a couple appeared, walking together. Jo and Andi stood at the door… waiting. Where was Sally? She *had* to come. They had not heard from her recently. Any mail sent could still be in transit. Jo felt nervously sick. Andi sat down on a chair. She was weak and wobbly. She tried to pray. She tried to claim the promises that Sally believed in, but every time words tried to form, her mind went blank.

Jo scanned the street below. She looked at the town clock on the hall down the street. She went and poured a drink for herself and Andi from the table laid with a water pitcher and glasses. Ladies sipped and balanced cups of tea, nodding knowingly as men discussed business. Jo jiggled nervously, tapping her fingers on a piece of paper that advertised some irrelevant event that had unaccountably made its way into her hand. They had done everything Sally had instructed. It's just she was not here. Not yet. Without Sally, there was no buy-back plan.

Jo stopped and quickly sat down by Andi and grabbed her hand.

"See there. The jacket!"

"What jacket?" Andi looked around confused. Trust Jo to become interested in clothes at a time like this! She hardly liked fashion at the best of times.

"Over there beside the morning-tea table... near the teapot. That's Sophie! And Jack is with her. Remember I told you about the shearer. She did it, just like she said she would. Oh man. Cat-fight coming..."

They watched carefully, as Mr Betancourt emerged talking congenially with the smartest looking suits and ties. As he turned around, Jack reached out his hand, and in his smiling, bush-boy's unguarded way, he shook Betancourt's hand. A look of confusion passed over his round, whiskered face as he registered that Sophie – his daughter, was here with this man in a business venture. His eyes narrowed as he looked at his wide-eyed, beguiling daughter, and he considered the wad of papers she held in her hand. There was a set about Sophie's determined jaw that helped him decide he would let them be.

Betancourt didn't even know Jack and that unsettled him. How could his daughter be with *him*? She had deliberately excluded him, and he didn't like that. What idiot would buy a place without knowing the facts, like he knew the facts? How could they possibly know what they were getting into? Eliminating as many unknown factors as possible was a business principle that drove him to have longer preparation times than many of his competitors. He noted with satisfaction, his auctions were better attended, his reserves higher and the sale prices far superior. Betancourt did not get attacks of conscience or feel uneasy often. Now his daughter had broken his composure by the element of surprise. That was not a good sign.

The young clerk stood up and tinkled a little bell mechanically. "Ladies and Gentlemen, five minutes before we commence. Please make yourselves comfortable by taking a seat."

Jo quickly looked out the window. Where were they? Jo approached the clerk. She seriously wanted to get some deep cleansing pore scrub onto his face. "Sir, I am expecting some friends, but they must have been held up… is it possible to wait a moment longer?"

He looked startled at such an audacious request. "Preparation for a serious bid would imply being early, not late." He paused, and then excused himself. "I'm sorry Ma'am. They've had as much time as every bidder here. This process is about equitable opportunity."

Jo laughed nervously. "Oh, and I thought it was about maximum money!"

"Mr Betancourt has rules about starting on time."

Jo grimaced. *Did power mongers with irrational rules run this entire town?*

He thought she must not have heard, so he repeated himself, very slowly. "It is import-ant to start the auct-ion on time."

Andi joined her friend. "You seem to know a lot about business. I think it would be especially difficult to know how to create such a healthy atmosphere of competition and spirit. That is such astute business. I would have thought an increased attendance…" She paused and took a breath, blushed prettily and giggled. She put stuck out her hand. "Sir, my name is Andi. It's just that my friend and I are quite inexperienced in these types of cut-throat business events. Yet we are very interested in learning how to handle them well from people who have experience. You look like a businessman of experience." She paused and tried to cover an internal swelling of shame at her blatant flirting.

The clerk did notice that the words "businessman" and "experience" had been spoken in the same sentence by a rather attractive young lady. He stretched out his lanky neck and pulled himself up importantly and cleared his throat. "Are *you* really interested in these matters?" he asked Andi, somewhat dubiously.

"Oh yes! Really…" she enthused, totally engrossed in a pimple on his forehead. "I was wondering if a smattering of flexibility gave the buyers a greater sense of confidence… and wouldn't that in turn, encourage them to spend more money? A serious student of business, like yourself, would know which principle holds more significance… where it counts… in the marketplace."

The clerk coughed and straightened his vest. "Well let me see… it is important that other businessmen take the proposal seriously. But you need to be seen as a person of your word and trustworthy. People want to know they will not be swindled. I agree with what you said about confidence… that is important. No purchaser, however financially positioned, will buy outside their comfort levels."

"Oh! What is an excellent point!" enthused Andi. "How fortunate that Mr Betancourt places so much confidence in you. Your responsibility …"

The mention of Mr Betancourt brought him abruptly back to reality, and Andi rolled her eyes as she realised she had successfully concluded stalling the proceedings. The clerk coughed again and excused himself. Just as he went to stand by the auctioneer, a party arrived at the top of the stairs. It was Sally. She had made it! Jo squealed under her breath and enveloped her in an enormous hug! "I was getting desperate! I thought you weren't going to make it."

Andi's shoulders relaxed. "You're cutting it fine… they're starting!"
Beside Sally stood Eunice with her father, Mr Glossop. There was another man in a plain dark suit with small reading glasses. There was a fading yellow bruise on his cheek. Jo beamed and steered them towards their unofficial seats, reserved by placing a shawl and papers over them. The auctioneer explained the terms of the

auction, detailed the virtues of the property for sale and opened the bidding.

Sally sat tense on her seat, her head down. She could not look. Mr Glossop was their bidding representative. He calmly waited for the eager frenzy of the opening candidates to settle. Bargain hunters dropped out as the price rose. Jim Glossop could have been at any horse auction. To him it was all the same. Know your position, know when to start, know when to stop. It was simple.

The auctioneer's deep voice echoed around the room as he identified buyers placing their bids. The clerk stood by his side scanning the room for the next bid. He looked as if he was going to wet his pants in the excitement of it all. Gradually the bidding slowed. Now there were three serious contenders left. Sophie was among them.

The bidders paused, and hurriedly consulted in hushed and low confidential tones. "Going once, ladies and gentlemen, going twice, going...." and Mr Glossop stood to his feet and raised his ticket. The pimply clerk called out triumphantly. "There, at the back!" The thrill of his single-handed discovery resonated through his announcement. People turned in their seats. The flow of the auctioneering garble did not pause. Horace Betancourt blinked. He had seen Jim Glossop come in at the last minute. He assumed it was for spectator's sport. He'd done that before. Now he was starting his bidding when the others were nearing their limit. It was a bold strategy that sent a definite message. Mainstar was his.

Sophie turned around in a panic. She had been so confident that she was in with a chance. Glossop looked bored – the whole this was as good as signed, sealed and delivered. He yawned quite deliberately and quietly indicated for Eunice to take over the bidding, just like the time they had bought Prince Tyron. Then he sat back down pleasantly amused. This *was* spectator's sport. More fun was ensuing here, than a day at the races… and that was saying something.

The gathering looked on with interest and watched the battle lines being drawn. Other bidding parties started whispering, and one by one they shook their heads in disappointment and withdrew. Sophie sat up straight and waved her hand in response.

Sally and Eunice looked at each other. They joined their hands and raised them together. The clerk screamed, the excitement transporting him away. The auctioneer acknowledged the bid. Sophie quickly reacted by waving her hand. She would meet anything they had to offer. Calmly Sally and Eunice responded with a counter-bid.

Jack looked around anxiously. He knew his limit was reached. This new, confident group-bidder intimidated him. His eyes met Jo's sitting beside Sally. He raised his eyebrows in surprise and glanced back at Sophie. He was concerned at the intensity of purpose he saw there. He wanted success too, but they had to be able to meet the commitment or they would be going through this process again in the near future, on the other side of the auction gavel. There would be other places, other auctions – or straight sales where he could negotiate sanely. He didn't want to risk his life's savings through an irrational, emotional moment. Especially when it wasn't *his* irrational, emotional moment.

Sophie went to bid again but he calmly held her hand. She raised her other hand, out of his reach. Jack reached around behind her and lowered her arm quietly at the shoulder. She wrestled free and slapped him defiantly across the face. He looked at her patiently, searching her eyes. What he saw made him shake his head. Slowly he took the wad of papers sitting on the chair beside him and tore them up. He let the pieces shower over her head and walked out. Their partnership was over.

Sophie stood frozen in the fragmented pieces of her shattered plans as she stared at her father. He secretly wished she had won. She had done all this without any assistance from him. The pride he momentarily felt was drowned in the humiliation she had inflicted on herself and her family. He never realised Sophie spilt over with the raw potential that was himself many years before. He had done it hard. He saw that same determination in her eyes that would cause her to relentlessly pursue the same path. Yet, if she could show control, if she was willing to be trained and groomed, he could teach her the ropes. If only the pride he saw reflected in her eyes will not stop her being willing to be taught.

He looked at his daughter and said, with surprising tenderness in his voice, "Go home Sophie." She twirled on the spot and walked out the door: the mortification of failure stinging her eyes. But she would return one day, she promised herself, one day – she would walk out of this room with her head held high.

The auctioneer announced the standing bid, the hammer fell and concluded the sale: Mainstar had new owners. Mr Betancourt quietly stood. For some reason the rush that the execution of each sale usually held, did not come. It was done. That was all, and the empty feeling in his chest, made him promise that his daughter would learn the ropes to fight like a Betancourt.

Sally and Eunice stood, still holding hands looking at each other with a profound sense of connectedness. They gave each other a solid handshake and then embraced warmly. "Partners," said Sally as tears fell unheeded from her eyes.

Eunice stood there, quietly amazed at their success. "Partners," she confirmed. How could they, two young women, thwart and outbid every man in this room? Yet they had. They had!

* * *

25.

Finally Sally and Eunice concluded the substantial amount of paperwork a purchase could generate. Sally went over it a third time with the man in the tiny glasses. It was imperative that nothing was missed. This was business. The excitement was high and the vision was fresh, and they felt that nothing could quench the exhilaration of their success.

Andi and Jo watched as a newspaper man introduced himself, and lined Sally, Eunice, Jim Glossop, and Mr Spottnick up against a wall and flashed their picture. "News breaking," he grinned, "Not every Betancourt lost out here today: lots of readers will be interested to hear how this sale went today." He licked his pencil tip enthusiastically, as he jotted down answers to his questions, in the hope that this story was his big break.

Andi tugged at Jo's sleeve. "That's Thomas Betancourt! Sophie's brother. He's the one who wrote the article and photo in the basket," she whispered in her ear. "The newspaper clipping… it gets printed tomorrow."

Finally, they climbed into their sulky. No matter how late, Sally couldn't want to wait any longer before going home. Home! Mainstar was finally home!

They pulled up at the homestead, lanterns bobbing on the outside of the sulky. Robert came to the door. They were back. Relief seemed to fill his lungs. He hadn't even been aware that he had been holding his breath. Sally ran up the stairs to him. "Robert – it's official! Now we can share our engagement with the world!" He looked at the exhausted excitement that flushed her cheeks, and he smiled in amazement that the expectation of sharing their life together covered all the trauma of losing Mainstar.

"You seem happy about that…" he said as he lifted her hand to his lips. He paused in confusion at the absence of her ring. "Your ring? You've taken it off? Did you need to travel *unattached* to go on your holiday?" Suddenly, all the tension and pressure of the last couple of weeks came crashing down on top of Sally. She had so wanted this to be a happy reunion and his accusation stung. She burst into tears!

Jo and Andi stood at the gate and backed up… okay… "Perhaps we should just crawl back to the hut for a good, well-earned sleep. We can catch up tomorrow," whispered Andi, and they quietly slipped into the shadows. Billy sneaked around to the kitchen where he knew Molly would have a special supper waiting for him. She always did.

"Bushrangers," sniffed Sally, "bailed up the coach. There was hardly anything of value… but they took the ring… I tried to hide it…" Sally had to again climb the mountain that the memory brought back. "I know it's only a ring, but it meant so much…"

"Oh Sal, I'm sorry." He hadn't intended to be so harsh. "I have been beside myself with worry, wondering why… the timing was appalling. There was so much to be done." He led her inside and sat her on the lounge.

Sally looked around this room. She had dusted and polished and cleaned every board and panel all her life, and she fell in love with it all over again. "You're telling me! There was no other time. It had to be now…" and through the tears in her eyes she smiled at him mischievously.

"Why do I think you reckon you have done something clever? Have you found a position already? Is that why it was so urgent?"

"Yes, I have actually. I went to Sydney to finalise some things."

"So that's why you went away... to find a job." The thought eased the vice of tension around his forehead that had been strangling him all morning.

"More or less. I've gone into business. A partnership."

He blinked hard. "A partnership? Without me? When? How?"

"This afternoon. It's all official! I'm in business – with a horse breeder!"

"Horses?"

"Yes… race horses. Arabians mainly."

"Are you mad? Without capital? What do you know about elite horses like that?"

"My partner knows horses... very well. But… "She sobered her voice… "Robert Madegan, I wanted to ask if you would consider working for me… I need a manager."

"Manager? Sally, you're not making sense. How can you go into business penniless?"

"Oh, Robert please say yes! I need you. This won't work without you!"

"Well, thank you for that… but you should have thought about that before you

committed yourself. It seems very evident you
have already decided what's going to happen.
And I happen to know nothing about horses
outside a fair farm horse! Not like that. I'm *not*
going to be pushed unwillingly into something I
know nothing about… married or not."

"Robert… how could I tell you? One slip,
however unintentional, could have jeopardised
everything."

"Huh!   The vote of confidence is
overwhelming me a little."

"I had to trust, that *you* would trust *me*
enough to follow this through. God did miracle
after miracle to see this happen. And now it has."
It was a bit harder to argue with God. She pulled
a scroll of rolled paper from under the leather
flap in her father's large wallet. She held it in
front of him… "Robert Madegan – please, trust
me in this.   It is the opportunity of our
life-time… please, work with me and my
partner?" He went to take the paper, but she
pulled it out of reach. "Please?"

He looked at her. How could he want
anything else? Not exactly the way he thought
things would be. Not that he had made plans
himself.   His mind, and time, had been

overloaded just getting this far. He sighed. "Miss McBride (soon to be Mrs Madegan, I might add) this hardly seems fair. Where do I need to sign?"

"Your word is good. That is enough for me!" and she handed him the scrolled-up document in her hand. "I need you to manage this for me, the pastoral branch of our agreement." He unrolled the paper looking her squarely in the face, trying to read exactly what she was scheming. He glanced down at the paper.

His gaze froze as his eyes ran across the words 'Mainstar Station'. His face went pale. Beads of perspiration ran across his forehead. How could his mind be playing tricks on him? Was he really so over-wrought that he was on the verge of mental collapse? He tried to focus afresh, but still "Mainstar" stayed firmly printed at the top of the document. He looked at Sally as if she was playing some cruel, macabre joke on him. "This is not funny." He put the paper down, his hands shaking.

"Robert, it is not a joke. It has really happened. I have gone into partnership with Eunice Glossop. We bought Mainstar together. It's ours. It's really ours. God saved it for us!"

And she told him of Billy's engagement present that had taken them from being paupers to sufficiently well off to make a substantial investment in reclaiming Mainstar. That is why she needed to go to Sydney - to get a fair price on the gems. "When the Cobb & Co was bailed up, one of the passengers gave me his card because I helped his wife. He was a legal man. He worked out the details and said he would act on my behalf. He came back to finish up the contract, and some business of his own, before he goes back to Sydney permanently to his wife's family. Oh Robert, our dream has come true! This is our home!"

* * *

26.

The girls lifted their dresses and walked through the blue bells under the light of a full moon, up to the verandah of the hut. "Do you remember how spooky this house looked, when we came?" said Jo. "We had no idea what was in here."

"Now it's like home. Every person we have met... it's incredible... amazing..."

"I still can't get over Billy – fossicking everyday... just doing his thing. Who would have thought that Billy would end up being the superhero of this place? He was insulted and dismissed by just about everyone and yet it was what he did that ended up being the very thing that has saved their home. Have you ever heard of a tin full of rocks being such an incredible present?"

"And do you know what is really awesome?" said Andi quietly, "It still would have been a fantastic present, even if they had been worthless...."

"Maybe, but that wouldn't have saved Mainstar."

"There would have been a way, because God meant it to be."

"Remember how Sally was so distraught when Billy hit us? She said people were telling her to send him away. I'm relieved that can't happen now that Sally has secured the rights for Billy and he can go on prospecting while he is living here."

"I don't actually remember much at the beginning…" Andi involuntarily rubbed the scar on her forehead.

"Or Eunice – how about that? Her selling her jewellery and most of her horses, as well as using her inheritance portion. Mr Glossop was right behind her, saying that since she is not engaged to Charlie anymore, there were no grounds to withhold it. The fellow might not put up a fight very often, but he's not one to argue with, once he has a mind to have his say."

"I think the bravest thing was for her to give up Prince Tyron as a breeding base for her own stud. It's a pity she couldn't raise enough money without selling him."

"Yeah, but her Dad bought him on the condition she gets four services when he is mature enough." Jo smiled elatedly. It *would* work out.

"What do you think will happen with Charlie?" asked Andi tentatively.

"Eunice's coming out tomorrow to go over with her father the plans to establish the stable." Jo lowered her voice confidentially even though no one was around. "She told me she is going to propose to Charlie."

Andi laughed at the thought. "There's no way he'll accept. He won't work for a *woman*."

"Well, Eunice is prepared for that possibility… but she's hopeful. She said when they last spoke, she had reason to hope."

Andi was sceptical. "As I recall, they had a big argument and refused to talk to each other. That doesn't sound too hopeful to me!"

"Charlie said he wouldn't talk to her again unless he could make her a genuine offer, without the charades. Eunice said he didn't want her money… but he insisted that while he had Mainstar and all its debts, he was not convinced she could know that for sure."

"Well, well, Charlie has less of the Madegan money-mining reputation than I thought."

They lingered on the swing seat hanging from the rafter on the verandah for a while longer, enjoying the moon-light dance shadows up and down the ripples of time. "Being here has made me love night-times so much."

* * *

Robert sat beside Sally for a long time, as she told him story after story. It seemed so surreal. Finally, she paused. Robert took her ringless hand. "I hope you kept one good sapphire to make a new ring."

Sally looked up at him, "No, I didn't... I never thought. I sold all of the ones that were worth anything at all. I needed every penny."

"Well, we'll have to ask Billy to do some more digging..."

"No, wait! There *is* one... a good one. Mr Holder at the jewellery store in town was not being reasonable so I took it back because it was worth much more than he'd offer. I took it to Sydney, but I left it in my little purse... it's still there. I forgot all about it!"

"Forgot you had a gem-stone lying around in your things? I can see how common place this has become for you!"

"But..." and Sally saw the teasing twinkle in his eye.

"Now, I would like permission from my new employer to ask if I could give her something I think she will like… a pre-wedding present." Robert stood quietly to his feet. "I still have no ring to give you, but I think that has been provided for once again. Close your eyes."

Sally obediently closed her eyes. What did Robert have… the keys to the house? She had them already… as the housekeeper… but no one locked up out here anyway. What it could be?

"No peeking," Robert instructed as he left the room. Sally sat in the dark, quietly enjoying the surprise. She felt him lay something in her lap. "Now, open your eyes…"

It a brown paper package tied up with string. "Welcome home Sally. This is something that is very precious to me. It was given to me a long time ago, and I want you to have it now."

Sally undid the string and her dark hair fell across her face. She tucked it behind her ear as she pulled back the paper to reveal an old worn large leather wallet with the initials "W. P. McB" engraved in the corner. Sally gasped and traced them with her finger. Tears brimmed around the corners of her blue eyes. She quietly opened the folder and took out a pile of yellowed pages, blotted with ink, scratched and corrected along the lines of poetry.

"Pa's poems," she said reverently. "His poems! I didn't know what happened to them! I looked for ages and never knew. I asked him once, and he said they went to a better place. I thought he meant he burnt them. I was so sad. I wanted to have one or two… but they're all here. Every one I remember, and some I've never heard. Oh Robert! No other gift could be more perfect! This is the grandest finale to the most memorable day ever."

He looked in wonder at the expression on her face. He closed his eyes in gratitude.

Sally held the pages gently. "Robert, I want to create a memorial. Something that will remind us how wonderful God is… how he blessed us beyond measure… something that we can use every day, so it will remind us and our children of the incredible blessings God gives us day by day… and it will be for those who follow us as well. We must not let them forget the heritage that they have in God!"

* * *

"You know Jo, I think I would've liked to have met Sally's Dad."

"We sorta have already. The poem in the basket… it tells…"

"It's funny, but I expected to read some of his poetry… the originals. All the other documents in the basket... I can account for them... but the poem?" She shrugged. "I asked Sally. She said all his poems have been lost."

Jo took Andi inside and opened up a little box. She unfolded a letter salvaged from the flood – water stained and smudged. There was the ledger that Robert threw at them and Sally's note about her holiday; even Charlie's letter to Eunice that she refused to keep and gave to Jo to dispose of. "It's all accounted for, except that poem. There has to be at least that one poem around somewhere. We have it at home in the twenty-first century."

Andi shook her head. She was tired. "Just now I want to sleep." She turned the lantern down low and headed behind the curtain to the bedroom. She stumbled on the uneven floor and grabbed at the curtain. She pulled on it hard to regain her balance.

"Andi! Look out!" Jo yelled. She tackled Andi to the floor as the beam supporting the

curtain gave way, hessian falling all over them.
Everything went black.

* * *

27.

"Jo? Andi? Hello? Oh my, oh my what has happened to you girls? Jo! Andi... Oh my!"

"Sally?"

"No Deary, it's June... oh my... this is so awful... oh my!"

"My head hurts..."

"Oh, Andi dear, don't move... you've an awful cut to the forehead... here..." June glanced around quickly picked up the tea-towel covering their picnic basket and placed it over the cut.

"My nose is bleeding..." Jo looked at the blood on her fingers as she wiped her nose and started giggling... "Billy, you made my nose bleed again!"

"Did you say Billy? Uncle Billy?" June paused for a moment and then shook her head as if to clear it of cobwebs. "There, there dear, you've had a nasty blow too: I think you are quite overwrought!" The serviette liner to their picnic became a pad.

"June? Oh I...."

"Just hold it on tight... there's a dear..."

"I'm okay... Andi? You're not looking real..."

"Oh dear, you are right. I need to get help… I can't leave you my dears… not now… but I need to… oh my! Jo, you keep checking her now, there's a dear…"

June left in a flurry and returned in double time with a man from the main house, and a workman. They carried Andi back to the house on a camp stretcher. When they got to the house they rang for an ambulance. Andi was made as comfortable as possible on a spare bed. Jo sat with her and looked at a gallery of sepia coloured photos in thick, carved wooden frames on the guest room wall.

A lady was there with June and helped bandage Andi's wound. She noticed Jo's fascination with the photos. "We've started hosting a farm-stay bed-&-breakfast. So many people have been really interested in the history of the station and I done as much research as I can using local records…" She paused and glanced over at June with a smile, who was absorbed in looking at a photograph that Jo passed to her. "Aunty June has helped gather quite a collection of these old photos," said the lady with a fond smile. "We've adopted June as part of the family. The connection of this place tends to make you feel like family here. This used to be a very successful horse-stud at the turn of last century."

"Three champions is quite an impressive record. Unusual story because two young ladies started it. They both married sons of the original owner. June's great-grandmother was one of those. The shearing shed was quite a good size for around here."

"And you wouldn't guess... there even used to be a sapphire mine! Our guests sometimes go down to the gully and fossick. It was quite productive for a while. The fossicking and mining rights belonged to a man everyone called 'Uncle Billy'. An eccentric old man, gentle as a mother hen. He lived in that hut for years and years. He didn't allow anyone else to work the mine right up until he died, but I've never heard anyone say a mean thing about him. We'll never really know the full story now most of the old-timers have gone. June is our only link with this history, and she has a very special place here at any time. That's Uncle Billy there when he was a young man... holding his little nephew... you can see he's as kind as a kitten..."

"Had a good left hook," said Jo under her breath, rubbing her nose.

"Here's a photo taken on the verandah one year at Christmas time. I love looking at their faces and wondering what they might have been like. I think it would have been a very interesting gathering." Andi struggled to sit up as Jo leaned over June's shoulder to look at the photo.

Sally and Robert stood tall with a young boy and a girl by their side; Billy held a little baby in his arms. Eunice and Charlie stood next to Molly and Bluey. Mrs Glossop and Aunt Millie were there, looking strained, like they could not possibly survive the imposition of a primitive "bush" Christmas. Uncle Herbert was distractedly patting a young black Labrador puppy in his arms, and Jim Glossop leant on the verandah post as if Christmas was the most intolerably tedious event on the annual calendar. You could almost hear him asking, "Why can't they have horse races all year 'round and just be done with it?"

"That's grandmother when she was six or so. And there's Uncle Billy... my great-great uncle really, but he never made me feel he was any older than me... even though when I knew him he was really old..." her voice constricted in a tight little gasp, and she sighed. "That's Uncle Wilfred..." June said stabbing the boy standing tall with an uncomfortable stiff collar. "And that's Uncle Bob," pounding the baby in Billy's arms. June started quoting names and partner's names and children's' names. Andi closed her eyes. Her head hurt, but somehow June's recital was comforting. It was a bit like the basket. The beauty of the decorations had faded and dated, but the essence of the heritage lived on in the next generation... and the next.

The lady tugged on June's elbow. "We might grab a cup of tea. The dear girl needs to rest. The ambulance won't be too long now."

As they disappeared out the door, Jo picked up an old, hard cloth-bound book lying on the bedside table. The spine on the volume was so faded the gold embossed print had all but disappeared. The front of the burgundy cover was blank, and the pages inside were yellowed and stiff. Was this a book that Robert and Sally had read? It seemed strange that this house and this room held so much of their lives even now.... three generations later.

She gently opened the cover and turned the page. Jo read aloud the thick, bold printing: "*BALLADS OF A BUSH PROSPECTOR - A selected Anthology by Wilfred Patrick McBride.* Andi! The Poems! There here - the poems are all here." The frontispiece was a black and white photo of a man leaning on a shovel in the bush, a pick and prospecting sieve at his feet. His walrus moustache and a shady felt hat concealing his sun-weathered face. "So, this is Will McBride," said Jo thoughtfully. He was a man she had never met, but who impacted so many lives. She even thought he had probably saved her life in a way… up a tree in the flood. Jo continued reading. "*For Dorothy, Wilfred and Bob — who never met their Grandfather, lovingly known by his friends as The Poet-Parson. Introduction by Sally Grace Madegan.*" She read on, the story of the poems and her father: a tribute of a much-loved man, who left a heritage in prose for his grandchildren, and great-grandchildren, and many others.

Jo caught her eyes filling with the memories of friendship. Somehow this last piece of the jigsaw, sealed the door to a very special room in the private lives of those at Mainstar.

Andi closed her eyes against the thumping in her head. How unfair that June had no kids to pass this on to. Then she realised, June had chosen them. Every time she asked them about their day or gave them a lift downtown, June was planting seeds from her heritage into theirs.

Andi held the basket tightly in her hands. In getting to know the people behind the layers, it symbolized everything her visit to Mainstar represented. She leaned back into the pillow and pictured a cream linen tablecloth, a kerosene lamp, an arrangement of gumnuts and wildflowers... blue-bells, red bottle-brush and a yellow bush-orchid, framing an old sepia photograph, like the one of old Uncle Billy nursing June as a little girl that sat on a dusty side board in June's living room. There would be sapphire blue serviettes lining the basket, bulging with crusty fresh herb bread, just like Molly used to make. She imagined June seated as her guest of honour in her best flowery dress, sipping homemade ginger-beer, reading a poem that was penned by her Great-great grandfather by the light of a campfire in the bush. And too bad if her teacher didn't get the significance of it all. What was really important was that...

The paramedics interrupted her thoughts. She squeezed her eyes tight against the flashlight as they asked her questions and took her blood-pressure, and then they wheeled her to the back of the ambulance. They drove off quickly. June scuttled off to retrieve her car.

Jo waited in the shade of the verandah looking out into the spreading arms of a tall gum tree, holding Andi's basket like a prized trophy.

Everything that had happened at Mainstar had generated so much hope inside of her, but really, it just seemed too tidy. Faith was probably okay for an altruistic mission like Sally saving her home for her disabled brother and other people's jobs. But what about something more personally ambitious? How does that play out? Would God really be okay with salvaging plans that are about individual ambitions? Huh. She doubted that. God would expect her to do the boring, dull, and dreary stuff... like being a missionary or something. There was no way she had that in her. She didn't know exactly what she wanted to do when she left school, but if having God in her life meant she had to eliminate any of those interesting possibilities, she was not up for that. No way in the world.

She looked up into the tree and spotted the long green-grey leaves of a bush orchid. It was pushing out a spray of tiny flowers against all odds, shining with all its might. Huh. Perhaps there were no answers to these big questions. Still. For now, Andi had her basket, and a way to approach her school assignment. And she thought of the words of a poem from the volume sitting inside on the bedside dresser…

Polish, shine and sparkle – yes, yes you must!
Because they're offering hope – these sapphires in dust.

* * *

Sapphire Blue
By Wilfred P. McBride

Caked dust on rubble scattered about
Rivers of sweat the prospector digs out
Through rock and thistles and grainy coarse sand
Persisting past pain and raw blistered hand
There's only a rumour of bluestone 'n fire
If that story proves good, the prize is sapphire

He's dreamt dreams - new lives and fresh starts
Prosperous living with his beloved sweetheart
None of the scraping, heavy hard labour
Of maids that he's met - cold hearts turned sour
A bequest of confidence, security for sons
Transforming dreams into living real ones.

Hope stays the power for days hard 'n long
When others cut out, the vision stays strong
When fragments of colour seem unbelievably small
Hope stands tall declaring, "That is not all!"
It's a mixture of skill and stayin' on track
We won't get the colour if we quit and turn back

It's the same with the way that I tackle my life
Look past disappointment, pain and the strife

God gives Hope of a promise that's sure
Stand firm and strong, 'There's definitely more!"
Just got to dig in the dust and the dirt
Knowing hidden beneath lies more than just hurt

So, I look in the blue of my baby son's eyes
Unsuspecting innocence echo deep anguished cries
It's a blue that is deeper than sapphire hue
And I know with conviction that's certainly true
God replaces sad spaces, and gathers each tear
Just dig in the dirt and the gems will appear.
Polish, shine and sparkle — yes, yes you must!
Because they're offering hope — these sapphires in dust.

Coming Soon

More *Gems of Australia*

#2 Rubies of Ambition

Jo and Andi travel back into another period, this time with a beautiful actress named Lillian Browning from the 1920's who suddenly returns to the town of Gum Ridge where she grew up. The prickly-pear plague is at its height and desperation has invaded the hearts of people on all levels.   How can Lillian find meaning outside her shattered ambitions? Will she ever reconnect with the people in her hometown who reject her pursuit of fame just like she rejected their humble community when she left?

#3 Emerald Dreams

Another time-warp journey finds Jo and Andi back in colonial times and they are horrified at the living conditions of those who had no choice but to live out the term of their natural life in Australia. Dreams seem a pointless exercise that belonged to their past. When the girls meet Polly, they start to see what is below the surface. Will Polly and her young daughter Jane, ever find a new way through the hardship to invest in their future dreams with anticipation?

Other Books by Olwyn Harris

Matt's Boys of Wattle Creek.

When Matthew Lawson's three sons were born, he wrote each of them a letter outlining his hopes and prayers for their futures. When he decided to give up his city job and move to the little town of Wattle Creek, he could never have imagined the effect it would have on his young family. As Matt's boys grow to maturity and find their places in their community, will his dreams and prayers come to fulfilment? Will his boys develop their own faith in the eternal God? And will they each find the kind of love that Matt holds for his beautiful Josie?

Praise for Matt's Boys of Wattle Creek:

I personally found the story beautifully presented, I fell in love with the story from page 1. I found myself seeing and living again my early life, the story entangled me, and it held me in complete interest, right through to the last page 691, you know, I became a member of the little town of Wattle creek for over 4 days as your book gave the complete story.

Congratulations!

I am, yours in the service of Jesus Christ,

John Stark

Maggie & Minotaur

'For Maggie, the mythical Minotaur represented Romance – half man, half beast. The Minotaur was a monster created from centuries of classical Greek mythology and no normal man could withstand its strength...... Sooner or later she would accept that Theseus, the hero, did not exist. She knew that she would have to battle through the maze of reality and confront it herself...."

Maggie Wick was shipped off to the city and high society life at the age of 12, where she would learn the ways of the rich and marry into a family of influence. What could have caused her sudden return to Henderson's Gap? Can she really settle back into life on the station, with all its diversity and challenges? Will she find fulfillment in her role as provisional schoolteacher? Will she ever figure out the "Captain", the mysterious, intimidating, station manager?

When war comes to her little haven and Maggie's world comes crashing down, taking her loved ones and the captain with it, Maggie needs to find a way to survive. Will her faith be enough to protect her, and what of the Captain? Could he really be the Theseus who would do battle with her Minotaur?

Praise for Maggie & Minotaur:

Another great book by this author. Maggie & Minotaur is a conflict-filled journey to the earlier days of Australia's colonisation. A time when racism and classism was rampant. This book uses historically accurate and yet, very confrontational language, especially around the issue of race, words we don't use in polite society these days. It paints an accurate - if unflattering - picture of early life in Australia. All that aside, however, this book takes you into the home and lives of a very culturally diverse society trying to come to terms with the changing expectations of the time, woven through with wonderful characters, loving relationships, and the ever-present grace of God. Olwyn Harris knows how to tell a story and this book is no exception!

Ann Smith